GIRL GONE
HOME

Kathleen O'Donnell

II **ITALICS**

Italics Publishing Inc.
Cover and interior design by Sam Roman
Editor: Joni Wilson
ISBN: 1-945302-41-0
ISBN-13: 978-1-945302-41-1

"She gives me love, love, love, love, crazy love."

Van Morrison

For my grandkids, Deja, Madison, Adelia, Amelie, Che Jr., and Sonio, all smart, funny, little jewels, who owe their original and eccentric personalities, in some way, both big and small, to the village that raised me.

For that village on the highway who loved and shaped me in ways I'll be forever grateful for and who aren't quite as odd as the people in this novel. They're all of the good, none of the bad.

For Ed, still.

ACKNOWLEDGEMENTS

Huge shout out and all kinds of love to my grandkid's daddies, Che Sr. and Paul, who love my daughters and their children. Love to Daniel and Kayla who grew up in and around our little highway town and who understand better than anyone how much love is there. Always for Marsha who is tireless in her quest to make sure I use hyphens and who still looks forward (so she says) to reading my work. A big thank you to Alex and the folks at Italics for their patience and their belief in my work. Love to Sandra Dillard and Christine Turner who read this book when it was a germ of a story and all my Ya Ya girls, Julie Wilson, Colleen Custer, Mary Snowden, Kathy Robinson, Monica Coleman, and Kitti Heaton, who cheer me on every day.

2005

CHAPTER ONE

"Willy Wally came to a bad end," Fran said. "Just like I predicted."

"Only you'd gloat over the dead at a funeral." I'd just walked in, looked at my watch. My mother irritated me in less than sixty seconds. A record.

"We don't do funerals, Delilah. The stiff puts a real damper on the festivities."

"Right. Memorials after the fact only."

"Who even knows where the nearest funeral home is?" Fran said, unimpeded by the Marlboro in her mouth, long ash miraculously still intact. "Okay, I know where it is, but who gives a highfalutin crap? Potluck and booze give whoever croaked a fine send off—this *is* a bar for Chrissake. You're back on the Highway. Better forget those fancy city ways."

From my spot bellied up to the bar I watched the sea of cowboy hats attached to heads full of rampage and Coors from the tap. They went whole hog at these things. The only commercial enterprise for as far as the crow flies, Vi's Place teemed with quasi-mourners spilling through both front and back doors to the overflow outside. The middle of nowhere meant good business for anyone with stuff to sell.

"No idea why I let you drag me to this thing," I said. "I'm still knee-deep in unpacked boxes."

"Still? You move in geologic time. It's the food. That's why you came. You've always been a sucker for the highway potlucks. Besides, won't kill you to show some respect for a guy you went to school with. Dead just like that." She'd have snapped her fingers if they weren't already occupied with the whole cigarette/ashtray/coffee cup situation.

"Nothing says respect like eating beanie-weenies while drunks heckle the bereaved," I said. "Good times."

"Good turnout."

"I should hope so. Willy Wally wasn't even forty." I stopped when I noticed Fran paid a lot of attention to my words. "Never mind."

She flicked her ash into the ashtray. "Doc Bates won't show. Accident or no, tough to look your daughter in the eye after you shoot her husband."

"Isn't Doc in jail?"

"You know he's not. Investigation's still on. Doubt it'll turn up anything criminal. Shit happens out here."

"Like there's gonna be a real investigation." I rearranged my butt on the hard stool, scooted it closer to hear Fran over the hootin'-and-a-hollerin'. "Unbelievable. What a fiasco. Whole thing's terrible."

"What do you care? You didn't even want to come."

"I don't and I didn't. Well, that's not altogether true. Of course, I care. It's sad isn't it? A young man killed?"

"Culling out the herd. You see Wally's widow, Wanda? Jesus, Mary and Joseph try to say that three times fast."

"I don't know. Probably wouldn't know her if I did."

Fran slipped her cigarette into the slot on the ashtray on the bar. "You'd know her all right—still two-bagger ugly. Wanda and Willy Wally Watkins. Why on earth poor Willy Wally didn't strangle himself with his own umbilical cord, I'll never know, with that dumbass name."

Nothing sordid happened that Fran didn't know about in great detail. Whatever the backstory, and there was *always* a backstory, she knew it and loved to tell me about the whole mess. I got zippo this time. Fishy.

"What do you know about this, Fran? You know something. I can tell."

"You obviously can't, since I know zilch, other than Willy Wally and Doc went hunting like always. Doc accidentally shot him. Makes sense to me. Willy Wally's schnoz made him look like a moose or some such."

"You're talking a mile a minute. Like you do when you're dancing around the truth."

"Shit happens around here."

"I'm aware. Fran, you—"

"Dee, aren't you a sight." Vi amputated my interrogation with a voice that sounded like someone dragged a cheese grater over her vocal cords. Her familiar shortening of my name gave me a warm fuzzy. "Been trying to get over to this end to say hey, but this crowd, no patience."

"Not much changes on the Fifty-Three," I said.

Including Vi who still looked like a jack-o-lantern left too long on the porch.

"If it did, I'd know it. Been behind this bar fifty years if you can believe that. But look at you. You're fresh as peach pie. Damn shame your TV show got cancelled," Vi said.

"Yeah, well thanks. TV shows come and go."

"She can still cook like the dickens though. What with that cooking class."

"Cordon Bleu is hardly a cooking class, Fran. I—"

"Now you're back home where you belong." Vi wiped down the bar with a snake-tattooed hand, pulled a frothy topped beer. "Where in Jesus's name are those good-for-nothin' bums I hired to help me out today? Goddamn-lazy-bastard-shit-for-brains..." She carried the mug to the other end, insults trailing.

"Is she wearing the necklace I gave you for your birthday?" I said.

Fran brushed crumbs off the front of her "Smooth Move Ex-Lax" t-shirt.

"Oh, that little bauble? Well, yes. Vi went on and on about how much she wanted it. I didn't—"

"Do you know how much that little bauble cost?"

Fran gave zero fucks about the cost.

"Never mind." I put a sock in it.

"Lord a mercy, Delilah." Margene Cox made a beeline, heaped plate in hand. "I liked to fell out when I heard you'd come home. Wondered when we'd finally lay eyes on you."

"Only been back a couple weeks," I said. "Still settling in."

Margene draped the silk sweater around her shoulders that I'd bought Fran last Christmas.

"Nice sweater," I said.

The sharp stab of Fran's elbow to my ribs shut my mouth.

"Fran give it to me. She's generous as always. Only fits if I don't wear it. So hot out here the devil up and left, but still cools down like the dickens at night." Margene stuffed a whole jalapeno popper into her mouth. I felt mildly surprised most of her teeth looked intact. "You out at the old Winston pig farm?"

"Mm hmm. No pigs anymore."

"You missed Jefferson Davis." Margene licked her greasy fingers. "Dadgum it. He's dyin' to bend your ear about that farm."

"My loss."

"You know Willy Wally passing the way he did near tore my heart in two." Margene wiped a nonexistent tear. "You dated him didn't you, Dee?"

"Mercy no," Fran said.

"Well, I swanee," Margene said. "Dee nursed a crush on Willy Wally ya'll could see from space back in the day."

"Emily dated Willy Wally," Fran said.

For once I didn't mind Fran's poking in.

"Oh, right. Emily. Land's sake." Margene pushed her plastic fork through the turkey tetrazzini on her paper plate.

"Where's Arthur?" I looked around for Margene's husband.

"Oh, honey, had his memorial right here a couple years back."

"Lots of memorials the last few years," Fran said. "I told you about Arthur's."

She probably did but I hadn't been listening.

"Not the same without Blanche and Edith, is it?" Margene squeezed in closer, set her plate on the bar. "Blanche dyin' of the cirrhosis after Earl died in that car wreck, drunk. Too many memories. And Edith with the Alzheimer's over to her sister's in Portland."

Before she could run on any more, Willy Wally's father hushed the gathered to thank everyone for coming. I wandered away from my lunch, Fran, and Margene's census update. A drunk blocking the exit got a free swat from me. Heat plus the pissy sour outhouse smells slapped me hard. Came as no revelation Vi still resisted indoor plumbing.

"You look just like you do on TV," a man said two seconds after I got out.

"Huh?"

The sun glittering off the rows of cars lined up on both sides of the highway made me squinty. I got closer. Strange man held out a too elegant hand, flashed a badge with the other.

"I'm Billy Dale," he said. "You're Delilah Diamond from *Fork in the Road*. Am I right?"

"Billy Dale what?"

Name like that usually preceded a Jim Bob or Buck Dee.

"Just Billy Dale."

"You're not from around here then," I said.

"Nope." He withdrew his unshaken hand.

Billy Dale's kick-my-ass-why-don't-you ensemble cheered me somewhat. His slicked-backed hair, *GQ* chin stubble, casual Friday Brooks Brothers khakis and pink polo made me want to open the bar door, throw him in to see how he fared. The small crowd milling around outside to avoid the teary farewells inside dispersed as if they smelled an unfamiliar no good cop. Nothing like stranger danger to speed folks along their way. Billy Dale peered over the top of his sunglasses, looked past me at the open vista, dirt, and sagebrush.

"Jesus," he said. "You could seriously get off the grid out here."

"What do you want?"

"Just making inquiries about the shooting incident."

"At a memorial? Willy Wally's barely cold."

"When I drove up didn't realize this, whatever this is, was going on." He gestured toward the food covered picnic tables.

I kicked up a puff of dirt with the toe of my Converse, shifted my weight from one foot to the other. Billy Dale studied the fly-infested open jar of mayo on a nearby table, waiting, silent, doing that let-them-talk-to-see-what-spills cop thing. He flicked an imaginary something off his shirtsleeve. His blank face and open-too-wide eyes gave him a real dimwitted appearance—the kind of guy who moved his lips when he read.

"Where's Rusty?" I said. "He's been the law out here forever."

"On a bender probably."

"No doubt."

"Mind if I do some asking now?" he said.

I let that hang like a corpse from a noose.

"You know," I finally said after the silence got too awkward even for me. "I just came back here. Moved away eons ago."

"So I heard." Billy Dale leaned against a clean sedan that must've been his. "Some say they're surprised to see you back."

"None more than me."

"You came back for the—this—potluck thingy?"

"No. Coincidence."

"Coincidences give me cramps," Billy Dale said serious as all get out.

Like I cared about his bowels.

"Willy Wally your old high school boyfriend?" He went on.

"Christ, no. He dated my friend. Emily. She—"

"You all right?" Billy Dale said.

I'd swayed to one side. The beer I'd chased lunch with gurgled its way up the back of my throat. I beat it back, steadied myself.

"I'm fine. This heat, outhouse smell, I'm not used to it anymore." I pulled away from the hand he'd gripped my arm with, snooty-like. He probably did it to help, but too bad so sad.

"Right. Well, Jefferson Davis told me you—"

"Oh you're already on a first name basis? Jefferson Davis and I haven't so much as cast shadows near each other in twenty years." Droplets popped up above my top lip.

"Right. Well, speaking of names. You call your mother by her first name?"

"Always have," I said halfway lying. "Fran *is* her name."

I'd replaced *Mom* with *Fran* when we moved to the highway, when she went full wacko, to distance myself from her in the only way I could then, to get under her skin. Joke was on me since her skin proved unyielding, but it stuck.

"Fran knows Doctor Bates well?" Billy Dale said.

"Everybody here knows everyone else well."

"Willy Wally too?"

"Yes, but they didn't exactly run in the same circles since Fran's old enough to be his mother."

We stared each other down. I wondered if he could see me sweat.

He blinked first. "Can you think of any reason Fran would've called Willy Wally the day before he got shot *and* the day of?"

"Who knows? It is a small town," I said. "Why don't you ask Fran?"

"Did. Said she doesn't recall."

"She's no spring chicken. Memory's going." I twirled one finger near my ear.

"Fran called Willy Wally four times the day before he died, twice the next."

"She's a talker," I said.

There it was.

Fran did know more than she'd admitted. I crossed my arms over my chest, shoved both hands under my dripping armpits, worked hard to keep my face from going funky.

"Not to mention six calls to Doctor Bates." He'd taken out a notepad, which I guess meant business.

"I'm sure for harmless reasons."

I turned on my heel. Eat my dust sucker.

Billy Dale hollered at my back, "I'm sure I'll find out."

CHAPTER TWO

"I wish you'd have made at least one dish for the potluck," Fran said. "Some of those fancy schmancy hot dogs. Everyone was disappointed." She rolled down the car window on the passenger side, fanned her smoke out. "I know you haven't had time to shop, but you're a professional chef, you could've whipped up—"

"Why'd you call Willy Wally the day before he died? Four times no less. Then twice the day he got killed?" I stomped on the gas to let her know I didn't intend to kid around or let her distract me.

"What are you blabbering about?" Fran docked her cigarette in the ashtray, clasped her fingers together—prayer like—that'd be the day.

"Don't bother to lie," I said. "Billy Dale's apparently got phone records. Don't pretend you're not familiar with Billy Dale."

She rearranged her "Where's the Beef?" shirt, stabbed out her smoke.

"Phone records, bah. That Billy Dale's a nosy parker. Down from LA you know."

"You and Willy Wally like this all of a sudden?" I held up crossed fingers.

"Called to talk to Wanda," Fran said. "You just drove past my house."

"Since when? You can't stand Wanda."

"I needed a recipe."

"You don't need a recipe for microwave macaroni and cheese. Wanda told Billy Dale you were the last person to talk to Willy Wally, besides her, before he went hunting."

Fran blew out smoke, didn't say anything, opened the glove box to rearrange whatever. "That cow doesn't know her giant ass from the hole through her husband's jugular." Now she sped up her words in a string. "And that Billy Dale know-it-all I'm sure you don't need me to tell you anything he already did."

"I want you to tell me. Shake a leg. I don't have all day."

Fran stopped shit surfing in my glove box and tilted her head to the side like Stevie Wonder at the piano. "Who remembers every single conversation?"

I flipped a sharp U. Fran's head smacked against the window. Take that.

"Billy Dale's not the brightest tool on the tree," she said.

"Brightest bulb."

She took a break from pushing my buttons to pull out maps, my insurance information and fast food detritus. Folded and refolded the brown paper napkins, fiddled with a couple straws.

"You still spend time at Doc Bates's place?" I said.

"Not so much. Who cares?"

"Angela died forever ago. I'm sure Doc's learned to do things himself. Why'd you call him umpteen times that day too?"

"If I'm going to the store, I'll pick up stuff for Doc." She stuffed some of what she'd taken from the glove box back in. Loose papers fluttered to the floorboard. "If I can help I—"

"Six times? You needed to get stuff from the store six times in one day?"

"You never know," Fran said.

"Is Doc your boyfriend?"

"Seriously? What do you think?"

I couldn't push her on that front.

Fran leaned down to gather the pile at her feet.

"Well," I said. "Why don't you just tell me why Billy Dale is suspicious about your sudden close relationship with Willy Wally who, in case you've forgotten, was shot dead?"

"Aren't you the picture of concern all of a sudden?"

"Roll the window up, you're letting the air conditioning out."

Fran did as I asked, then resumed her paper shuffling.

"He said he's suspicious?" she said.

"Not exactly," I said. "But he'll get to it. He's not drunk Rusty, which is disturbing in itself. Means someone thinks Willy Wally's death needs a real looking into, a job Rusty can't do, so they brought in a real cop. The guy showed up at Willy Wally's memorial just to ask questions and eavesdrop. I'd say he's working up to something."

"People die," Fran said. "Heart attack, gunshot wounds, whatever. Natural causes are dull." Her tone implied she'd died of both gunshot wounds and a heart attack so knew the preferred method. "Why would anyone suspect me of anything? Why would I give half a shit about Willy Wally?"

Right on both counts. Still.

"I know you, remember?" I'd turned off the highway onto the short dirt road in front of Fran's house. "Something stinks."

Fran shuffled with diligence through her glove box finds. She unfolded more paper. "Who's Matthew Hardy?"

"What?" I slammed to a stop in front of her gate. Fran flew forward. Take that too.

Before I could stumble for an answer, or grab the paper, Fran recovered then said, "You're stalking again?"

"What are you reading?"

I turned off the engine, snatched the offending paper.

"Says Restraining Order right at the top. Whoever this Matthew Hardy is, you've been stalking him, haven't you?"

"Misunderstanding. Don't worry about it."

I folded the thing up, dropped it on my lap.

"I know you too. Remember?" Fran said. "You haven't done anything stupid for Chrissake?"

"Never mind Fran. Whole thing's ancient hist—"

"Is he ... this Matthew whatever ... why you came home?"

"No. Maybe. Partly."

Fran smoothed the cigarette she pulled out of her bra.

"You know how needy you are Delilah. First there was that Cajun guy, the one who yells wham or bam or what the hell, then that red-haired Casanova goofball with the TV star wife. Ex-wife now. Thanks to you."

"They're not just guys or goofballs, Fran. They're chefs. Famous celebrity chefs."

"Married famous celebrity chefs that you had affairs with then followed around like a lunatic when they cut you loose. They always cut you loose."

"Yeah well I got my own show, didn't I?" I said under my breath.

Fran's knack for illuminating my shortcomings never failed to infuriate me. My inability to keep my trap shut about my conquests always bit me in the ass. When I was younger the notches on my headboard made me feel important, star-like. Now I felt, I didn't know what for sure, but not good. I knew Fran wanted to say something else but didn't. Her lips pinched together, back and upper lip stiff. My mother'd never been prone to hissy fits. We sat. Neither of us made a move to get out of the car.

What a mistake I'd made coming back to the highway. Why did I think Fran would act as a balm not a burn? The windy sound of Fran's lighter brought me around. She looked so small and frail sitting there, too fragile to bear all she'd suffered, or all she'd wrought. I admired her moxie. She could look the hard thing in the eye and never blink. The heart I'd willed into hardening over the years softened like it always did where Fran was concerned.

"Matthew Hardy and I used to date." Why not throw her a bone? "He produced my show. Our relationship ended. Not well. I got fired."

"Fired? Not cancelled? I suspected as much." She mulled over whatever else she suspected before going on. "Why would you get fired for that? What'd they care?"

"Matthew's wife found out. Her father owns the network."

Fran pushed her glasses up to press her lids down with the hand not holding a cigarette.

"Fran, what the—"

She couldn't possibly be tearing up? Not in this lifetime. She pressed hard on her eyes, turned away to face the passenger side window.

"You never did get over your dad running off, or us moving here after, my marrying Hank, and all that … well, all the rest."

"Fran, don't."

"All those cooking classes—"

"Cordon Bleu. How many times do I have—"

"You've slept your way to the bottom."

That hurt.

"That's quite a turnaround. You told me once that a girl's gotta take care of her own, remember?"

"I was wrong."

"Fran, listen. It's fine. All that, well, all that's in the past."

"We're all about the past though, aren't we?"

CHAPTER THREE

Fran's house remained a monument to Giving Up. Dirty white paint still peeled in the same places, yard bare in some spots, overgrown in others. The tin roof over the lopsided concrete patio dipped in the center and the raggedy screen door shrieked like a fishwife when I opened it.

Fran busied herself at the coffeepot in the tiny kitchen, with its cracked counter tiles and peeling linoleum, while I sized up the living area. She'd replaced the new sofa and loveseat I'd bought her a few years before with two folding chairs, a plastic table meant for the outdoors, and a stack of TV trays. The dining table and matching chairs I'd given her when I bought my new house had disappeared too, replaced with nothing. The original wood flooring, now scuffed and scraped, groaned under my feet like my weight caused it pain. One wall boasted loud floral paper but only in part. Fran must've lost interest in the project midway. Not a single thing hung on the other walls.

"This is over the top even for you," I said. "Cost a fortune to get all that furniture moved way out here." I could hear my voice raising too many decibels. "What was I thinking? I knew you'd gift it all to some Joe Schmo. Nothing means anything to—"

"Oh, those old things?" Fran bustled in with two mugs. "Margene went on and on about how much she loved that dining set. And Vi, well you know how she gets about matching upholstery."

I cried uncle like always, dropped the subject, took the hot coffee from Fran even though something cold would've been better. She drank coffee all day all night in all weather. We each took a folding chair. Fran moved hers farther away from mine, checked to judge the distance, then moved farther, which tweaked me. No one can chip off a chunk of your soul without saying a word like your mother.

"Fran, I don't want you to worry about Matthew. I shouldn't have said anything."

"I'm not worried."

"In the car," I said. "Well, you seemed so sad, especially about, well, years ago. I—"

She sipped her hot brew. "Can you believe Margene? Still trying to foist Jefferson Davis off on you?"

"Fran, really, I—"

"You know, all Margene's other little presidents paired up. Like any of those slowpokes woulda been mistaken for presidents. Anyway, everyone except Jefferson Davis," Fran said.

"Okay, Fran. Whatever."

I counted to five in my head.

"Yep," she went on. "James Madison, John Adams—"

"Don't tell me Teddy Roosevelt found a willing bride?"

"Got the prettiest one," Fran said.

"Bully, bully."

Fran's laugh made my ears feel good.

"All of 'em live on the Cox's turkey farm. Place is huge, like one of those cult compounds. You can't fathom how many thousands of birds they've got now." Fran shook her head in wonder. "Anyway, Margene's the only one doesn't know Jefferson Davis isn't playing for the home team. If you know what I mean."

"Jefferson Davis? Gay? Here on the Fifty-Three? Poor bastard."

"Margene thinks he can't find the right woman." Fran laughed louder. "I told her Richard Simmons never did either. That woman thinks the South rose again so whatcha gonna do?"

For a few glorious minutes I reveled in Fran's company. How light and lovely it felt to be with my mom, to drink coffee, gossip and giggle, without our painful history to encumber us. I wished it could last forever. I knew I should grill her some more about Willy Wally, Doc Bates and that creepy Billy Dale, but didn't.

"Hey, I almost forgot." I pulled my phone out of my pocket. "I can't get any signal up at my house. Haven't checked my messages since I arrived."

"Won't here either."

"What? You're kidding."

"Nope. No cell service out here," Fran said. "Don't even think about the interwebz either."

I stood up, held my phone out while I walked around the house. Hoped changing spots would get me a signal.

"Give it up, Dee. Nada, nyet." Fran drank more coffee. "This is the highway not the fancy pants wine country you're used to."

"Shit. No cell, no internet? Now what?"

"You'll live. We've all managed." Fran set her Folgers down to pick at her cuticle. "If you drive up to the turnoff to Kearny, you'll get cell service. At least that's what Vi says."

"That's ten miles away."

"More coffee?"

"No. Guess I'm going to the turnoff. Last thing I wanted to do." I schlepped the short distance toward the door, stopped at the kitchen sink, nodded toward the house next door through the window. I'd seen pictures of third world country huts that looked better. Fran planted herself next to me but didn't speak. We stared at the abandoned house next door.

"I half expect Edith to come over angling for a dinner invite," I said.

Fran embraced herself with both arms, tight.

"Window's still broken," I said.

"Nobody around to fix it now."

I pointed at the empty pen in Edith's yard. The eight-foot tall chain-link fence enclosure still stood, ghosts of tragedies past its only occupants. "She never did get new dogs."

"No. She never did."

1985

CHAPTER FOUR

"What're your dogs' names?" I said.

"You and You Too," Edith said.

"Funny."

I laughed even though Edith's dogs scared the bejesus out of me. I didn't normally have a reason to talk to our next-door neighbor with the mean-as-crap looking animals. Didn't have one now—just a creeping curiosity that bit and hung on like a snapping turtle. Like most teenagers, grownups didn't interest me as a rule.

The skin-stinging heat on the highway already beat down and it was only early May. You could hear it in a near constant buzz. I'd been out about two minutes but my long hair already stuck to my neck in a stringy chokehold. Not hot enough to keep me from watching the Yous in their pen though, fangs bared, slobbering, churning up clouds of dirt. Edith shoved her sausage fingers through the chain-link pen to touch their fur as the Yous swirled by pawing and nipping each other.

"How come you're not scared of 'em?" I said.

"They're my babies."

Edith's voice didn't fit—whispery sweet as Cool Whip. I expected a booming foghorn, like the evil nemesis in a comic book, since Edith Smalls was the fattest, butt-ugly woman I'd seen in all my sixteen years. Mrs. Potato Head brought to life.

"What kind are they?" I asked.

"Pit bulls," she said.

"You ever let 'em out?"

I'd seen her in with them plenty but never out. I watched, wary. No lock on their cage just a U-shaped latch that rattled in warning whenever the dogs butted the gate.

"Oh, no. Can't take the chance. They only like the ladies. Not sure how they know the difference, but darn if they don't. Oh, they'll yap a little, butt their heads against ya, but they don't mean it. You can pet 'em if ya wanna."

"Oh, okay." I stepped forward but wasn't excited about it. "I—"

On cue the dogs bounded up on the pen with their lips stretched. Both spewed globs of spit and meat. Their fleshy bits of lunch spotted Edith's haggard housedress. I stepped back again, but quick.

"See there? They was smilin' at ya," she said.

She patted their mud colored flat heads the best she could. No way she could squeeze a whole ham shank-sized hand through the links. I inched close enough to see her bluish-green eye, swollen cheek. A few months back she sported a cast on one arm. If Edith bought those dogs to keep her from harm, I couldn't see they helped. The fwap of a screen door made us both jump. Well, I jumped. Edith jerked. Her considerable girth kept her grounded.

"If it ain't the Princess next door."

Edith's husband Smalls swaggered over, easy as you please, doused in sweat and booze. Whatever first name he'd been blessed with no one remembered so everybody called him by his last name, even Edith. The Yous rammed the pen, crazed. Edith gnawed her bottom lip, crammed as many fingers as she could through the pen to calm her babies.

"Delilah's just wonderin' about my puppies." Edith looked at me, not her husband, eyes wide like she'd been goosed.

"Princess Deeelilah," Smalls said his voice squeaky and high, mocking me. "Ain't you neighborly all of a sudden? Most times you're too good to talk to us. You and yer highfalutin ma." He kept a respectable distance from the yowling dogs. Too bad Edith didn't keep the Yous in the house.

"Her ma's a nice lady," Edith said, emboldened with the Yous behind her chomping at the pen, enraged.

"My ma doesn't want me talking to trash like you."

I looked Smalls up and down, not a long trip, his name suited. Not much taller than my five-feet nothing he looked more grasshopper than man with his inverted triangle head, stringy combover, bulging eyes. Hard to fathom he held such power over his wife who could crack his skull like a walnut with her thighs if she were so inclined.

Inspired by my smartass, Smalls Spiderman'd up the eight-foot walls of the pen, screeching. You and You Too shot up and down like bullets ricocheted under their paws. Drool flew. Their agitated growls turned frenzied, shrill, their vampire teeth snagged on the metal links. A tornado of dirt filled the cage. Their cocky prey stayed safe, out of reach, swinging hand over hand around the outside of their pen with acrobatic precision.

I had to hand it to Edith. She hadn't moved a lard-covered muscle. I crept back a hair more. With one last yodel Smalls let go midswing sailing through the air with the greatest of ease. He hit the ground, rolled the way they tell you to do if you've caught fire, then popped upright, agile as a Flying Wallenda.

Squealing rubber scrunching over rock announced my mother's assault on the perimeter. She piloted her hulking station wagon like the Queen Mary, churning along the dirt driveway beside our house, ramming to a stop just shy of the fence.

"What the devil—" she pushed the paneled car door shut with her butt, purse on her forearm.

"It's just Smalls acting the fool," I said.

"I told you to stay away—"

"Hey, Fran, been to town?" Edith hollered over without a care, like she didn't know she'd married a dickhead.

"Yeah, took Blanche for groceries." Fran's voice turned melted sugar. "I was going to ask you if you needed anything but then, she, Delilah—you know how teenagers can be."

"Me?" I said. "Oh, right. Saint Fran would never forget to come to the aid of her unfortunate neighbor if it weren't for her dunderheaded daughter?"

"Hush," Fran said.

Edith lumbered over. Fran yanked the station wagon's rear door open, pulled grocery bags out. I automatically scooted into position so she could hand them off. Smalls stood stock still where he'd landed, sneering. The Yous quieted.

"You sure do a lot for Blanche. She couldn't get along without you," Edith said.

"Oh, I don't mind. They've only got the one car and Earl's always got it so I do what I can. You know me, do unto others as—"

"You remember beer?"

I hadn't heard Hank, Fran's second husband, come up behind me. His voice erupted deep and slow like it worked its way up through a volcano. He threw a long shadow. Fran heaved a clanking bag at Hank's chest, pissed he'd cut her off mid-gloat.

"Take it," Fran said.

Edith stared down at her men's loafers, slit at the sides for more room, mum.

"Did you fix that leaky faucet?" Fran said. One way to get rid of Hank was to bring up one of the many jobs he neglected. "That old plastic tub under it's overflowing."

"I emptied it," I said.

"Did you put it back?" Fran stuffed another bag in my arms. "The grass underneath gets flooded if you don't, mostly washed away now."

"Doc Bates came by looking for you," Hank said.

He kept on toward the backyard with his beer, kicked the dripping spigot on his way by. No way he'd do chores instead of malinger in his shed where his buddies gathered to drink free Coors and belch out kneeslappers like, "I had a girlfriend like that once," or "Pull my finger."

When Hank plodded out of sight Fran and Edith convened out of my hearing, heads together. Something in the air shifted. I felt like an intruder not party to my mother and Edith's private discourse. I trotted toward the house with as many bags of groceries as I could.

Smalls vanished.

****

A slim curl of smoke floated up from the skillet. I plopped a knob of butter onto the black cast iron, stepped away while it spit and hissed, a vipers' nest of foaming ooze. I loved the rich perfume of butter pooling on a hot surface like popcorn at the movies but without those pesky kernels of air-filled corn.

A survivalist, I'd learned to cook. Getting an edible meal on the table fell outside Fran's scope of accomplishments. Plus, she didn't much like it. I watched old cooking show reruns on TV— that Galloping guy who drank a lot and the hunchbacked old lady who looked like a man and sounded like she just sat on a pair of tongs. "If butter makes you nervous use cream," she'd warble.

I learned how to get a crunchy crust on a piece of chicken without burning or drying it out and how to scramble the perfect eggs—light pale meringue-like curds, damp, not dry. I pulled out all the stops.

"Goddammit Fran, if I wanted any cheap shit out of you, I'd unscrew your head and dip it out with a cup," Hank said.

I dragged a pork chop through seasoned flour, fantasized about leaving the Fifty-three.

"Hank," Fran said. "All I said was—"

"Do I look like I give a rat's ass what you said?"

Another good thing about cooking, it served as at least a minor distraction—elevator music of sorts—during the fights. I turned my chops, studied their breaded beauty without a glance into the living room. No need for visuals with the audio.

"Hank," Fran's voice slipped into an almost whisper.

I opened the refrigerator door to get some milk for my gravy. They didn't notice me. If they did neither missed a beat.

"I'm sorry," Fran said. "You're drinking so much. So much more than you used—"

Hank slammed his recliner into its upright position.

"Maybe you need to stop looking," he said.

I turned in time to see him lick two of his nicotine-stained fingers then smear them over her glasses to blur the lenses. She squeezed her eyes shut, rubbed her hands together in her lap.

"I'm going to bed," Hank said. Fran kept her head down. "Anybody in there?" he thumped her on the forehead, hard. Her head jolted back. Fran kept silent, her tight lips turned lilac colored. "Nope, nobody home." Hank spun a half turn on the carpet, weaved to their bedroom like the drunk he was.

I bit the inside of my cheek, turned the flame down under the perfectly cooked pork, so I wouldn't see my mother with that look on her face anymore. The one that made the inside of my mouth taste like aspirin and kicked my stomach into a high burn.

"Just you and me for dinner again," she said like nothing happened.

Fran pulled off her glasses, scrubbed them with the bottom of her "This is Your Brain on Drugs" sweatshirt with a puff-painted fried egg on it then fingered her reddened forehead. I could think of nothing to say of any consequence so I cranked up the heat under my unfinished dinner. Fran fluffed her mussed hair, planted herself in front of the kitchen window.

I rescued Hank's unfinished beer from the end table to toss the remainder in with the chops. It fizzled up, a malty sauna. I'd seen those TV chefs throw in various kinds of wine. Once I'd seen a stew made with lager, which I found out later was just a fancy name for beer. So I figured Hank's Coors would do. Fran peered out the window while I wondered how to tell when the alcohol burned off enough to get on with my gravy.

"Look at that prickass." She jutted her chin toward the Smalls's yard.

I poured milk over my culinary chaos, fidgeted with the flame so I could join Fran in her favorite pursuit—not minding her own business. Smalls lay prone on the lawn that resembled his scalp—balding with thin wisps covering it here and there.

"Worthless drunk," she said.

"It's contagious," I said. She didn't take the bait.

Edith hobbled out of the house. Smalls didn't budge. She swayed on her elephantine legs toward her darlings' pen with a plate of bloody something teetering in one plump hand. The Yous hopped up, ecstatic. Edith swung the gate open, slogged into the pen to the dogs' howling delight.

Fran lit her cigarette. "Thought she got those psychotic animals to keep Smalls in line. Now I think she got 'em because she just likes them. Why she bothered to get two, who can say?" She blew a perfect, smoky O. "But that's Edith. Picks dogs like doughnuts. Why take just one?"

"Maybe she's working up to it," I said.

"Working up to what? More doughnuts?"

"No, the dogs. Still too scared to let 'em loose on Smalls. For now." I considered my recent interaction with the happy couple. "Smalls won't let on he's scared of the Yous so he won't make her get rid of them. One of these days Edith'll catch on. A flip of that latch, at the right time, Smalls is the dogs' dinner."

Roused as if he heard me, Smalls made a running vault up onto the outside of the pen, a repeat of his earlier feat, while Edith caressed the Yous inside. He hit the chain-link so hard she lost her balance. An achievement, considering she had to outweigh him by a hundred pounds at least.

Jack Sprat could eat no fat, but he could kick the shit out of his wife. The plate of raw meat fell. The dogs raged, bypassed the food, desperate to get a piece of Smalls soaring by. In their frenzy the Yous knocked the already wobbling Edith to the ground, scrambled over her mountainous form and whirled dirt in her face. Smalls kept swinging across the cage—hand over hand like Tarzan's chimp through the jungle.

Fran sucked in deep drags, watched the spectacle outside.

"Only a moron would put up with a man like that," she said.

A silvery Mercedes rolled by, slowed like it'd stop, drove on a few feet then backed up. With a quick glance over her shoulder toward her closed bedroom door Fran hustled out.

"Stay here. It's nothing." The screen slapped behind her.

My pan-fried mess bubbled. I dropped a lid on it to watch Doc Bates struggle to get his gut out of his car. Fran closed the gate behind her, met Doc before he got to it. Smalls dropped from the pen to ogle the good doctor's wheels. Any car not on blocks signaled success on the highway, but a Mercedes trumpeted unheard of riches. Edith struggled to her feet, brushed grit out of her greasy hair. She abandoned the Yous to their dinner to stand near our fence to stare at Doc Bates and Fran. Bored, Smalls spit in his wife's direction then trooped into the house. Edith stayed.

I couldn't see behind Doc's car but Fran no more than walked around it when Doc got back in. In three steps she stood on our side of the gate again while Doc cruised off. I busied myself in front of my now overcooked chops swimming in boozy milk. No clue what I'd just witnessed. Looked underhanded or something like that, though.

"Well, let's eat." Fran pranced in clapped her hands together. Before I could say "soup's on" she'd disappeared into her bedroom. By the time I'd put the chops in their serving dish she waited at the dining table that took up half the living area.

"I'm starved," she said.

I plunked the dirty skillet into the sink. Edith still loitered at the fence, studied our house like she expected God to come out.

CHAPTER FIVE

"Don't worry about it. I'll let you have mine," Fran said into the phone. "When I come get you for Hazel's memorial, I'll bring it with me. No, better yet, I'll have Delilah bring it up this afternoon. No, no, I never use it. Well yes, but that was unusual."

I'd left the door to my bedroom open, turned the volume down on my new cassette—the better to snoop. After Fran said goodbye in that gooey, fake, distracted, I-was-only-listening-to-myself way, I heard her plonking around the cupboards for the rotisserie.

"Delilah, run up to Blanche's for me." Fran hollered from the kitchen.

"Whatever," I hollered back.

I wanted to go, but why make it easy on her? I leaned back against my wicker headboard, arms behind my head like Cleopatra on her barge, yawned, unmoving. Wynona and Naomi Judd gave a little love in the background.

"What are you waiting for?" Fran poked her head in. "A gilded invitation?"

I gave in, swanned out past her. "Keys?"

She pointed toward the kitchen where the keys hung on a hook by the door, sacrificial rotisserie under one arm. I yanked it from her, hard, so she'd know she'd pissed me off but good.

"Why don't you just tell her to back a truck up to the front door?" I said. "Oh, wait, Earl's always got the truck. You'd have to give her one of those too."

"It's my rotisserie. I'll give it to Blanche if I want."

"You know, I use that rotisserie," I said. "In fact, I was the one who used it last."

Fran's Helen Keller impression was spot on.

"Never mind." I huffed out.

Fran followed me. "Don't dawdle—"

I lifted the latch to our chain-link gate with an elbow, slogged to Fran's wagon like I'd been summoned to the electric chair. My performance got coldcocked when Smalls fell out his front door on all fours with a dull grunt. The Yous started up where they'd left off.

"If he doesn't beat all," I said. "It's only ten a.m."

I shifted the rotisserie to the other hand to open the passenger side door. Smalls crawled in the dirt, a long rope of drooly snot swung side to side from his chin.

"Don't look," Fran said. "It'll only encourage him."

That did it. I looked.

Smalls rocked on hands and knees, tried to gain momentum to move ahead. One grimy arm came up off the ground. He froze mid-crawl then collapsed like a pinpricked inflatable doll. Something didn't seem right. Jesus, had he died?

"I think something's off," I said.

"You list everything off with Smalls we'll be here all day. Now scoot." Fran yelled over at the Yous, "Shut up you fool dogs." They did, then sat on their haunches like waiting for their next command.

Edith had heaved herself outside. "Oh my. What in tarnation. Fran—"

"Edith, I'll be over in a minute."

"What can you do about him?" I said. "Maybe you should call an ambulance or something."

"Probably nothing. You know it takes at least an hour to get an ambulance out here. Besides, nothing's wrong with that jackass anyway. No cure for stupid. Now go," Fran said.

Edith waddled closer to the fence. "Fran, do—"

"Be there in a sec, Edith." Ice cream wouldn't melt in Fran's mouth. "Delilah, do I have to take that damn rotisserie myself?" All of a sudden, she sounded a lot less friendly.

My curiosity didn't trump my yen to drive unchaperoned or to see Emily to tell her about the latest act in the circus of my life. I dropped the rotisserie on the passenger seat, slipped the key in the ignition while Fran and Edith conferenced over the maybe dead Smalls. Their foreheads almost touched. Their lips moved fast. Fran looked my way like she was about to yell something at me, her mouth opened.

The roar of the engine drowned her out.

****

Free at last. Free at last. Thank God Almighty, I'm free at last.

I sped along the barren highway toward Emily's, windows rolled down, radio blasting a little ditty 'bout Jack and Diane, two American kids doin' the best they can. I'd gotten good at one-handed steering while I dug around under the driver's seat for my hidden pack of stolen Marlboro Lights from Fran's stash. She never knew the difference, not like she counted. I pushed the car lighter in, rapped the pack against the dashboard, pulled one out by the filter with my teeth—a pro. Oh yeah, life goes on. Long after the thrill of livin' is gone. I bopped my head up and down to the beat.

The car lighter popped out, I held the cigarette between my lips, pressed the smoldering end to its tip, sucked my cheeks in and out like I'd seen Fran and Hank do. I settled back, took a deep drag, arm hung out to get scorched by the already burning sun. Between hits on my smoke I smiled to myself. Delilah Diamond— the coolest breeze to blow through Bumfuck since, well, maybe ever.

Out of nowhere another vehicle zoomed up on my side like it intended to pass. But instead it stayed with me neck and neck.

Shit. Fuck. Shit.

Hank.

His old silver GMC pickup truck kept pace, his view of me across the truck seat unobstructed. He motioned for me to pull over.

Busted.

I pulled over but puffed away on my cigarette in a feeble attempt to retain my rebel posturing. Who was I kidding? The jig was up. Hank got out of the truck cab one long leg at a time. I blew wobbly smoke rings, plumbed the depths of my courage to keep from bawling.

How long did it take to walk from the truck to the car for Chrissake?

I died a thousand times, but still took another long leisurely drag, fingers shaking so much I could barely hit the mark. I felt faint. Hank hunkered down in front of the passenger door, reached in through the open window with one endless arm to turn off the radio.

"Afternoon."

"Afternoon," I squeaked, pretty much the opposite of badass.

"Think you forgot something."

Then I saw it in his hand—the plug end of the rotisserie cord.

Holy mother. In my fervor to get away I must've slammed the cord in the car door and dragged it down the highway.

I blurted, "No way."

"Way," he said.

Hank opened the passenger door to free it up and slammed it shut again, walked around the car at a glacier pace, opened my door. In over my head, I took one last hit off my cigarette, dropped it in the dirt in front of his size thirteen Timberlands, got out of the car then ground it out with my size five Nikes.

Do. Not. Cry.

He dug out my hidden pack of Marlboros from under the seat like he'd known all along, hurled them across the highway deep into the sagebrush, then reached into his shirt pocket for a nearly new pack of Camels no-filters. He handed me one, put the rest under my driver's seat.

Silenced, I watched him fish out his lighter, flick the roller. He held the flame out. For lack of something smarter to do I put the no-filter Camel to my lips, brushed it against Hank's waiting blaze, took a deep breath. The filter-less tar and nicotine hit my lungs like a blowtorch. I felt engulfed in flames. Tried like the devil not to cough, but couldn't pull it off. The inside of my nose and ears burned. I choked, gagged, thought the top of my head might blow off.

"If you're gonna smoke have the balls to do it like a man."

Desperate to draw in breath I croaked out, "I'm not a man."

"You're goddamned right you're not."

In no hurry at all he walked back to his truck, reached into the bed, held up a long, flattened rattler's corpse.

"Watch out for snakes," he said. "It's the season."

CHAPTER SIX

"Willy Wally called," Emily said first thing.

"What did he want?" I dropped the rotisserie on their kitchen counter.

Emily didn't even glance at Fran's latest offering. We traipsed to her bedroom. The trailer squeaked and moved with every step as if it was about to give way at any precarious second.

"He wants to go bowling in town." Emily stretched out on the floor, hair fanned out over the orange and yellow shag carpet squares. She reached far under her bed. "Smoke?"

"Just put one out." My mouth tasted like an old ashtray. Chest still burned. "Bowling? Weird. You like him?" I dropped onto the bed.

"He's okay."

I picked at a string on Emily's quilted bedspread.

She arranged her smoking paraphernalia on the floor in front of her. "He's pretty cute, don't you think?"

"For a dumb jock, yeah."

"Dork City name though. How his parents came up with that humdinger. His sisters all got such pretty names—Grace, Faith, Charity." Emily stopped to light a half-smoked cigarette. "If I date him, I won't call him Willy Wally. Too embarrassing."

"You can't change his name just because you don't like it," I said with too much force.

"Calm down. I wouldn't change it exactly. I'd use Will, or William, maybe."

"Yeah, that's better, I guess."

"Hey," Emily sat up. "What's up? You're making a weird face."

"It's not his name you know."

"What isn't?"

"William. It's Willy Wally, not short for anything."

Emily's laugh made me want to pinch her.

"That's even worse," she said.

"Don't blame the messenger."

"Are you all right?" Emily climbed up on the bed next to me. "You don't like him still, do—?"

"No," I said. "Never did, really. Not a lot. Besides, that was, like, a million years ago, right after we moved here. He wouldn't give me the time of day."

I looked down at my disappointing chest, then at Emily's more promising one.

"Well, I'll tell him no." Emily flopped onto her back. "I couldn't care less."

"Don't turn him down on my account."

"School's almost out for the summer. I'll think about it. Might get bored enough to give him a whirl."

I intended to tell her about my run-in with Hank and the soap opera I'd abandoned at my house. Emily loved hearing about Fran's escapades. We usually enjoyed hours of entertainment at my mother's expense.

I didn't feel like telling her anymore.

****

"Oh, for heaven's sake," Blanche picked the rotisserie up off the counter, put it down again after a two second examination. "I didn't mean for Fran to give me the fool thing. Just said I thought it probably came in handy."

"Does it matter?" I said.

My gossip session with Emily ran out of steam after the Willy Wally thing so we made our way to the front room.

"I know she means well—"

A horn honked out front.

"It's Dad," Emily said.

Blanche yanked her suede-fringed bag off the back of the kitchen chair. "Gotta run into town." She stopped. "Don't tell your mom. She offered to take me again. Told her I didn't need anything." The trailer door flapped closed behind her.

"Are you going to Hazel Davis's memorial tomorrow?" Emily trudged down the narrow hallway lugging the rotisserie.

"Fran said so." I followed.

"My mom too." Emily stopped in front of the hall closet door. "Poor Hazel. Guess the cancer finally got her."

"You didn't hear?"

"Hear what?"

"She fell off the combine. Ran her over. Fran said the blades sliced her like a pepperoni pizza with extra sauce."

"Now that's how you die on the Fifty-Three," Emily said. "Well, Hazel told my mom she hoped she didn't die of cancer."

"What luck then."

Emily swung the door open wide. The cramped space bulged with Tupperware, plates, bowls, casserole dishes, and clothes—all booty from Fran.

"One more for the crazy closet."

CHAPTER SEVEN

"These things sure bring out a crowd," I said.

"Freaks," Emily said.

I looked out across Vi's Place through the smoky congestion at those gathered to remember Hazel Davis or to get a free meal. The buffet tables lay in ruins, an explosion of dirty plates, tattered napkins, half empty beer glasses, Corning Ware crusted with burnt Velveeta, crockpots slicked with congealed chili beans.

"Wanna see what I got outside?" Jefferson Davis had somehow made his way over to us, a pair of scrawny legs wearing a giant Stetson and a platter-sized silver belt buckle awarded from a-ropin' or a-ridin' competition. "It's alive."

"Speaking of freaks," I said.

"Whatcha got little man?" Emily said, nicer than me. She tipped his hat up by the brim, exposed his freckles and buckteeth.

Jefferson Davis was a few years behind us in school, an uncrossable divide in adolescence. We were cool. He was not.

"I got me a—"

"Boy," Arthur Cox's back-of-the-house voice made its way to its target. "I'ma open up a can a whoopass on you right here in front of God and all these good folks. Leave them gals alone. Help Thomas Jefferson with 'em kegs. Margene," he yelled to his out-of-sight wife. "Keep a leash on this kid."

Face pink as a radish Jefferson Davis pushed his way back toward wherever he'd come from before his dad could get out the can opener.

"Vi, I brought you a present." Fran said. She, Blanche, Emily and I had taken stools in front of the bar. "These were my dad's, a deck of cards from World War II. Look, every card has Betty White on it—in the nude."

"Looks younger but you can tell it's her all right." Vi peered down her nose, cigarillo slung from the corner of her chapped lips. "I can't take these, Fran. They belonged to your father. Might be worth some money. Wouldn't be fittin'."

"Course it would. I don't want those old cards," Fran said a little louder, with an edge. "Dust collectors if you ask me. The guys down here'd get a kick out of them."

"Hank'd probably get a kick out 'em," Vi said.

I didn't dare look at Emily or we'd laugh our asses off.

At the end of the bar, Hank struggled to keep upright, using the pool table to steady himself. Emily's dad, Earl, pushed him up every time he slid downward. Only thing Hank got a kick out of came out of a bottle. He and Earl had squatted at Nellie's all day, warming up for the mourning.

"You don't want to hurt my feelings, do you?" Fran pushed the deck toward Vi.

"Don't make her drop her halo to twist your arm," I said.

Fran rewarded my contribution to the debate with a stiff poke. Vi scooped up the cards, stuffed them under the bar. Emily sucked the last of her Sprite through a straw with a loud slurp.

"Doc Bates." Blanche jerked her head toward the front where the good doctor regaled the widow Winston with what looked like some sort of interpretive dance. "Ever since Angela died he's on the prowl."

"He's fairly young," Vi pulled another beer for Blanche. "Reckon it's hard, Angela only in her thirties, dyin' like that. Gotta raise Wanda alone."

"If he's lookin' to add pigs to the raisin' he's on the right track with ole lady Winston." Blanche gulped her Coors, wiped the back of her hand across her foam moustache. "Who knew a woman Angela's age could have a stroke?" She reached for her cigarette case.

Fran shook her last Marlboro out of its packaging. "You know Angela took to drink. That and her weight." Fran crinkled up the empty pack. "Nearly fat as Edith. Recipe for a stroke if you ask me."

"It's good of you Fran to make sure Doc's got groceries and all," Viola said with a politician's skill, steering the conversation to more complimentary waters. "Hank said you run errands for him."

"Well, you know me—do unto others. I don't mind." Fran puffed up like a blowfish. "I do what I can to help out. That Wanda is worthless and Doc Bates is awfully busy with—"

"What with all the dieters on the highway," I said.

"Delilah, you know Doc's practice is down in LA," Fran said with a tone that implied everyone down in LA smoked crack and swapped wives.

"Look who crawled outta the woodwork," Blanche said.

We all followed her eyes toward the door.

"Smalls and Edith," Fran said. "Eyesores."

A very-much-alive Smalls crossed the threshold looking much more alert than when I'd seen him last, toppled over in his yard. Edith hoisted up the rear. Smalls zipped in on the balls of his feet, stopped quick, parked in front of Fran with a creepy leer. She shrank back like a demon hit with holy water. Smalls stood his ground several seconds, then moved on.

"What was that about?" Blanche said, then lit her cigarette with the still smoking butt of the last one.

"Who knows?" Fran said.

****

"Earl, you know what the doctor said." Blanche crumpled the paper tablecloth she'd yanked off one of the buffet tables. "Take it easy on the booze and the Camels. You're smoking like a house on fire."

Earl's face shone red as barn siding. "I've only had—"

"Enough is what you've had." Blanche smashed the trash down with both hands.

Fran gathered dirty paper dishes. "Hank, help me with this folding table."

"Goddamn women." Hank leaned on his pool cue. "Give us another round, Vi."

"Hank, please." Fran's arms hung like dead weight at her sides.

"If I wanted any cheap shit out of you, I'd unscrew your head. . ."

Hank's favorite refrain got lost in translation. He steadied his cue against the pool table, took a few unsteady steps toward Vi.

Fran's mouth cut a rigid line through her face. "Hank, it's late, let's—"

He cuffed her on the back of the head on his way by.

Fran jutted forward, her glasses jumped.

I'd busied myself folding chairs, propped them like dominos. I heard someone take in a sharp breath. Probably me. I started toward Fran. Earl moved back. Blanche kept her eyes on the cracks in the floor.

"I won't have that in my bar," Vi said. "Take that shit home or I'll call Rusty to haul your ass outta here."

Fran straightened her glasses. Her bloodless lips folded into themselves. Before I could get to her, she walked out the door. Blanche held an arm out to keep me from following. "Leave her be honey." Blanche looked about to cry.

"Mind your knittin' Delilah." Hank bounced his empty beer mug on the bar top, his Frankenstein sized head rolled forward. Vi snatched the glass out of his way before he could land on it, face down.

"We'll see to him, Dee," Earl slurred. "Go on now, drive your mama home."

"Just leave his drunk ass alone. Let's clean up so we can go," Blanche said, hands on hips. "Where's Emily? She's supposed to help."

"I'll find her," I said. "And my mom."

The last I'd seen Emily she'd schlepped out the back door with potluck wreckage stuffed in Hefty sacks. I retraced what I thought were her steps. Night had settled in on the highway but the clearest, starry skies were a highpoint. I could easily make out the dumpster. The white propane tank that powered Vi's Place glowed like a beacon. I started toward it. A low murmur to the left needled the hairs on my neck. Like a cat tracking mice, I followed.

"Shh," I heard someone say then giggle. I sidled low to the ground to hide behind the tank.

"No one can hear," a male voice said. "They're drunk, or gone."

"I've been out here too long. I've got—"

I stepped around the corner about to say "Emily," when I darted back. Eyes adjusted to the darkness I recognized Willy Wally. When did he get here? I'd looked for him all day on the sly but never saw him. Did my best Agent 99, crouched, hidden by the side of Vi's Place and the propane tank. Willy Wally's shadowy form covered Emily's smaller one. Their kissing sounds made me feel sick, all the potluck I'd eaten wrestled with my intestines. I hunkered down for what felt like eternity.

"I gotta go," Emily said.

"I don't want to sneak around," Willy Wally said.

"Too bad."

"No one cares."

"Delilah cares. She went totally quiet when I told her you'd called."

"So?"

"She's my best friend in case you forgot."

Hearing my name made me nervous. Afraid I'd get caught I scooted in the other direction hunched over, toward the outhouse. I didn't realize I'd started to sweat till it dripped down my face. Once out of earshot, away from Romeo and Juliet, I straightened up. The stars blinkered, crickets chirped, like any other summer night only it wasn't.

I'd wiped my wet face, screwed up my courage to head back inside, when the outhouse door opened with a low creak, its rectangular bulk illuminated in the moonlight. I scooted back around the corner again in full spy mode. Fran stumbled out. I started to call to her, but the words snagged in the air.

Smalls jumped from the outhouse right behind her zipping up his pants, sprang past like a jackrabbit toward the highway, light as fog. Before I could move, or make any decision at all, the back door of the bar slammed behind Fran.

2005

CHAPTER EIGHT

I'd driven two or three miles before I realized Fran had outmaneuvered me. I'd told her everything (well almost). She told me nothing. "You don't need to tell everything you know," she always said. If I've learned anything from Fran, it's that. To say she keeps her cards close to the vest doesn't cut it. They're strapped to her like a suicide bomb. Try to pull one from the deck and she'll blow.

I knew she'd never tell me what she knew about Willy Wally's untimely death. Whatever I felt I needed to know about his shooting I'd have to find out through other means. Exactly what other means I didn't have a clue—almost impossible to nose around on the highway without Fran knowing. Thinking about Willy Wally made me squirmy so I pushed him out of my head. Getting crowded in there anyway.

Like a shark I surged along the Fifty-three toward the turn-off. The sun dipped downward. Passed a lot of nothing on the way to more nothing if you didn't count the alfalfa. Most farmers on the highway raised alfalfa. I'd heard some outlier was going with carrots, and one rebel planted apple trees, which alarmed the locals as anything new did. They wished them well then had a good laugh at their idiocy with a beer at Vi's. I rolled down my window to get a cleansing breath of one of the best smells on earth. Wet alfalfa. Nothing smelled more like summer and clean-living innocence than that. Row after row of sprinklers whirled with that unmistakable continuous hum and click.

Right that second if felt so good to be exactly where I was—home. Home before the whole thing went to shit.

Glanced down at my phone with one eye, but couldn't tell for sure if there were any bars indicating service. Didn't look like it. I slowed to veer into the turnoff, crunched to a stop. Hurrah! Service bars lit up my cell screen.

The weird, computerized voice inside my phone told me eleven new messages waited for me. I jabbed the appropriate key "Yeah … Matthew. . ." said a woman. I think. The message cut in and out. "Don't ignore me," a woman said, definitely a woman, probably Matthew's wife again. "Delilah, where are you?" Then, "Delilah … not the end … world … we," said my agent, Max. I hadn't talked to him since I got fired. Couldn't face him, disgraced as I was. He'd showed up at the door a few times before I moved, but I pretended I wasn't home. Then I left town. Curious, his voicemail made me wish my messages came across clearer. But not enough to do anything about it, like call him back from a land-line somewhere. Maybe he called to deliver good news? Had the pissed off father/network owner forgiven me? Could I get my show back?

Then I remembered the reality of my situation. Fran was right. I'd slept my way right out of my once-in-a-lifetime career. Before I could prop my hopes up, I deleted Max's message and every one after it without listening. I poked the phone off. No news was good news. I plunked my phone into the center console, flipped a U, rolled down the rest of my car windows then steered toward my new pig farm home.

CHAPTER NINE

Doc Bates's efforts to woo the widow Winston those many years before fell flat. She'd bailed, and the remaining family either died out or lost interest. Their barren farm now belonged to some preservationists down in LA whose ignorance-is-bliss idea of preservation involved doing nothing.

The guy I'd talked to on the phone said, "We don't care much what you do out there. Just let us know if you find a barefoot banded gecko or any kind of lizard you don't recognize."

Like I was a lizard expert.

"Feel like cleaning the place up we'll reimburse you for material costs and lower the rent. Makes no difference to us."

The last caretaker, who might've made a run for it in the middle of the night, left behind a smattering of furniture in the main house. Nothing to write home about, but it was clean, paint job fresh, wood floor blemished but buffed. Decent enough.

My appliances took up most of the kitchen floor space. I'd pinched Fran's old freezer a while back, before she could foist it on a protesting neighbor, but due to its unwieldy size the eighties era appliance ended up out on the screened back porch where its too-loud electric drone didn't disturb.

I scooted one of the four cases of wine my neighbors had given me as a goodbye gift across the porch floor, not sure where to store it. Like I wouldn't drink it all pronto. My generous winemaking neighbor's vineyard had abutted the carefully curated rose and herb gardens of my dream house. The one I didn't own anymore. Here, on this time forgotten pig farm, nothing abutted me but dirt, sagebrush, an endless number of rot smelling sties, the pig wrangler and farmhand cabins, and several big barns. No neighbors for miles. I'd gone from wine country to The Grapes of Wrath.

About to pop a cork on an award-winning Pinot, a big-ass truck roared in—from the sounds of it, the monster kind. The gravel road from the highway to the Winston place led around to the back-porch door, not the front, where dirty feet wouldn't encounter the living room first thing. Margene Cox busy-bodied her way over from the passenger side, scrawny cowboy hat wearing driver in tow, a whirligig of dust in their wake.

The dreaded drop-in.

"Merciful savior this place needs work." Margene buried her capable arms, wrist deep, into her doughy love handles. "Jefferson Davis'll set ya right. Don't look like it but this boy could tote a barge."

Margene stepped to one side to let her barge-toting boy take center stage. Jefferson Davis looked so different from the scrawny, lanky, freckled, Adam's apple almost as big as an actual apple boy he'd been twenty years before—I nearly gasped. He'd turned into a man, a clean living, good looking grown-up, which nonsensically surprised me. Though not usually a fan of the cowboy hat, his Stetson looked good on him, no more wobbling on a pinhead. Ah, but still shy. He stared at the toes of his Tony Lamas, yanked his hat off like his mama'd taught him. I could smell his musky sweaty nerves. He met my eyes with his, unflinching. That surprised me more than his, dare I say, handsome looks. His appearance plus steely gaze didn't match my memories of him, even close.

"What a surprise," was all I could think to say that wasn't rude or cougar-ish.

Margene twisted around taking it in. "'Bout passed by your turnoff then thought we'd pay a call. Gal way out here alone could be every which way but loose. Could be in a mighty bad way, and no one knowin' any better. Specially a citified one." She jerked a stubby thumb toward her son. "Jefferson Davis's yer man. Keep ya company, plus help ya put this dump back together. Nothin' he can't do with a hammer and nails."

Margene had been here less than five minutes and had already moved Jefferson Davis in. Good Christ. Good looks aside, that preposterous idea deserved a cutoff at the knees. Certainly he'd do it so I wouldn't have to. Wouldn't he? Jefferson Davis didn't have much to say way back when. Still didn't. Made sense, with a bulldozer, nonstop yakker for a mother. Before I could make up my mind what to say, Jefferson Davis spoke.

"Delilah. Been a long time," he said with quiet, detached, confidence. I couldn't say exactly in what way, but his sudden coolness discomforted me. "Thought you'd moved on for good."

"Well, I—"

"Never did get yourself a husband, did ya?" Margene said.

Plenty. Just not one of my own.

"Got a career instead." I should've shot her down with a withering rebuke but I'd always admired Margene's shoot-from-the-hip style.

"No babies then?"

"Nope."

"All my boys got hitched up," Margene said. "'Cept this one here." She jerked both her chins toward Jefferson Davis. "If he'd give chase, he might catch a gal if she moved slower than a herd of turtles, but even then, it'd be neck 'n' neck."

"Stop it," Jefferson Davis said. A vein popped up on his forehead.

"Never got a gal even at that fancy college he ran off to. Why, if this young'un even went on one date, the shock'd hightail me out the nearest window."

"Headfirst?" Jefferson Davis's bulging vein grew a twin.

"Just gal talk. Delilah knows I'm joshin' dontcha?" Before I could say no, Margene went on, "Why don't you give us a tour? Ain't been out here in a coon's age."

"Mom, she's got things to do. Let's—"

"She's on backcountry time now." Margene crowed. "No hurry. Right Dee?"

Great. Now I'd need to find time to fire up some dog shit on Margene's porch.

"No. No hurry, Margene. Haven't looked around much myself," I heard myself say, resigned to their company, and now more than a little curious about Jefferson Davis who might've grown a set. Gay? Doubtful.

We took a quick go round through the house. In the five minutes or less it took to show the place wall to wall Margene offered up homesewn curtains with a matching tablecloth, volunteered Jefferson Davis's services for cabinet refinishing, building repair, interior painting. Before she could get him to carry me over the threshold wearing her mother's wedding gown, I led them back outside.

I'd been on the highway a couple weeks but never thought to give the outer buildings more than a cursory look-see. The barns and sties went uninspected. We started through the first barn door held open by a chivalrous, but annoyed, Jefferson Davis. Margene followed close. My move forward got thwarted by Jefferson Davis's muscular forearm block to my chest.

"Shh. Hear that?"

In a faster-than-the-speed-of-sound move he pulled his boot-cut jean leg up, jerked out a small pistol from what I later surmised was his boot.

A slight rustle drifted up, then a sizzle. Jefferson Davis pivoted on his boot heels like a weathervane in the wind, gun poised. Under the straw on the ground, a ripple spread. Jefferson Davis fired. I let out a noise somewhere between a yelp and a scream. Margene, cool as an aging Bond girl, sauntered over where the noise'd come from then kicked at the straw.

"What the hell?" My heart thumped like an Ethiopian drum.

"Snakes." Margene held up the dead specimen.

"It's the season. They're after the mice," Jefferson Davis said. "You remember, Delilah. Lots of snakes on the Fifty-Three."

I licked my chalky lips. "Oh, um, yeah. I remember." Sweat pooled underneath my bra. "Let's go look at the sties then."

"Jefferson Davis, that there's the first order of business—gettin' rid of all them vermin. Where there's one there's more." Margene brooked no argument. Her quick-draw son put his gun back where it came from. Margene gave him the reptilian corpse, it's head nearly shot off. He slung it over one arm.

"Do you want to, ah, get rid of that?" I said after collecting myself.

"Nah, I'll take it home." Jefferson Davis held his snake-covered arm aloft. "Make a hat band or something." He looked pretty pleased. "Let's see whatcha got out here." We meandered toward the pigpens. Me still not sure what the hell just happened.

"These things look in pretty good shape up close. Not that I'm a pig expert. Except after they're dead," I said. The sties all still stood, a number of them, far as I could see. Feeders lined the fencing close to the ground.

"You could farm pigs, Delilah." Margene chuckled at her own joke.

"No woman's gonna farm pigs, Mom." Jefferson Davis, still sexist at least, shook the railing, headless rattler swinging to and fro. "These are sturdy, though. No doubt about it."

"How many pigs could they hold?" I leaned against the sty nearest me.

"More than you could handle."

Margene wiped the back of her neck with the hanky she kept at her waist. "What in tarnation would you do—"

"Charcuterie." I smiled without showing teeth.

"Charcootawhat?"

"French—for flesh cooked." Lording it over Margene was wasted, but I did it anyway.

"You're gonna fry up a mess o' pig flesh?" Margene made her scorn plain. "We call that pork chops."

"She's a chef, mom. It's a chef thing for Chrissake," Jefferson Davis said.

"It's a highbrow term for preserved meat products like sausage, bacon, salami," I said to no one who gave a shit.

"Oh, right. Them wieners, or whatever you're famous for charcootering."

"One of the things I'm famous for." I bragged like an insecure loser.

"I wouldn't need to fill all these sties. Could just get a few," I said.

She snapped her pudgy fingers. "Jefferson Davis can help with 'at too." She turned toward him. "Pigs, turkeys, what's the dif? Critters a critter. Don't matter which kind." She looked back at me, not interested in Jefferson Davis's input. "He'd be thrilled to do it. Ain't that right?"

"We'd need to come to terms. Compensation," Jefferson Davis said, all of a sudden a captain of industry. Since when did Jefferson Davis say things like compensation? That fancy college must've stuck.

"Barter later." Margene linked her arm through mine. "Everything's gonna work out fine and dandy."

Jefferson Davis had gone from mouse to the most interesting man in the world in the time I'd been away. Somewhere between getting out of his truck, shooting a snake between its eyes, and his disdain for Mommy seeping like an infected wound, my interest in him piqued. He might be a good source of information as well. It was the only explanation I could think of for my response.

"You know Margene, you're right," I said. "Jefferson Davis'll work out dandy."

****

After I managed to pry the Coxes loose, I headed home and drove to the turnoff, pulled over, pressed my cell on to listen to messages. Only two.

"...talk to you." Even with static I recognized my long-suffering agent's voice again. Give it up, dude.

Delete. Next.

"I know he's with you." Definitely a woman this time. "You lying cun—"

I stabbed the phone off, jumped out of the car. Always a believer in fresh starts I threw my phone as far as I could into the acres of juniper and sagebrush. "What you don't know won't hurt you," is what Fran would say. But what you do, might.

I purred back onto the highway, thought about how to compensate Jefferson Davis when I could barely compensate myself. He could help me make some improvements which would lower my rent…I'd figure out something. I'd have to. Manual labor wasn't my thing. Where could I get a Pigs for Dummies manual?

My hoity-toity German car sailed down the Fifty-three at a good clip. Engine so quiet I could hear myself breathe. For the first time I felt satisfied and sure of my decision to move back to the highway, my skin loosened, relaxed. Weirdly, my car's leather interior still smelled new, even though it wasn't. Was that a sign my new life back at home would work out for the best?

I'd heard home is where you go when no one else wants you. I laughed a little to myself at that. Then the memories rose like the iceberg that sank the Titanic. My relief was short lived.

Here's a newsflash. Home doesn't want you either. Especially if you know where the bodies are buried.

CHAPTER TEN

I heard Fran's heap before I saw it, the Impala's old motor sputtering, exhaust pipe dragging, tires spewed out rocks like artillery from a Gatlin. She stopped, shot out of the driver's side. In two shakes she stood in my living room, the tag of her sweatshirt peeked out at her collarbone.

"Fran, your shirt's on backwards," I said.

"I know. Front's dirty." Fran brushed off the front of her pants, licked her palms, ran them over her hair and face like she'd just crawled across the Sahara. "Christ on a cracker, you're out in the middle of nowhere. Hardly anybody remembers this dump is even out here."

"From your lips to God's ears," I said.

Fran and I faced each other three feet, and lifetimes, apart.

"So you're a pig farmer now?" Fran said.

"Wow. Didn't take long for that to spread. I plan to eat some, sell some. I need to make money, Fran. No job, remember?"

"How much money can you make selling a few pigs? I'm no finance wizard but even I can see that won't pay."

"Which is why I'm gonna ask Vi if she'd let me cook at the bar a few days a week."

Fran dropped her cigarette back in her bra to clap. "Really? That'd be wonderful."

"Think so?"

I hadn't seen Fran so happy since Hank died.

"Vi's too old for all that bar foolishness every day of the week. We can finally take the camper to Yosemite."

"We?"

"Sure. You know us old ladies. We stick together."

She followed me into the kitchen. "What's Jefferson Davis gonna do? Sing show tunes?"

News traveled at NASCAR speed on the highway. "Heavy lifting." I handed her a mug of coffee. "He knows more about livestock than I do."

"What's Doc gonna do?" Fran made herself comfortable at the tiny kitchen table.

"Doc Bates?" I stopped mid-sit down. "Why would he do anything?"

"He's out there with Jefferson Davis."

I rushed out to the porch. Sure enough, there they both were, out on the horizon but not too far away to see them scurrying around the barns in a flurry of activity.

I resisted the urge to barge over, demand an explanation. Fran knew too much of my business as it was. Then muscle memory kicked in. Fran probably knew more about it than me.

"Why isn't Doc in jail yet?" I said to Fran, who naturally followed me out, freshly lit smoke in hand.

"You haven't heard?"

"You know I haven't, or you wouldn't have made the drive."

"They found the smoking gun."

"Didn't know it was lost."

"Figure of speech for Chrissake. No such thing as a smoking deer."

I heaved myself up to sit on top of the freezer. "I'll bite. What smoking deer?"

"They found the deer carcass. Doc said he'd shot at the fool thing when Willy Wally managed to jump in front of the bullet, as morons will."

"You're kidding. How on earth? You didn't tell me that."

"Through and through—Willy Wally's neck to the deer. Wounded the deer but didn't kill it at first. Ran off, died later. Rusty found the damn thing. Who thought he'd actually go looking?" She took a theatrical drag off her Marlboro. "Must've been up there whacking off, found the thing by accident."

"Unbelievable." I stopped eyeing Jefferson Davis and Doc fiddling with whatever.

"Exactly like Doc said it happened all along," Fran said.

"I didn't know Doc said anything all along. You never mentioned—"

"Nosy parker Billy Dale can kiss our hairy—"

"Did Billy Dale tell you about this convenient find?" I said.

Fran was like Obi Wan when it came to intel, knew all and sundry. She inhaled and spoke at the same time. A real skill if you ask me.

"Nosy parker told Doc. I just happened to be there when—"

"Of course you were."

Fran flicked her cigarette to the porch floor, ground it out with her Ked.

"By all means, Fran. I don't mind you mashing your cigarettes on my porch at all."

"Listen miss, just be glad we're rid of Billy Dale."

"Doesn't matter to me one way or the other," I said.

"Does too or you wouldn't be back here on the highway, hiding." Fran crossed her arms over her chest. "I think you're the one who knows more than you're telling."

I twirled the ends of my hair like the day was halcyon.

"Damn thing's still loud as the dickens." Fran finally noticed her giant, noisy freezer I'd been sitting on for several minutes. "Probably needs another new motor, it's so old. Think Jesus owned it first."

"Can't hear it in the house from here."

"Dumb place to put it."

With that final pronouncement and a wave, she pushed through the screen door to leave. In bold, black lettering her back read "The Golden Years Suck" mucked up by a brown coffee stain.

1985

CHAPTER ELEVEN

I drove Fran home, my lips sealed. We left Hank face down on the bar to Earl and Blanche's generosity. Thought my floozy mother might notice I'd stopped talking to her, but she didn't, just stared out the window at the full moon, lovesick for her new boyfriend I supposed. The outhouse of all the sleazy places. Fitting, though, if I thought about it. Quite a ruse Fran had going, pretending to hate our nasty neighbor when she … I couldn't bear to think about it. For kicks, I drove off the road to see if she'd snap to. She didn't. Left me in the truck without a word after I parked in front of our house.

I'd stomped to bed, half expected her to inquire or comment. Nothing. Betrayal tasted sour as a slug of vinegar. I rolled over on my stomach, mashed my face into the pillowcase. Who'd have thought Fran could have any worse taste in men than Hank or my dad before him? Smalls beat all.

I turned over again, then again, like a dog trying to get comfortable. Visions of Emily and Willy Wally all over each other, my mother and slimy Smalls, competed in my head. Salted tears ran into my mouth and ears, made soft plop plop sounds on the pillowcase. I'd be glad to go to school so I didn't have to face Fran but then Willy Wally and Emily would be in my face, but in two weeks school would be done. No end in sight for either situation.

I'd needed to pee since we left Vi's Place, but didn't want to leave my room unless I knew Fran had gone to bed. No matter. My bladder didn't care. I crept out, door whined open, padded in bare feet to the bathroom. On my way back the sound of running water in the kitchen gave me pause. I looked in.

Fran stood at the sink, Marlboro clamped between her lips. The moonlight lit her through the window. She stared out toward the Smalls' house, white smoky clouds curling up around her face, a femme fatale in a "Keep on Trucking" t-shirt.

"Dee?" Fran said without turning around. "What are you doing?"

Trapped, I stopped.

"Going back to bed. Had to use the bathroom."

"Damn dogs finally quieted down."

Everything I wanted to say, to ask, stuck to the underside of my tongue, tamped down by shame. I knew I could never say anything about Smalls. If she didn't die of embarrassment, I might. In a few steps, I planted myself next to Fran.

"Don't you ever want to go back?" I said.

"Back where?"

"You know, the city."

Fran, roused out of her semi-trance, gave me her resting bitch face. "To that little apartment?"

"Yes."

"Heavens, no." She flicked ashes into the sink. "What for?"

"Our old life. Just me and you," I said. "No men around."

"It's better now. We're a family. I don't work so I can be home for you."

I gathered my loose pajama bottoms in tight fists at my thighs. "You think this is better for me? A drunk for a—"

"You won't understand until you're a grown woman with children of your own. A woman needs a husband. Children need fathers."

"Any man will do?"

Fran stabbed out her Marlboro on the bottom of the wet sink. "Hank loves us. He's here every day, which is more than you can say for your deadbeat father, who never looked back."

"Hank's here because he never has a job. It's not like—"

"He's got his retirement," Fran said.

"You can't possibly love him," I said.

"Good heavens, Delilah." Fran's cigarette rolled to the drain, then stalled. "Love shmove. A marriage based on love can't go the distance. Wish I'd have known that before I married your father."

"What on earth is your marriage to Hank based on then?"

"You don't know how lucky you are." She rinsed out the sink. "My father—" She squared her shoulders to look me in the eye. "Hank would never hit you."

"What about you? He hits—"

"I'll never forget," Fran's voice turned dreamy on a dime. "My brother John had just come home from the war. He stuck his gun right above Daddy's ear, told him if he ever hit any of us again, he'd kill him." She chuckled like she'd relayed a treasured memory of a family singalong. "It worked for a while. A luger's got a way of improving a man's disposition. Shame he didn't have a gun held to his head every day."

I didn't know what to say, so I didn't say anything. Minutes ticked by in the quiet.

"He wasn't all bad," Fran said. "He used to say I was the only one out of the ten of us kids who could mix his drink the way he liked it. I'd help Daddy out at the butcher shop after school, the only one of us girls he'd let work there. My sisters all got so jealous. On Fridays he'd stop at the tavern instead of going straight home. Daddy was so protective, never let me go into a bar, so I'd sit in the car and wait."

I started to point out the flaws in Fran's thinking but she went right on.

"In the winter—oh it's down-to-your-bones cold in the Midwest. He'd come out to the car, give me his coat so I wouldn't freeze. I'm sure I was his favorite even though he never said." Her eyes looked so dark and deep I thought I could see her soul. "Why, I was the only one who did what he wanted before he even asked. Soon as he crossed the threshold, I'd hand him his whiskey and the paper."

"Are you kidding me? He—"

"Look." Fran pointed outside.

"I know, I know, that stupid faucet's still leaking. We've got other things to—"

"Not that." She turned my face toward the sky by the chin, closing my mouth in the process. "The moon."

The bright white sphere loomed large in the sky, surrounded by twinkling stars.

"Remember what I told you? If you look hard you can see Mickey Mouse, upside down, on its face."

I strained to see, rotated my head sideways. Not sure I saw what Fran did, but I tried hard, harder than I'd ever tried to do anything before, desperate to share something silly and sweet with my mom. If I crooked my neck and squinted just right, I could make out one big ear and Mickey's gloved hand held aloft in silent homage. For a few seconds, peace settled on me. The heat from Fran's body warmed me. The last thing I wanted was to cry, but I started anyway. I reached for her arm to hold on as long as I could. Standing there on cracked linoleum, searching for a nonexistent mouse on the face of a beautiful moon, I let myself forget everything else and love her.

Earl's truck crunching across the dirt broke the spell.

Fran let out a breath so deep I thought it might be her last. She stared ahead at the Smalls' yard. Wet pooled under her thin lashes. My heart felt unattached, like it could drop to my belly. I wanted to turn away, or run. We could hear Earl fiddling with the gate, mumbling, Hank barking nonsensical words. Neither of us looked or moved. Fran crossed both arms across her chest, the skin across her knuckles bloodied and torn.

CHAPTER TWELVE

On the highway nothing screamed party like separating a bull from his balls.

Every year, summer kicked off with a swarm of locals raining down on Arthur and Margene's turkey farm carrying country hams, potato salads, chocolate sheet cakes, and clover rolls—the usual grub to go with the mountain oysters and various other cuts of fresh-butchered beef. Castration as a bonding exercise used to crack me up, today not so much. I'd even forgone the obligatory stroll around the action near the barns where I'd usually make faces and barfing noises. Truthfully, I didn't have to exert much effort into that ritual since the whole barbaric thing made me nauseous. I hadn't felt like going, or doing much of anything, since I found out about my mother and Smalls ... seeing the two of them, even in my head, filled me with ick.

When we arrived, I ignored Fran's orders to help carry the cupcakes and potato salad she'd bought at Safeway then emptied into Tupperware to pass them off as homemade. She'd expected me to make stuff, but I feigned illness till it was too late, which forced her to make an emergency run to Kearny. Hank had warmed up for the strenuous activities ahead by downing a shit-ton of beer before noon. Think I bailed out of the station wagon while it was still moving.

I marched a straight line to the picnic tables, vowed to stay away from them both all day. On the way, I made small talk with a couple of the little presidents, who cut me off to get back to the blood and gore, chatted with patronizing adults only when cornered, waved off a couple school friends. No Smalls sighting so far. He didn't usually make time in his wife-beating, dog-taunting, neighbor-seducing schedule to attend social events but who knew now?

Normally, Emily and I stayed together like Chang and Eng at these things, poking fun, running amok and giggling about boys. Not this time. I'd seen Emily only briefly before she raced back to the waiting arms of Willy Wally. I'd managed to finish out the school year faking my ass off with Emily. But she knew I knew so she wasn't putting up a good front anymore about that situation— one made worse because I was partly to blame. She'd given me the opportunity to fess up about my unrequited feelings for him. I declined. Who was I kidding? What would've been the use? He'd have welcomed my attentions like a poke to the eye.

So I filled a plate with barbecue and wandered toward the nearest shade tree, sat away from the pack, feeling quite sorry for myself, idly wondering why no one noticed my solitary pouting.

"Hey, I wanna show you something." Jefferson Davis crashed my pity party. "Lookie here." He cradled a pretty good-sized cardboard box in his spindly arms.

"Get lost, freak." I was in no mood for this hick. I didn't know who I wanted to notice me, other than Willy Wally, but it sure wasn't pesky Jefferson Davis.

"Aw come on, check this out, Delilah." He'd poked several holes in his mystery box, written his name in red ink on all sides. "Come on, just look fast. It's worth it."

So out of sorts, I gave in and peered over the box top Jefferson Davis had flipped open. I jumped back. The tiny snake inside slithered all over.

Jefferson Davis giggled like a girl. "Scaredy-cat. It's just a baby," he said, a goofy smile on his mug, the shit eating kind.

Arthur Cox stalked toward us. "Goddammit boy, I told you to keep that snake away from all them gals." He pulled his belt out of the loops on his pants as he walked. "Git on outta there."

Jefferson Davis slapped the top back on, took off like a cat sprung from a trap, his belt-swinging dad in hot pursuit.

****

After Jefferson Davis sprinted away with his baby snake, I loitered around the picnickers still at the picnic tables to pass time, attempted another halfhearted search for Emily with no results, when I noticed Fran and Doc Bates separate from the rest, thick as thieves. I snuck closer, eyes on the ground. Like an ostrich I thought maybe if I couldn't see them, they couldn't see me.

"Let me know if you need … " Doc Bates said.

Or I thought that's what he said. I couldn't hear them well so I took a few more steps forward.

"Oh, okay. I will," Fran said.

"Anything she needs." Doc patted her arm. "Nothing worse than—"

"Hey, where've you been?" Emily drowned Doc out, scared the crap outta me.

"Shh." I held a finger to my lips.

Too late—Fran and Doc spied us. Their chitchat ended. He bowed at the waist like Rhett Butler in the library at Twelve Oaks. "I'll see you next week. Grocery time," he said in parting. Fran gave us her phoniest smile, started our way but Margene saved the day by calling her over for blah, blah, blah, in the opposite direction.

"What's wrong?" Emily said. "You look weird."

What's wrong? Could I give her an earful or what? She didn't know a thing about Fran and Smalls's outhouse romp or that I'd seen her and Willy Wally's spit swapping session. I'd laid low since.

"Nothing," I said.

"Dee, come on. I know you're upset about Willy Wally and me. I really wasn't gonna go out with him. He's persistent. I—"

"How many times do I have to say it's fine?" I said.

"You just yelling that means it isn't fine at all."

"You see Smalls and Edith?" I said.

"What? Where'd that come from? No. You know they don't come to these things," Emily said. "Why?"

"Never mind."

We looked away from each other arms across our chests. We weren't used to not getting along. The last few weeks were the longest we'd spent apart since we met. I wondered where Willy Wally'd gone but didn't ask.

"Hank's hollering for your mom, stumbling around all over," Emily finally said. "Fell on his drunk ass near the branding irons. Almost caught fire."

We busted up laughing.

"All the alcohol in him—he'd blowtorch the shit outta this place," I said.

We laughed harder. I'd missed laughing with Emily. For a few seconds our relationship felt normal. Might as well forgive her now since I'd forgive her later anyway. "Let's hit up the desserts," I said. Swallowing my pride with a banana pudding chaser made the prospect more palatable.

"Fran, goddammit. Where are you?" Hank clomped around. "See? There he goes." Emily said. "Thought he might've given up by now."

"Francis, you better show yourself," Hank cut a swath through the crowd.

Fran scurried over in full cower.

My barbecue weaseled its way back up to the back of my tongue. Emily and I stayed put, waiting. Fran's mouth opened and shut like a fish looking for food at the top of the fishbowl, but no sound came out. Everyone stopped, quieted. Margene took a step toward my mother as if to protect her. Even Arthur stood at high alert ready to intervene if necessary. He'd had to last year. Felt like the whole world held its breath waiting for the inevitable rain down of insults and abuse. I gripped Emily's hand not sure what to do.

Hank shot out one hand to Fran—she flinched. We all flinched. "Dancin's about to get started. Let's show these leadfoots how it's done."

****

The barn closest to the Cox's house shone, spiffed up, fresh dirt packed hard on the ground. Dozens of chairs lined the rough walls already half-full of pooped, stuffed to the gills, partiers. One of the little presidents turned up his stereo. The windows of the house thrown open to better hear the music. Early yet, the sun still up but sliding. Some of the younger kids ran wild outside while their parents lingered to enjoy the cooler temperatures. Cutting started early so the day stretched long. Only the ones with stamina still intact made their way to the barn where the annual tribal ceremonies commenced with the dance.

Emily and I followed behind Fran and Hank expecting the worst. Fran walked like the guillotine waited. Every few steps she'd look up at him, eyes wide, trepidatious. No one knew what would happen, but we knew what could happen, what had happened in the past. Fran stopped at the entrance, skittish. Hank pulled her forward. I'd started to sweat in fight-or-flight mode.

We no more than crossed the threshold when Hank yanked his cap off, shoved it into his back pocket. Smoothed back his hair with Goliath sized hands, bobbed back and forth like he might pass out. He draped one big paw on Fran's waist, steadied himself. "Do me the honor?"

"Never seen Hank dancing drunk," I said to Emily louder than I wanted so she could hear me over the music. "Puking drunk, yes." Neither Fran nor Hank seemed like they heard.

"I don't know whether to laugh or cry," Emily said. "What in heaven's going on?"

"No idea. Whatever it is can't be good. Can it?"

Please God, let it be good.

Fran's arms stayed straight at her sides. I couldn't decide if the odd look on her face made me happy or sad. She hadn't uttered word one since Hank's invitation. "Now, come on Fran," Hank said, less slurred than I expected. "We gotta show these klutzes a thing or two."

Whatever Fran felt on the trek to the barn—dread, fear, both—melted. She smiled—small at first, then bigger. Her arm circled Hank's waist, then they hit the dance floor. I couldn't remember the last time I'd seen Fran so happy. Relieved, everyone let out a collective breath, kept time with the music, with bobbing heads, clapping hands or tapping toes, but no one joined them to dance. All in attendance knew the dicey situation could take a turn on a dime. But while everyone else wondered, Hank and Fran danced.

They looked magnificent, without a worry in the world, or a history of violence. Still gripping Emily's hand with all my might I wished this moment would never end. Hank used his hands to hold his wife close, not as weapons against her. In all the years they'd been together, I'd never seen them share affection. If I had it'd been long forgotten. Hypnotized, I watched Hank circle Fran around the barn, his eyes crinkled up at the corners.

I stood, riveted, while they twirled and dipped around the barn, in perfect time. They whirled passed me, laughing, and I saw Hank as he must've been before the better angels of his nature got their asses kicked by the darker ones. Before he became a man who could use a gun held to his head every day.

2005

CHAPTER THIRTEEN

"Fran told me Willy Wally's case is closed. Doc's cleared," I said to the peeping Billy Dale through my porch screen. A whiff of aftershave mashed up with dirt and old manure tickled my nose. Not necessarily in a bad way.

"Wrapping up some loose ends is all," Nosy parker said from the other side.

"How'd you know where to find me?"

If Fran told him I'd throttle her. Billy Dale skimmed the grounds hand over brow like a sailor in a crow's nest.

"Wasn't easy. No one here is exactly a fountain of information, but I managed." He craned his neck to try to see around me.

"Welcome to the Fifty-Three. They talk plenty to each other, more so behind your back, but never to outsiders with questionable intentions."

Billy Dale smiled like he had all day to talk through a screen, didn't budge.

"It's nice out here. Peaceful."

I'd just peeled garlic and screwed the cap off the chili flakes for a quick pasta dinner when his knock stopped me. I'd left the front door open to avoid any more blindsiding by gossipy uninvited neighbors like Margene, or worse, Fran.

"No point standing around all day out here." I opened the door wider. Billy Dale trailed me through the porch, then inside.

"Coke? Beer?" The highway must've already grown on me. I'd turned right neighborly.

"Oh, Coke is good. Thanks."

I handed him a can of Coke, sat on the small sofa. Billy Dale followed suit, popped the top with a crack. I jumped. Billy Dale dwarfed my living room. A man with a badge imposes. He must've gotten the hint his last visit, changed up his outfit choices accordingly. Nothing pink, not a pleat in sight. Still didn't blend. Even in jeans and a simple button down you could tell he listened to NPR and knew the names of obscure jazz musicians.

"I'm not interrupting anything am I?" he said.

I didn't bother to answer, wouldn't matter anyway. Billy Dale took a few leisurely sips.

"Must be tough out here in the middle of nowhere," he said.

"Why?"

"Well, after big city life."

"I didn't live in a big city," I said. "San Ysidro Valley, about three hours from here. Wine country." Why I blurted that out was anyone's guess. This guy flummoxed me.

"Before that you lived in New York, didn't you? Then Vegas?" He flung his head back, gulped Coke.

My hand went to my breastbone, an auto reflex. I could feel the thumping under it. Sneaky bastard checked me out. "Why does any of that interest you?"

He shrugged. "I'm a detective." He smashed the empty can in his hand. "Finding things out about people is what I do."

"Maybe I should sauté you with a little olive oil and garlic, or make a nice pâte out of you. Since I'm a chef and that's what I do."

Billy Dale laughed. "Actually, I did come here for a reason—not to impress you with my trivia."

"You don't say?"

I could feel my back gathering sweat. My cotton tee felt warm as a sweater all of a sudden. I wiped my wet palm on the nubby sofa cushion. The tinny rattle of the window mounted swamp cooler was the only evidence cool air blew in. It felt like at least a hundred degrees.

"Seems like folks around here have a lot of accidents," he said. "Fatal ones."

His tone implied he thought accidents meant anything but.

"Lots of drinkers around here," I said. "Every day someone doesn't die is an accident."

"I've heard."

"Guess somebody was a fountain of information," I said.

Billy Dale pursed and unpursed his lips, like kissing practice. He laid the smashed can on the coffee table, with the other he took his pad from out of his shirt pocket along with a short pencil, licked the tip. "In no particular order ... Willy Wally, Theodore Smalls, Hazel Davis, Hank—"

"If you're gonna read a running list you'll be here for days."

So Theodore was Smalls's first name. Huh. I never did know.

"That's ancient history," I said. "But it's weird you're bringing it up and weirder you're bringing it up here in my living room. Nothing but bad luck caused all those accidents, just like Willy Wally's."

"Says Rusty."

"You say different?"

"Like I said, wrapping up loose ends."

"Like I said, I haven't lived here for decades."

"I didn't realize you were here the day Willy Wally got killed."

"I didn't realize that was any of your business." Why I never felt the need to reel in my claws when the situation screamed for it, I didn't know. My contrary nature never served me well. "A week or so. Not sure you can count that as ... as anything."

"You see him? Talk to him? You know, before."

"No. We'd have nothing to say to each other. Not like I've got a lot in common with anyone around here anymore."

To my surprise nosy parker Billy Dale didn't comment. He returned his pencil and pad to their resting place, got up, hopefully to leave. "You've been gone a long time. You might have a different perspective on all things Fifty-Three now."

"I don't. Nothing changes here. Ever."

"I never did resolve your mother's chattiness with the deceased and Doctor Bates. All those phone calls the day he got killed. For recipes."

"Small town, people still trade recipes here."

Would the man ever go?

"Neighbors trading recipes, young couples in love, agreeable in-laws. This place is heaven on earth, perfect."

"There you go. Perfect."

"Except for the corpse with a bullet through his throat."

I decided to take the lead toward the door. I'd had enough of Billy Dale. He got the hint, took a few steps in the right direction then stopped, took out his pad, pencil and tongue for licking again.

"Emily." He looked up from the dreaded list. "Your friend, right? The one who dated Willy Wally in high school?"

"What about her?"

Jefferson Davis pulled up with a truckload of pigs aborting any further conversation. I rushed out to greet him leaving Billy Dale no option but to do the same.

"I don't know what you're gonna do with sixty pigs," Jefferson Davis said, truck door slammed behind him. "More coming tomorrow."

"Eat 'em," I said, admiring my snorting livestock, so cute at eight weeks.

"Can't eat that many." Jefferson Davis eyed the strange guy studying the pigs.

"No, but I'll make sausage, cure bacon. Sell some whole ones. They'll be gone before you know it. Vi's gonna buy a bunch for the bar. I'll cook them right up on the grill. If it goes well, we can think about more." I'd warmed up to being a pig farmer. Why not?

"You're working at Vi's?" Billy Dale said.

"Not yet, but soon. Three days a week. Not that my job is any of your concern either."

Billy Dale took out his infamous pad again, made a quick note, then introduced himself to an unmoved Jefferson Davis. He paced around the truck, slow, deliberate, unreadable, a suspicious Jefferson Davis close behind.

"Well, you're in the right spot for pig raising," Nosy parker said, unfazed by a pig delivery.

"I'll take 'em over to the pens." Jefferson Davis swung his truck door open. "What'd you say brought you out here?"

Billy Dale put his hands on both hips, gave Jefferson Davis the onceover. "I didn't. But if you're asking, I'm just—"

"Wrapping up loose ends," I said for him. If he repeated that one more time, I'd lose my shit.

"Right." Jefferson Davis didn't like Billy Dale. I could tell. Stranger danger. I'd seen that same face right before he shot the snake in my barn. "Last I looked loose ends don't grow out here."

"I'll keep that in mind."

Jefferson Davis nodded, lips parted like he wanted to say something else, but didn't. Instead he pulled off his work gloves, stuffed them into his back pocket. Billy Dale, the space invader, kept eye contact with my farmhand.

"Since you're here—" Jefferson Davis jumped into the driver's seat, left the door open. "Some asshole set fire to some dog shit on our porch. Coulda burnt down the house."

I petted my piglets. Noisy buggers.

Billy Dale looked like he was trying not to laugh. "Definitely a Rusty call."

"Right, the highway drunk. Thanks for the tip." Jefferson Davis slammed the door, stuck his head out the open window. "Good luck with your loose ends. Hope they don't hang you."

I waved the dust kicked up by Jefferson Davis's truck tires away from my face, ready to get rid of my unwanted guest to get back to my abandoned dinner.

"If I wasn't such a nice guy, I'd say Jefferson Davis just threatened me."

"If I wasn't such a nice girl, I'd say man up." On my way up my porch steps I said, "Don't let me keep you."

"Wonder why we never ran into each other before," Billy Dale said.

That stopped me.

"Why would we have?"

Billy Dale traipsed to this car, opened the door.

"I'm from San Ysidro too," he said. "Still live there."

CHAPTER FOURTEEN

After spending a few hours as the nails on the chalkboard of Jefferson Davis's nerves while he fussed with the pigs, I decided a reprieve was in order, so I left him to it. Convinced Fran outed my location to Billy Dale, I'd driven to her house to give her the what for, but she wasn't home. Figured I'd cruise over to Vi's Place to firm up my work schedule, then make another run at Fran's on my way back. Not a lot of daytime business during the week at Vi's, but enough to keep it open. Still too early for lunch, only two vehicles parked out front—one was Fran's Impala.

Once inside, eyes adjusted to the cave-like interior, I waved to Vi who I could see flipping a couple burgers on the grill in the back. I pulled myself up on a stool next to my mother, nodded to Margene who wielded a mop near the pool table in the back. In recent years Vi'd hired her to clean. However many times a week, or month, I didn't know. It wasn't enough. The stink never went away.

"Since when do you hang out at bars, Fran?" I said.

"Since I feel like it." Fran sipped coffee from a mug with her name painted on it.

"Bring your own mug?"

"Vi gave it to me, keeps it here."

"Well, you must be quite a customer to—"

"What are you doing here?" Fran pulled the cellophane off a new pack of Marlboros.

"Stopped by your house first. Came here to talk to Vi about my workdays." I leaned my head toward Vi, red-faced putting burgers together.

"My house?" Fran said. "What for?"

I gave her the rundown about Billy Dale's visit plus his list sotto voce so Margene's flapping ears wouldn't pick up any signal.

"How'd he know you're out at the Winston's old place?" Fran said. "Sure as hell wasn't me who told him. I wouldn't help Billy Dale across the street."

Before I could get her take on the list situation Vi plopped the saddest cheeseburger on the planet in front of Fran. The bun looked prehistoric, the meat like rubber, sliced cheese (I suspected Velveeta) not melted. Fran took a bite, chewed with gusto, while Vi did the same with the one she'd cooked for herself.

"Reckon ya'll heard the latest?" Margene leaned her mop against the bar.

"Doc's cleared," Vi said mouth full.

"No. The cheatin'." Margene leaned in.

That perked me up.

"Cheating? Who?" I said.

"Wanda." Margene leaned back like she expected some serious collateral damage from the bomb she just dropped.

"Wanda?" we three said at the same time, half eaten cheeseburger dropped out of Vi's mouth.

"You've lost it Margene," Fran said. "Wanda's coyote ugly. You ask me—"

"No one did," I said.

"Willy Wally stopped that bullet with his neck on purpose," Fran said, then resumed tackling her lunch.

"I swanee," Margene held up one palm in the Girl Scout salute. "Been seein' some guy over to town is what they're sayin'."

"If she was, Fran would've known," I said sure of myself. "Doc tells her everything."

"That's right," Fran said. "Doc doesn't shit if I don't know 'cause I buy the toilet paper."

"Who's doin' the sayin'?" Vi plucked the pickle off Fran's plate, popped it in her mouth whole.

"All my sons' gals say it's true," Margene said.

"Nope, can't picture it," Vi said end-of-story like.

Before I could pile on, Doc barreled in. We probably all looked guilty as sin.

I hadn't seen Doc close up in years. Like everything else from childhood, he seemed smaller than I remembered, but much the same. Shifty as ever. Despite his Jabba the Hutt shape and his surprisingly good head of McDreamy-ish hair flecked with silver, his demeanor rode the razor's edge of reptilian. His tiny pink tongue darted in and out of his tiny pink mouth when he licked his lips, which he did an Olympian number of times in the space of ten slithery steps from the front door to where we'd all gathered.

After the obligatory round of greetings and glad-to-see-you-back-home mini-convo he settled in on the stool next to me, beer in hand. Vi hustled back to the grill to incinerate the steak he ordered. Margene ditched her cleaning supplies then took her bad poker face on home. Fran and I let the small talk dwindle. I hoped he hadn't heard us yakking about his secret slut, homely daughter.

"Word is Wanda's got herself a fella," Fran said. "Two-timed Willy Wally."

Before I could fall off the stool both Fran and Doc burst out laughing like fools. Doc actually slapped a knee.

"Much as I hate to damper your jocularity," I said. "What's so funny about Wanda cheating on Willy Wally?"

Why I'd forgotten Fran's habit of blabbing out whatever came to mind, I didn't know. The only thing that should've surprised me was that I was still surprised.

Doc got a hold of himself. "I love my daughter more than life and she's got some wonderful qualities. Ambition isn't one of them—wouldn't make the effort. Plus, a looker she's not."

I waited for Fran to blurt out something with as a mud fence in it but she didn't.

"Maybe someone thought Wanda was beautiful on the inside," I said with fake generosity.

"That's what they say about ugly people," Fran said.

For a second, Doc looked pissy at Fran, as if he wanted to slap her down for the gone-too-far nasty comment about Wanda. Fran sipped her coffee with la-di-da smugness. He clenched and unclenched a fist then turned to me. "Nope, no clandestine rendezvous for Wanda. Only thing Wanda's lookin' for is whoever's stealing her husband."

We all nodded in unison. Even Margene saw the sense in what Doc said. Wanda's frequent trips to Kearny to hunt down her womanizer husband, and not to shake her moneymaker with someone with a fat fetish, we could buy.

"That SOB Willy Wally on the other hand—only time his eyes weren't wandering was when they were closed."

"Now that wouldn't surprise me. He was a man, wasn't he?" I got up to leave. "I wouldn't say that to anyone else if I were you, Doc. Sounds like motive and Billy Dale's still sniffing around."

Doc's smile pushed the fat up around his slitty eyes. "Noted."

I had to ask. "Who on earth would Willy Wally cheat—"

"Not homegrown. She's over to Kearny. One of those town women." Doc said town like Fran said down in LA.

Vi plopped Doc's charred steak and fries in front of him. "She got a name?"

"I'm sure she does, but I don't know it. Tried like the dickens to find out but never did."

I stopped at the door. "What makes you think you're right?"

"Nobody taught Willy Wally a damn thing about subtlety. Made a lot of trips to town to get this and that, came back with nothing. Some things you just know. Wanda cried many a night at my place over his affair. She knew it. I knew it." Doc sawed into his steak.

Fran snorted. "Please. You two could throw yourselves on the floor and miss. You didn't know crap all about anything."

That was weird. Fran and Doc getting all up in it with each other. Maybe some things did change.

"Doesn't matter now, I guess," I said before Fran could throw more insults.

"Not in the scheme of things," Doc said between bites. "I drove Wanda over to her aunt's place in Sun City. She could use the change of scenery and I could stand not looking at her sourpuss all day long, what with the crying and the grieving. Makes me nuts."

Especially if it's your fault I wanted to say.

Vi hustled toward me. "Here's your schedule for the rest of this month. Let me know if something doesn't work for you."

I'd forgotten all about the reason I'd come.

"Right. Well, I've got pigs to—"

"Before you take off," Doc said, mouth full. "Billy Dale's sniffing around you too, just so you know."

"Hardly." A muscle in my cheek flexed. "He was just at my place a few hours ago. Talking nonsense."

"Bastard just left my house right before I drove over here," Doc said. "Said he was just wrapping—"

"—up loose ends," I said. Christ on the cross, didn't Billy Dale know any other phrase?

"Seemed mighty interested in you," Doc said to me. "Asked if you had a beau."

"He did not," I said.

"Nosy parker dog wants a date?" Fran said.

Doc's brows and lips jumped toward his nose. Never occurred to him Billy Dale's interest in me might not be professional. Didn't to me either. Nope. Didn't ring true.

"Hope you told that jackass to keep to his side of the street," Vi said.

Doc laughed. "I think that particular jackass might be queer as a three-dollar bill."

"Why on earth would you think that?" I said.

A pink polo didn't make a man gay. Plus, he'd been wearing pretty nondescript clothes when he'd dropped in. What was it with the gay thing up here? These people needed to get with the times.

"No straight guy watches cooking shows." Doc hacked off another bite of steak. "He knew everything about yours. Means he's either a nancy pants or checking you out."

1985

CHAPTER FIFTEEN

Fran and Hank cooed like lovebirds so we'd left them to it. Already past midnight, Emily drove me home, but didn't stay. Said she'd need to go back to Vi's to drive her soused parents home. I knew her speedy departure had everything to do with Willy Wally but didn't press. I didn't want to upset our new balance. I wanted my friend more than I wanted Willy Wally. Or I'd decided to try to. Didn't want to ruin my barn dance high.

After Emily peeled out, and the Yous shut up, I turned off the water cooler and opened most of the windows in the house to let in the cool night air, a hot weather ritual. Got into bed all set to dream about a happy home. I'd almost drifted off when Hank's truck roared in, doors opened, slammed, jarred me fully awake. The Yous started up again, their yaps sharp, but didn't last long. Seeing the same old neighbors quieted them down.

"Hank, I don't know what Smalls told you but I—"

"Shut up, Fran."

My nerve endings felt fiery. Honeymoon was over—again. I bolted out of bed, raced to the kitchen window to better see, as well as hear, the fighting.

"Hank, I—"

"All over him … stink on shit … "

Hank's tumble into the metal trashcans, and the Yous loud, but quick protestations, cluttered up the last of his sentence.

"No, it wasn't like that."

"Smalls … 'xactly like that." Hank righted himself as much as a drunk could.

"Why on earth would he tell you, of all people, if that were true?"

"Didn't. Heard him brag."

I stumbled for the door, opened it to storm out to help my mother, but too chicken, I peeked out instead. The small porch bulb offered the only dim light in the dark. Hank's bulk blocked Fran's way out of the passenger side door. She must've lost the wrestling match over who'd drive. I could see her flailing, trying to get out around him.

"Goddamn whore, make a fool outta me," he said, his words slurred but clear, even over the Yous who barked more out of habit than alarm. They were used to domestic disturbances on all sides.

"Let me out, I'm gonna be sick." Fran tried to duck under his apelike arm. He jockeyed, kept her prisoner.

"If you're gonna slut around you better learn to hold your booze." He jerked away from the door. Fran tumbled out like dice on a craps table, hit the gravel on hands and knees. Hank made no move to break her fall. "Get up. Get your tramp ass in the house."

I wanted to go to her, but couldn't. I felt hobbled. My bare feet seared to the cracked tile floor. Fran retched, tried to pull herself up. Before she could Hank kicked her back down, knocked the glasses off her face. She stayed on all fours feeling the ground for them. Hank's boot, headed in Fran's direction again, spurred me on. I flew out the door, spine finally intact.

"Leave her alone," I heard myself spit out the words. "Don't. Please, don't."

"Mind your own goddamm—"

"Delilah, go back in," Fran said still on her knees.

I snatched her glasses off the dirt. Heard Hank open the gate latch but didn't turn my head. I wanted to get Fran on her feet. I helped her with her glasses, checked for wounds. Dirt covered her pant legs. I grabbed her hands. She snatched them back, her eyes darted back and forth fast. No lights on at Edith's house. Edith and Smalls apparently slept like the dead, thank god. All we'd need is Smalls out here to finish what he started. What he and Fran started. I checked to see if Hank had gone inside. He stood with his back to us, swaying, close to the patio table.

Fran took half a step toward the house when we heard it. The sound of Hank's drunken lead weight hitting the patio echoed loud, brutal. Bone and flesh smacked the concrete with a crack like a pool cue hitting the eight ball into the corner pocket.

The Yous howled at that.

Fran froze. Hank lay flat on his face. I started over when he shifted and got up on all fours, forehead and nose running blood. On hands and knees he crawled all over the patio, going nowhere, looking for nothing.

I led Fran forward. "Let's go in."

We limped to the kitchen door, leaving Hank to slobber and blabber.

"He can stay on his knees for once," Fran said pulling me along inside.

A sloppy splash, like a fat kid belly flopping in the pool, kept me from shutting the door behind us. Hank sprawled face down in that plastic tub, filled to overflowing from the leaking faucet, his big head displaced half the water. The cold didn't revive him. He lay still. Fran sighed but didn't move. We both did nothing. Hank's torso and legs stuck out behind him like a giant rag doll, the leak still dripping pellets onto the plastic edge of the tub. The dogs kept up their bawling.

"Goddammit, shut up," Fran hissed to the dogs. They shut up.

Only a few feet separated Hank's salvation and me.

An electric shock of pictures struck my brain. Hank's big hand holding up the rotisserie cord, lighting my smoke, his arms around Fran's waist. I started forward, then stopped when reality dashed my fantasies. Whatever leeway Hank had earned got the heave-ho when he kicked my mother into the dirt. But could I let him die? I started toward him again. Fran threw her arm in front of me, like she did when she slammed on the brakes when I rode in the passenger seat.

"Fran," I tried to push her arm. "He's drowning."

Fran went firm jawed. She pulled me to her, grip desperate, immovable. She turned us both so we faced the house, not Hank.

We stood together waiting. I wriggled but Fran held on with the strength of an army. With the iron hand that wasn't keeping me in place she pushed her bent glasses up her nose.

It dawned on me Hank would die, right here, right now. Another quick vision of Hank and Fran floating around the barn, looking love-struck, hit me again. He'd smiled the whole time. Was that already a world ago? I opened my mouth to breathe in deep. I felt faint.

"Fran, please," I said. "Please."

Feeling my anxiety, Fran ripped her glasses off, faced me. Her naked vulnerability held me in check. I'd given in, started crying. She didn't talk, just stared, silently pleading for me to let this go, make the easy way out possible. I tried to wipe my wet cheek by rubbing my face on my shoulder. But couldn't move my arms in her stranglehold.

I wondered how long it took to drown. Surely, he'd come to, save himself. Wouldn't he? Before another thought could wriggle its way through, Fran let me go with such force I stumbled. She marched over, grabbed Hank's nape, wrenched his face out of the tub. His head fell to the patio again, hard. He gave no sign that she'd saved him. Fran knelt down to hold her ear to his mouth. She stood upright, pushed his head with her foot, walked fast to the kitchen door where she pushed me in, turned off the porch light and clicked the door shut behind her.

"It's late. Get to bed. He'll sober up."

2005

CHAPTER SIXTEEN

"Jefferson Davis." I handed him a bottle of beer. "You've done way more than I pay you for. I'm starting to feel bad."

"Doubt it." He put his beer on the counter, finished wiping down the new kitchen cabinets he'd made and hung on the wall of my kitchen. "You don't strike me as the feeling bad type."

Mincing words wasn't Jefferson Davis's style. Not anymore.

"Well, you do live in that cute cottage here for free," I said.

"It's not that cute, or free. No such thing as free. More than one way to pay." He nodded at the handmade cupboards.

Jefferson Davis's contempt for me, and pretty much everyone else, intrigued. Made him a badass, fascinating. His unexpected intelligence disturbed me. I wondered what it meant. Like Siegfried and Roy's tiger, a lot went on under his surface. Exactly what I didn't know. Nor did anyone else as far as I could tell. Perhaps to our detriment. But he knew how to work, hard, which I needed.

"So we're making headway. Lots of projects done," I said. "Looks like you don't need Doc's help after all."

I'd been so distracted by Billy Dale's uninvited visit and the Wanda/Willy Wally saga I'd forgotten to needle Doc when I saw him at Vi's about why he'd been at my place without being asked or talking to me at all.

"Doc didn't come to help. Came to pass time. Told you that already," he said. "But I'm gonna put him to work. If he's bored, might as well get some free labor outta him. If that passes muster with you."

I noted the snide tone, like getting a root canal with no anesthetic was a more pleasant endeavor than answering any questions of mine. Guess he didn't recognize inane small talk. I don't know why I insisted on making conversation with a guy who didn't converse. But there I was, gabbing away. Not only was I not really the type to feel bad I didn't need to be liked either. Guess I wanted to peel the Jefferson Davis onion, at least a layer or two, for amusement if nothing else.

"You said you had hardware for these cabinets?" Jefferson Davis pushed two of the wine cases I'd never found a spot for farther along the wall. "Might find stuff if you'd unpack."

"Might." I pushed a box marked Kitchen Stuff toward him with my foot. "Think they're in this one." Jefferson Davis cut through the packing tape while I scooted another box alongside the first. "If not, they're in this one."

"I'd think you'd wanna get settled before you start at Vi's Place. That job plus fixing this dump up and the pigs'll keep you pretty occupied."

"That's why I hired you," I said.

He pulled out a newspaper wrapped something or other. "Light fixture?" He dug around again, unwrapped something else. "Another … light fixture? You rip these outta the ceilings or what?" The wires dangled out the bottoms.

"Never mind. Put those back in the box. We'll hang them later." I grabbed the scissors he'd put on the floor and opened the other box. "Here they are." I pulled out two handfuls of drawer pulls and cabinet knobs. Beautiful, cut, light pink glass knobs and vintage flour bin pulls.

"You rob a hardware store?" He pulled out some more fittings.

"No, I brought them with me." I laid my treasures on the floor. "From my house in the Valley."

"Thought you sold that place."

"You don't have to include everything in the sale, you know."

He held up a doorknob and a light switch cover. "Even these?"

"So what?"

"You stripped the place didn't you?"

"I wouldn't say stripped. It was mine after—"

"Foreclosed?"

My flushed face gave away the truth, my mouth didn't need to as well, so I ignored him to open a case of wine.

"I wondered why you already had all those fancy appliances and that doohickey I put in the bathroom." He stood up, leaned against the kitchen counter, sipped his beer in no hurry at all.

"That doohickey is a custom-made sink cabinet."

"Hit the skids, did you?"

I popped the cork on a bottle of wine as an answer. Unwrapped a wine glass but didn't bother to wash it out.

"Expensive wine for someone who's broke," he said.

"What do you know about wine?"

"What do you know about me, or what I know? We're not all hillbillies around here."

"Not that it matters, but this wine was a gift. From my neighbors. A very nice couple who wouldn't look twice at all the hillbillies up here."

He made a sound almost like a chuckle if I didn't know better, plus that wouldn't have fit his current expression. "Well, you must've been good at hiding your inner hillbilly."

I pouted a little, realizing I did want Jefferson Davis to like me. Of course. No one more attractive than the one who doesn't want you. I tossed that around in my head a few minutes in the sudden silence. So, of course, I said the perfect thing to put an end to our little tiff.

"You know everyone thinks you're gay."

He started it.

"Not everyone," Jefferson Davis said, like he covered this topic daily, without missing a beat. "My mother still keeps the faith."

I had to laugh even though I was still super irritated at his brazenness.

"Well, are you?" I said assuming he'd tell me to fuck off.

"Not yet. But the highway isn't a gay free zone. We're not that backward."

"As if. Who's gay on the Fifty-Three?"

"You wouldn't believe me if I told you. Besides, does it matter?"

Before I could say no but I want to know anyway he blurted, "Almost got married once."

Wow. One layer peeled and what a layer.

"Who was the lucky lady, or man?"

He tossed his empty beer can into an empty box.

"Wanda."

"Shut up."

Jefferson Davis made that chuckle sound again, but this time he actually smiled.

"Willy Wally's Wanda?" Like there was actually another Wanda.

"Well, if you say it like that."

"I don't believe you."

I had to sit for this so I eased down onto the hardwood floor on my ass balancing my glass and bottle of wine.

"Long, long, time ago."

"Your mother never mentioned it."

"My mother didn't know shit. No one did. Wanda and I went to the JC over in Kearny together."

I didn't know what shocked me more, Jefferson Davis and Wanda as a couple or Wanda as a college student, or Jefferson Davis admitting it. Before I could ask what happened to their romance, he said, "I went on to Cal State, she came back to the highway. Willy Wally took up where I left off."

Blimped up plain Wanda in polyester elastic waist pants and knockoff Birkenstocks came to mind. Talk about a bullet dodged.

"That was before," he said.

"Before she got fat?"

"Yep."

Seized by temporary Tourrete's I said, "And ugly?"

"From the front."

I filled my glass for the third time.

"Best I can say about it is I learned a lot."

"Like what?"

"Like how to live without her."

"That's something, I suppose." I drank.

"I never could beat out Willy Wally," he said.

"Didn't know you tried."

"He got my high school crush too."

Scrawny, freckled, dorky Jefferson Davis had a high school crush? Why did that seem so unlikely? I'd have guessed sheep were as close as he got to crushing, or dating, back then.

"Emily," he said.

That sobered me into silence. I traced the rim of my wineglass with one finger, shifted my weight from one haunch to the other, but didn't comment.

"I wasn't the only one with a high school crush who didn't know I was alive." Jefferson Davis eyed me close. Made me squirmy.

"What are you talking about?"

"You."

"Me?" I poured glass number four.

"You and Willy Wally. Everybody knew you had it for him bad."

"Hey ya'll, hope you're decent." Margene's barge-in cut off my protests.

Just about to say, "We're in the kitchen" when she appeared there. I had to admit I found comfort in Margene's presence, even when she annoyed me. She smelled like yeast and chocolate chip cookies straight from the oven.

"Great, it's you again," Jefferson Davis said. "How often you gonna drop by? I might as well've stayed on the turkey farm."

"Boy, you best find your manners," Margene said. "Don't think I—"

"Why don't you pull up a chair, Margene?" I said.

"Can't stay but a sec." She clapped her hands together. "Just stopped by to give you some good news."

"Your mole's changing?" Jefferson Davis said.

I elbowed him. He mumbled a gripe then polished cabinet hardware, his back to us.

"You had a visitor," Margene said.

That was the opposite of good news.

"Who? Where?" I said. "Had?"

"Well, she was at Vi's Place. You know we don't like strangers wanderin' the highway without an invite. Bad enough that Billy Dale nosed out folks about poor Willy Wally. Vi told her she didn't know where you were, you'd moved a long time ago. So she left."

"She?" That surprised me the most—she not he. "Did she have a name?"

"Lordy be, my mind's like a screen door." She tapped her forehead with a short finger. "Hardy. Something Hardy."

CHAPTER SEVENTEEN

I'd brushed off Margene's news of a mystery visitor. Said I didn't recognize the name, must be some sort of mix-up, not worth the gas to Vi's to check it out. Even though I doubted Margene bought my bad lie, she didn't push for once. No one disliked surprises more than me. No way I'd stroll in like the village idiot into a booby trap set by Matthew's wife, what's-her-name. I welcomed public scenes like a sledgehammer to the head.

Figures.

You want to get shit done, get a woman. I should've known if the Missus wanted to find me badly enough, she would. But she knew the worst. I could add nothing new. Plus, I'd lost. She'd emerged victorious so what else could she want?

I didn't dare look at Jefferson Davis who'd not only grown a backbone but bat-like radar for all things bullshit. Margene left wearing a definite something's up face. Jefferson Davis and I both carried on all day, business as usual, although there were a couple times I thought he'd press the visitor issue but didn't. I'd see him staring at me with a look that'd shave the hair off a coconut. I did my best to pretend I didn't notice. He finished my new cabinets, we both did pig stuff, then went to our respective residences on the farm.

I felt mildly comforted when Fran didn't show up. Till I remembered Fran never missed a trick. Had I gone brain dead in the time I'd been away? Of course, she knew all about the Missus Hardy's pop in. If Vi knew, Fran did too. Fran's absence raised my hackles. No reason under the sun why I hadn't heard a peep from my mother, rooting out details. No good reason anyway.

So when I heard a car pull up, then the knock at my front door, I assumed it'd be Fran. Except she always burst through the back porch and never in a million years would knock.

Jesus H. Christ.

Missus Hardy must've found her target. I peeked out the too-girly chintz curtains Margene had recently made and hung. Yessirree. The woman scorned found me and parked her S-Class Mercedes in front of my house, audacious bitch.

I knew I looked like I'd been yanked through a windsock. I smoothed my frizzed curls, pulled my t-shirt down to cover my stress-eating muffin top and wondered if I could lose a quick five pounds if I ran to the door. Resigned, I brushed the dust off my Levi's, then faced the music.

I yanked the door open. There she stood in an avalanche of glory. Smug, smiling like the wife who ate the mistress, oh so triumphant she'd run me down.

Well, she didn't get the absolute last laugh. Missus didn't look good. Dumpy came to mind.

Yoga pants at her weight? Girlfriend could've used a dye job too. Cover up that firebreak at her roots. Not a natural blonde, I surmised. Felt insulted she'd made no effort. Confident she was my better in every way, with or without those cankles, the Missus didn't feel the need to dress for the occasion. We gave each other a quick up and down, the way only women can. I knew she thought as many unflattering things about me.

Before we could sniff each other's assholes, I said, "What do you want?"

"You're hard to find," she said the obvious, in her private school, WASP, upper-east-side tone. "When you leave you do it right."

"Apparently not."

I remembered the humiliation when she showed up at my house during filming, ranting like a fishwife, the red-faced crew scattering like roaches, Matthew the wimp, cowering, denying, crying. Not long after, the terse phone call from my boss, her father. The restraining order served. The little money I'd saved lasted about six months. I was never as good at saving as spending. I lost everything after that.

I should've slammed the door in her flat face.

Shoulda, woulda, coulda.

Instead, I opened the door wider. "Well, don't stand out there all night."

She pushed past me, sat on the couch without an invite to take a seat. I watched her soak up her humble surroundings, all the while looking down her rich, snooty nose. Not the penthouse in NY Daddy bought her. Wench.

I stayed standing, alert. I waited for her to say something. She did the same. Minutes ticked along. I wanted to ask how she'd found me but, apparently, I'd been hiding in plain sight. I'd lost interest in the hows or whos. I felt sure that no one from my TV life ever knew I lived here on the Fifty-three. I'd never shared details. TV chefs, with the rare exceptions, weren't that kind of famous. The kind the public, or Google, showed a lot of interest in. Plus, I wasn't glam enough. Lookswise I'd say I was somewhere between Ina Garten and Giada De Laurentiis.

"Where is he?" Missus Hardy finally said, breaking my reverie.

"I haven't the faintest idea. Nor do I care."

She jumped up, roamed around the small house like a kid playing hide and seek. Before she could get any farther, I said, "You're wasting your time. He's not here. But by all means, lurk around all you'd like."

"If he's not here, then where?"

"Are you deaf? I said I don't know. You're the one who wanted to hang on to him. Guess you should do a better job of it."

She considered me. "I don't believe you."

"Makes no difference to me what you believe."

"I think you lie every chance you get. If something's happened to him, you—you're the reason."

"What makes you think something's happened to him?"

To my surprise she plopped down on the sofa and cried. With no intention of feeling anything but scorn for her, I felt sorry instead, a little at least. In the dim lamplight I realized my first pass over her appearance might've been harsh, wishful thinking. Her beauty was the offhand kind of those born into the right family, right neighborhood, and the right class. My opinion on her leggings didn't get more magnanimous, at any rate. She could afford to be casual about pretty much everything. But she'd learned the hard way she couldn't afford to be so casual about her man.

I let her cry while I stared. I wondered if Matthew had ever wiped tears off her cheeks, brushed her long hair away from her face to get a better look, or kissed the spot on her throat that she currently, idly, covered with one manicured hand. The thought of those small intimacies rebroke the bone.

"I don't even know your name," I lied. I knew more about her than I'd ever admit. It's what stalkers do—find out shit.

"Penelope," she said to her lap.

Naturally. When I'd first heard her posh name I'd laughed and laughed. Until I cried. I'd always known I didn't stand a chance against a Penelope.

"Matthew's been gone for weeks," she said, gathering herself. "I have no idea where else to look if he isn't here. But I'm not convinced he isn't around here somewhere and you know where."

"He's a big boy. He's not lost." I sat next to her. "If you can't find him it means he doesn't want to be found. He's left you I guess."

If I was gonna be mean, might as well put a shoulder to it.

"I talked to your neighbors about you," she said. "They told me a lot about you and your ways."

"What neighbors? What ways?" Like I didn't know.

"The vintners. Karen something or other. The one with the pilot husband."

Of course, she'd say vintners, all grand. "How would you have talked to her?"

"Eons ago. Before I knew for certain about you and Matthew." She dug a crumpled tissue out of her jacket pocket.

"I barely knew them. Neither would have known anything of interest to tell you."

She barked a bitter laugh. "You're a thief, for one. You stole cases of their most expensive wines. Flirted with her husband right in front of her. She knew you were doing him too."

"Philip? Good god. That lump? Brother."

"She saw Matthew going in and out at all hours too. You steal wine and men."

"They weren't close enough to have seen anything or anyone. Karen was pulling your chain." I stood up. "I'm sorry to disappoint you Penelope, but I can't help you find your husband. He's your problem."

She jumped to her feet. "I'm going to the police to report him missing. Expect a visit."

"Can't wait. Now get out."

She did.

1985

CHAPTER EIGHTEEN

After the annual BBQ at the Coxes and Hank's near drowning, I made up my mind to live and let live where Emily and Willy Wally were concerned. I'd try to be happy for her, or at least try to not be outwardly pissed and jealous. I needed my friend back. So much happened that I needed to share. Luckily, Fran found some doodad not nailed down to give Blanche so I volunteered to drive it over. Emily and I sat cross-legged on the floor of her bedroom, Madonna assuring us of her virginity on the stereo.

I told her everything.

"I can't believe it," Emily said. "Your mother and Smalls? Gag me with a spoon."

"Tell me about it."

After a few seconds of digesting this disturbing information, Emily's face fell. "They looked so sweet at the dance. Your mom and Hank."

Just as my eyes started to well up Emily said, "She really tried to kill Hank? That's, like, attempted murder, isn't it?"

"No. Not exactly." Worry pricked me. Did I tell Emily too much? "She just didn't want to save him. Can you blame her?" Then in a rush I said, "She did though—of course. She couldn't hurt him, much less let him drown. You know that, right?"

****

You don't often hear sirens on the highway.

I didn't think to turn the radio on in the car, preoccupied with my talk with Emily. The one cut short by Willy Wally's phone call. I'd felt relieved to dish with my best friend like the old days until his interruption, which she allowed by taking the call. I realized my understanding of the Willy Wally/Emily situation wasn't as generous as I thought. Emily didn't steal my boyfriend, per se. But, still. Then there was her on-the-money comment about Fran's stunt with Hank. I knew what it was, or almost was, but hearing murder jolted me. Still a stretch to call it that, I soothed myself. Besides, he still lived.

The sirens' wails howling in through the open car windows cut short my mulling and piqued my interest. My eyes shifted to the review mirror—nothing behind me. The high-pitched screeching roared louder, then stopped. I kept driving. Lucky enough, both sides of the road were mine for the taking. I took my half out of the middle, kept vigil as far as I could see, but didn't notice anything out of the ordinary. No car wrecks, or fire, or even smoke to indicate a fire, none of the usual tragedies that brought anything with a siren to the highway.

When I turned off the highway onto the short street that led home, I saw them—fire truck, ambulance, sheriff's car, and a couple handfuls of people—a lot considering not many lived near.

Something must've happened to Edith. Smalls finally got her.

Or Fran. Maybe Hank remembered she'd almost let him die.

I slammed on the brakes, careened to a stop in the middle of the road and leapt out. The small crowd tittered. Men I didn't recognize in various uniforms darted in, out, and between the more familiar faces of the neighbors, moving at lightning speed. Most neighbors had one, or both, hands covering their mouths. They'd come to see the fuss but looked sorry they'd made the effort.

I pushed closer, elbowed through the crowd. Arthur Cox stood straight, soldier-like, next to a pit-bull carcass, shotgun in hand, a second dog not far from the first. The Yous lay dead, a few gory feet apart—their heads nearly blown off, pulpy masses of bone and something else glutinous, gummy. The yard a fury of blood, flesh, and clumps of—Jesus, clumps of what? Scalp? A dirty wrinkled finger, ripped from its hand, pointed skyward from the dirt, tendons trailing. Meaty carnage lay strewn across the sparse dead grass, smeared red, the human indistinguishable from the canine. Pungent air settled around me like an executioner's hood. I felt smothered. Breathing didn't come easy.

Edith heaved and sobbed over her headless dogs. She pushed Rusty away, shaking her giant head—he motioned to the paramedics who shut the ambulance doors. I knew Smalls lay in the back of that ambulance—at least one finger short. No budging Edith if she didn't want to move.

My eyes finally found Fran, parked by the chain-link fence looking just like she did when I left for Emily's, wearing her "Takin' Care of Business" t-shirt.

Relieved she looked all in one piece, I said, "What happened?"

"Who knows?" Fran yelled over the departing sirens. "Only caught the ending."

"How? This mess is practically on our doorstep." Not quite, but close enough. "Edith finally let the dogs out," I decided.

That finger. I closed my eyes but couldn't unsee it.

"Smalls is most likely dead," Fran said like she just bought canned peas, two for one. Not that her tone meant anything. A devastated Fran usually acted like a delighted Fran.

"She finally got up the nerve to let out the Yous," I said. "'Bout time."

Then I remembered. Fran and Smalls. Lovers. The memory made me almost as sick as looking at the Smalls' battlefield of a yard. I stared at my mother's face, looking for I didn't know what. Heartbreak? Sorrow? Even horror. Nothing. A blank, colorless slate. Then I saw her eyes, hidden a little behind her glasses. If I didn't know better, I'd have thought she'd been crying. I looked closer. She turned away.

"Edith was up the road at her sister's. The prickass went in," she said not looking at me. "At least that's what Arthur Cox said. The door latched behind him is what it looked like to him."

"That'd be almost impossible."

"Almost, but not quite, apparently."

True.

The heavy metal U-latch could fall into place if hit right. Smalls shimmying up the outside of the pen was one thing, but going in? He didn't seem keen to do that, but who knew what a drunk like Smalls would do? He could've fallen in from the top mid-monkey imitation. I'd bet on that one.

"Maybe he accidentally wandered in on his way to a Mensa meeting," Fran said with a surprising lack of bite. Like she felt she needed to fling her usual insults but ran out of oomph. She lit a Marlboro with a tremor so slight only someone like me, looking for signs, would detect it. Held the flame at its tip too long, pulled at the bottom of her t-shirt.

There it was—a flicker of something unpleasant, painful, flickered across her face. I saw it. Quick as it came, it was gone. Obviously still crushing over her now-probably-expired traitor boyfriend.

Before I could investigate Fran's true emotional state further, Arthur ambled over, shotgun lobbed over his shoulder, flecks of god-knows-what splattered on his legs and shirt. "That mighta been the nastiest piece of business I ever seen. A fluke I passed by. Hank left his wire cutters up at the house after the barbecue. Margene sent me to deliver 'em."

"So you saw it?" I wanted details.

"Yep," Arthur hung his head. "Heard it too. Lord as my witness, the hearin' was worse than the seein'. Won't forget it long as I draw breath. A man torn limb from limb by dogs." He spit out a black stream of Copenhagen. "That's something you never want to witness. Oh lord, the screamin'. I jumped outta the truck with my gun. Smalls and the dogs were inside that pen. Couldn't tell where Smalls started and the dogs ended, all a tangle."

Fran picked at her cuticles, smoke suspended at the edge of her lips.

"You went in?"

"Course. With my little friend." He held up his gun. "I flung the damn thing open fast as I knew how. Damned if them dogs didn't head out with Smalls between 'em. Didn't give a cracker's ass about me." Arthur stared over at the empty pen. "They wouldn't let go for love or money. Kept a yankin', tearin' and pullin' him. I'm hollerin' and kickin' at 'em but them animals kept right on. Shot quick as I could, lucky I didn't shoot Smalls."

"Lucky," Fran said with zero enthusiasm. She seemed to shrink the longer Arthur went on. I wondered if she'd break right here, in front of God and everybody.

"The whole mess was over before I could even call the ambulance," Arthur said. "Damned if that mean old coot's heart was still beatin' when they hauled him off. Said they didn't give him a frog's hair of a chance. Don't know who called Edith over from her sisters but there she is a-wailin' like a bear with his leg in a trap."

Her a-wailin' hit a crescendo in the background.

Rusty, doing his usual trying-not-to-let-on-he-was-drunk act, waved Arthur over. More locals pulled in. Word spread fast. A few ladies tried comforting Edith, who refused it. She yowled without ceasing, eyes heavenward.

"Show's over." Fran flicked ashes to the wind. "Let's go in."

"Hank's not home yet?" With all the commotion I'd just noticed his truck wasn't parked in its usual spot.

"Nope," Fran said.

"How'd you miss it?"

"Miss what?"

"Are you in shock or something?" Now she really seemed out of it. "Smalls and the dogs. From what Arthur said, you would've heard."

Fran shrugged, stepped on her cigarette.

"Fran," I said. "Arthur Cox heard it from his truck, with the engine running, driving by."

"Guess he's got superhuman hearing."

I persisted. "We can hear the dogs from inside our house even when they're not tearing up a human."

"Those damn dogs are always raging. Who notices anymore?" Fran dumped out the plastic tub under the leaking faucet. "Besides, looked to me nobody could've done a thing about it even if they heard. From what the paramedics said, Smalls fought the dogs and the dogs won."

"But still—"

"Why don't you cook up some chicken fried steak and gravy for Edith? You know how she loves that."

Fran smiled, a weird, creepy, I-need-medication-and-a-straitjacket kind of smile. "They might've killed her dogs, but nothing kills her appetite. That woman can eat no matter who gets slaughtered in her yard."

CHAPTER NINETEEN

"Do you think your mom had something to do with it?" Emily said from her usual spot at the end of her bed.

"I don't know. She sure acted weird." I rolled over onto my back on the floor holding one of Emily's many crocheted, hand-made pillows tight to my chest. "Weirder."

The Fifty-three folk talked about nothing else. Dog mauling was a particularly vicious event, even for the highway. Edith had been hustled off to her sister's down the highway so at least I didn't have to hear her constant caterwauling. Not over her chew toy of a husband, but the Yous.

"Geez, first Hank, now Smalls." Emily looked smashing like usual—all that lush hair, perky boobs, jeans and t-shirt casually cool.

"Huh?"

"Well, Fran tried to drown Hank. Now she might've killed Smalls."

Why couldn't I keep my mouth shut? Laughing at Fran's usual escapades, eccentric and self-serving, was one thing. But criminal behavior was another. Fran was a wacko mother of the highest order but she was the only wacko mother I had. Come to think of it, Fran was all I had in the world. Sure, I rationed out bullshit in her direction on the daily, but wasn't that an unwritten rule in the Asshole Teenager Handbook? Fran didn't leave. My dad did. Hank would, in fact maybe soon, if he couldn't forgive Fran for her momentary loss of sanity. I'd never admit it to anyone, especially her, but I needed Fran. The end.

"I told you, she didn't try to drown Hank. He did it to him-self, she just wanted to teach him a lesson, that's all." I sat up. "Besides, she'd have never gone near the Yous. They were scary as fuck." As soon as I said that I remembered Edith saying they only liked the ladies. But you'd never know it as far as I was concerned. No way any lady with a brain would risk it. "And Smalls isn't dead. Yet."

Word was Smalls hung on like a trooper. In a coma, but hanging on by however many fingertips he had left.

"Maybe Hank somehow got him in there. He's the one with motive." Emily pulled out her smoke stash from under the bed.

Words like motive made me squirmy. How hard had Emily been thinking about this?

She went on, "I mean, you said he put the beat down pretty hard on Fran when he found out they were—"

"Don't say it." I couldn't stand to remember my mother and Smalls's liaison or her beat down. "Hank wasn't home, remember. He was at Vi's. Where else?"

"We're back to Fran then. She must've been so pissed at Smalls for blabbing about their—"

"Why is everyone forgetting Edith? Talk about motive. She could've lured him in there easier than anyone." I felt relieved to have suddenly thought of what should've been obvious to everyone.

Emily took a deep drag off her cigarette to mull that nug-get over. I could tell she hadn't thought of it either. She went on smoking several seconds. I kept quiet (better late than never). Emily blew a couple smoke rings then, "At her sister's. Isn't that what Arthur said? Edith wasn't home."

Shit. Right. "Yeah, I forgot."

"Besides she's had those dogs for at least a year. Doubt she'd ever get up the nerve to let 'em out." Emily flicked her ash into an empty tin can. "You know she was too scared of Smalls. She could've bought ten pit bulls and a twenty gauge. Wouldn't have mattered."

That made sense in its nonsensical way. We all knew Edith.

"Whatever happened to accident? I think he fell from the top doing his ape impression. It's the only rational explanation." My ire started up. Emily's accusations were getting on my nerves. I only had myself to blame. How I wished I could roll this partic- ular boulder back up the hill. I kept feeding the fire hoping she'd say something comforting that I hadn't thought of, that would settle things for the better in my mind. She did the opposite. "You know——"

"Hey," Willy Wally interrupted my desperate explanations. "Wassup?"

Emily leapt up from the bed. My heart about leapt from my chest. I wasn't sure what to do. Well, I should've left, but how to pull that off without feeling like the pimple on the ass of my own dignity, I didn't know. I couldn't help but stare while I thought over options. The only thing unattractive about Willy Wally was his name. He looked like what he was—captain of the football team, basketball team and voted Most Likely to Become a Movie Star in last year's yearbook.

Emily had flung her arms around his neck. I guess she forgot she was trying not to rub my nose in it. Thank god I didn't have to see her face. Sadly, I was witness to Willy Wally's face and his arms going around Emily's waist in a natural, sensual way. He pushed her long hair away to put his hands under it. Unwittingly mesmer- ized, I was just about to look away and get up to get the hell out, when Willy Wally mouthed over Emily's shoulder, "I'll call you." Then he puckered his lips at me in a silent kiss.

2005

CHAPTER TWENTY

It took Fran two days to come around asking about my unwanted visitor, which not only surprised me, but made me nervous as hell too. Fran not acting like Fran was cause for alarm, for any number of terrible reasons.

"I didn't send that woman up here,' she'd said as soon as she zoomed through the door. "I think she drove up and down the highway asking anyone breathing till someone gave it up."

"She didn't stay long," I said. "I didn't have what she wanted."

"Her husband, I suppose?" Fran didn't sit down. She watched my mouth with interest every time I spoke. Like I was in one of those campy karate movies where the audio dubbing didn't match the way the actor's lips moved.

"Good guess."

"Don't get sassy with me. I know you've done something foolish. I didn't want to know at first, tried to mind my own business—"

"Since when?"

"I'm old, Delilah. I don't need any more drama. I'm done with that."

"That's convenient. Could've fooled me. Why, I'll bet three years haven't gone by since—"

"Stop. I want peace and quiet for the rest of my days. But no, you keep—" She stopped.

"I keep what?"

"Never mind." She moved closer to me. "If you're in trouble, if you've gone and done something stupid, tell me now so we figure how to get your dumbass out of whatever man mess you've gotten yourself into again."

I took her by the shoulders. "Fran, I didn't do anything to Matthew. I honestly don't know where he is."

Her eyes never left mine. "You're sure?"

"I swear."

We stared at each other for what seemed like an hour. Finally, she turned toward the door. "I don't care what you say. You're hiding something. I gave you your chance, now I don't want to know anything about it."

"You should talk. You—" I said to the slamming screen door.

If I were hiding something no one would want to know more about it than Fran. Before I could dwell much more on the never-ending list of peculiarities embodied by my mother, or get back to my kitchen chores that she'd interrupted, Billy Dale came calling.

Fuck all.

Always a glutton for punishment, I let him in. He followed me to the kitchen but didn't sit down. I plugged in my 750-meat grinder. Picked up my cleaver like Billy Dale didn't exist.

I took a good whack at one of several hunks of meat. Billy Dale reached out to steady the cutting board I'd spread it out on. Still not talking.

Like he probably hoped, I folded.

"What are you doing here? For an open and shut case you sure spend a lot of time around the highway." I hacked harder for emphasis. "Doc's moved on. So should you."

"I got a visit from your ex-lover's wife. Penelope," he said, right out front.

I couldn't say I was surprised to hear.

"That makes two of us." My cleaver sliced through its target.

"You know her husband's missing?"

"So she says." I stuffed meaty hunks into the grinder. "I'll tell you what I told her. Don't care. He's not my problem anymore."

"No idea where he is? Where he'd go?"

"We fucked. Other than that, I know nothing about his habits."

He glanced around, unmoved by my crudeness.

"Go ahead, search the place. I assure you he's not hiding under the bed."

"When was the last time you saw him?"

"The day before he served me with a restraining order. If you need a date, look it up."

He'd taken his trusty pad out. Licked the tip of the pencil, then wrote whatever.

"Your neighbor, Karen, is it?"

"Karen, yes. And Philip? The Bonds." That almost made me laugh. The Bonds. Shaken not stirred. "What've they got to do with it?"

Penelope had already enlightened me on that score so I knew the answer, but what the hell?

"Penelope thought you were having an affair with Karen's husband as well as hers." He flipped through the pad. "And that you stole a few cases of expensive wine."

"Penelope's free to think what she likes."

"Karen denied saying any such thing, you might be surprised to know. Said you were the perfect neighbor."

I slammed my cleaver through a slab of bone and meat. Pulled a stuck chunk off the blade. "Of course she did, none of it's true, and I was a good neighbor. Minded my own business. Doesn't surprise me at all."

"She did say you had a boyfriend, though. Saw him."

"As you must already know, my show was filmed in my house. The entire crew was male."

He rifled through his stupid pad. "No, this was after your show got, um, cancelled." He cleared his throat like he felt embarrassed for me. "And well after you were served with the restraining order. Matthew make one more stop for old time's sake?"

"No. She's wrong."

"You sure you don't have any idea where Matthew is?"

"Absolutely." I brought the cleaver down hard. "Why is this an issue? He's a big boy. He can go where he pleases, can't he?"

"True, true," he said. "But if a guy goes out for a pack of smokes and doesn't come home, well, that's, uh fishy."

I stopped mid-cleave. "Really?"

"Not exactly, but you get it."

I went back to butchering.

"Nobody out there's got security cameras either. Odd, considering the wealth around that area, your TV show, local fame and all. At least it didn't look like you did. Or Karen."

"The Valley's not that kind of place. No need. You should know that, living there yourself."

"They're moving. Did you know that? House, vineyard, and winery all up for sale."

"Good luck to them. Those huge vineyards and wineries are hard to unload."

"Your place has new people living in it."

That gave me a pang. I had so loved that house.

"I'm not surprised. That vineyard was Philip's vanity project. I don't think they made any money. Karen probably got sick of it. I got the impression he lost interest and she bore the load of the place and didn't appreciate it."

"So you do know something about them."

"Never said I didn't. They were my neighbors."

Billy Dale wrote and wrote some more.

"Look," I said. "First you come out here 'wrapping up loose ends' on the Willy Wally case, which wasn't a real case anyway. Not around here. Now you're the missing persons department? I think I'm out of patience with you." I turned the grinder on. Hoping he'd leave. Too bad the professional grade grinders ran quiet.

"When I get a complaint, I've got to look into it."

"Consider it all looked into. Satisfied?"

"No, but time will tell."

I turned the grinder off. He tucked his pad and pencil back into his shirt pocket. For the first time since he'd arrived, I noticed his outfit. He'd given up on the city slicker duds and moved into a city slicker's idea of cowboy wear. Complete with cowboy boots. Dork.

"What are you doing, anyway?" Billy Dale watched me feed more meat into the tube.

"Making sausage." I pointed to the sausage stuffer at the other end of the counter.

"I thought those pigs were still too young to make anything out of them?"

"They are." I pushed more meat through, the ground up meat oozing back out onto the board I'd cut it up on. "Jefferson Davis brings me all kinds of livestock scraps from their place, Vi gives me some scraps, I throw in my own leftovers, whatever's around. I grind it up and make sausage to feed the pigs."

"Pretty spoiled pigs."

I laughed. "True that." I turned the grinder back on.

He watched me a few more minutes. "You're good at that, at all this." He gestured around the kitchen, arms wide. "Considering you don't have any formal training."

I felt my heart drop like a pig shot between the eyes. After a couple seconds or years, I turned the grinder off. "What are you talking about?"

"Well, you didn't really graduate from the Cordon Bleu."

CHAPTER TWENTY-ONE

B illy Dale nailed it. I'm not a formally trained chef. I'd lied for years about the Cordon Bleu. It's amazing no one ever bothered to check. Just took me at my word. Of course, I had to prove I could cook, and that I could do. I'm an artist. I learned at the feet of Julia Child on TV. Everything else I learned on the job. Much the same way a person learns to drive by grabbing the wheel from the passenger seat when the driver drops dead.

It didn't hurt that I blew the boss.

I fled the highway like a prison break and before you could say "Shawshank Redemption" I fled the highway in a beat up, secondhand car, pulling a U-Haul behind me. Fran in my rearview mirror, both of us trying not to look happy I was leaving. I ended up in New Orleans for reasons that didn't work out, but stayed because it seemed like a fun place to live. That's the decider when you're barely eighteen.

I needed a job and a place to live or I'd have been on the street. To make a long story short, I groped, fondled and screwed my way through various restaurant kitchens for more than a decade to pay the rent, only telling I'd been trained if asked. Why I bothered to lie, well, I just did. No good explanation. It wasn't, and still isn't, unusual to become a chef under the tutelage of another chef. Which is how I explained it to that nosy parker Billy Dale in my best bite me tone.

I didn't say I used my own definition of "under the tutelage."

My big break came when I jumped ship from the mom and pop (Pop had a wandering eye, thank god) diner to the hottest new restaurant in town. Lucky for me, the owner/celebrity chef took a fancy to me. His wife did not. Still, I managed to work that situation a few years before the gumbo hit the fan and it all got kicked up a notch.

I can't name the chef. Our nondisclosure agreement prevents me from dishing details. I can't complain. He taught me to make andouille and that's how sausage got to be a mainstay of my career. The great thing about making sausage is you can pretty much mix up whatever you dare and put it in a casing. Most of the time it tastes fantastic, and presto, you're a sausage genius.

Armed with cash from our agreement not to mention our hide-the-salami get togethers to his missus, I headed to New York where I did enroll in Le Cordon Bleu. But, why stick it out when a hummer here and there gets you further with less work or hassle?

Well, there was that thing with one of my instructors and his nosy wife with a connected daddy, but we managed to work out terms acceptable to all parties. With more cash, I headed to Vegas.

I landed a chef job (an added cost to my instructor for me keeping my mouth shut was a glowing, not entirely true, reference. If I'd slept with someone higher up I might've gotten that diploma) at a flashy, high profile casino restaurant where I entered one of those goofy TV cooking contests. That famous BBQ guy with the red hair and a Ben Affleck accent strolled in, on the hunt for chef participants for his team. First prize to the last chef standing was a TV show.

I gave it a go.

Worried my gourmet sausages wouldn't be enough I concentrated on the BBQ guy's sausage instead.

I won.

My quirky show, Fork in the Road, caught on. I reimagined the recipes I'd learned on the highway. Stick to your ribs farm food, upscale. Pretzel salad made with muscat jelly and handmade marshmallows. Chicken fried steak using beef filet, panko crumbs and new baby potatoes sautéed whole with rosemary and sage topped with red wine gravy. Finally, my claim to fame, weird as all get out if you think about it, was my sausage. Inspired by an old recipe I'd gotten from a 4-H cookbook I'd found buried under Fran's old TV Guides and Reader's Digests, and altered for the more sophisticated palate. I made countless combinations for pastas, sandwiches, grilling, fancy pants versions of casseroles, sausage in the casings, or out. Dried, cured, sliced, whole, you name the meat—I made it into some sort of sausage.

The BBQ guy, with a bit of prodding, agreed it'd be best if I did my thing, no matter how popular, from afar. Far from him and his TV actress wife. I agreed to move. I bought my dream house in the Valley with the money he paid me off with even though the price fell way beyond my means. Just because you're on the tube doesn't mean you're rich, but headed there? You betcha. I got to film in my own state-of-the-art kitchen. They came to me. I rode high.

I'd written four successful cookbooks. A line of cookware, and a ridiculously lucrative deal with an organic grocery store chain for my sausages and charcuterie, was in the works. Everything I touched seemed to turn to gold. Well, at least silver. Then, up to my old tricks, Matthew caught my eye and I finally scored the fuck up I couldn't come back from. After I got canned my royalty checks from the cookbooks kept me afloat, still helped now, but they'd slowed with no show to keep them bolstered. Anyway, with so little income I couldn't make my high mortgage payments, so I stopped. The bank took my house back (minus everything I stripped out of it) and that was that.

My mother hit me hard with the truth. I had slept my way to the bottom.

But what would you expect from someone named after a biblical slut?

1985

CHAPTER TWENTY-TWO

The Yous did maul Smalls to death, but no one told him. They were six feet under, but Smalls could only wish he was.

"Jesus Christ," Hank said. "They kicked that asshole out of the hospital already?"

"No," Fran said, puffing like a madwoman on her cigarette. "Edith checked him out soon as he woke up from the coma. Says she can nurse him better than they can. All of a sudden she's Florence Nightingale. No money or insurance is what I'd guess."

"Yeah, she's doin' a damn good job of nursing," Hank said.

Pinned to the patio we all watched Smalls maneuver his way around his still bloodstained yard. I wondered if they'd picked up that severed finger. I hadn't seen it anywhere, but I made a point to not look too closely.

"Dumbass can't even get eaten by dogs right," Hank said. Whatever hatred simmered under his skin, Hank was as mesmerized by the hideous sight as much as the rest of us were.

Smalls roamed like a zombie from an old movie with "Living Dead" in the title. A one-man freak show, looking like he'd just crawled out of the grave to eat rotting flesh. Emaciated, he lurched, holding his pants up with the one hand that still had most of its fingers. From the looks of it there were either a few more hidden in the yard or the dogs had eaten them. Edith said his one eye worked pretty well, but most of his upper lip got torn off and what was left of his mouth was twisted into a permanent scream.

He hadn't said a word since the dogs ripped his throat out.

Miraculously, Fran wasn't a for-better-or-worse kinda gal when it came to her half-eaten boyfriend. Under normal circumstances, she was one proxy away from Munchausen's. She saw sick people as a means to her indispensable end. I would've expected to see her jump on Smalls like Clara Barton on a Civil War amputee. The only thing Fran loved more than a deadbeat was a deadbeat invalid. More times than I could count I'd seen her dispense medicine, nurse injuries, and sit bedside vigils with a song in her heart and a spring in her step. She'd sit perched at the edge of her seat, ever ready to administer the Heimlich or donate an organ.

God willing.

She wouldn't have lifted a finger for Doc Bates if not for his fat, sickly wife and the "atta girl's" she got for tending to her. Now she wouldn't put Smalls out if his ass were on fire.

Hank took his cap off to see Smalls better. He hobbled toward us, pulling his lame foot behind him like a sack of dead racoons. "Edith told me that foot's about gone," Hank said like Smalls had gone deaf along with everything else.

Fran straightened out her "I'm with Stupid" shirt. "Fun as this is, I'm going in."

"He's makin' me sick," Hank swaggered off to his shed. "Smells like a three-days-dead squirrel."

I hadn't heard another word pass between Fran and Hank about Fran's unfortunate fling with Smalls. I didn't know where that fiasco stood, but I knew silence rang golden. Maybe Hank's drinking made him foggy on the details. A brain swilling in liquor couldn't retain much.

Really all I could think about was Emily's attempted murder accusations and Willy Wally's "I'll call you." So far he hadn't. Probably wouldn't. I felt no obligation to tell Emily. She'd probably never believe me anyway. She'd get hot under the collar quick enough though. No way I'd gain anything by tattling on her pig boyfriend. The pig boyfriend I wanted.

Smalls leaned against the chain-link fence. He reeked. A fusion of beer, urine and sweat clung to him like a hair shirt. Plus, a sweet, rank smell like something rotten. With the few fingers he had left, he poked his hands through the chain-link and stared at our kitchen window. I turned to see what caught his one eye.

Fran.

She stood at the sink, curtains drawn back, in plain view.

Smalls rattled the fence, frantic. Spittle flung out from the hole that used to be his mouth. He made gurgled, choked sounds and jerked his scarred head back and forth. I stepped back, even though I wasn't close. Fran flew out.

"Get away from the fence." She clenched my arm. "Come in the house."

"What do you think he wants?" I said, heading in.

"To bitch. He can't even talk but he still manages to bitch," Fran said. "The dunce could barely put one foot in front of the other, now he's Marcel Marceau."

That was the most I'd heard Fran say about her beau since his run-in with the Yous. From the living room window, I saw Smalls reel past. Whatever he wanted he'd given up and headed toward the highway.

For someone who a month before had been doggie dinner, Smalls got around.

I didn't know if he escaped on his own most days or if Edith opened the front door and wished him luck. He drifted. No one, including Edith, knew where he might turn up. Almost daily one of the locals brought him home, often from staggering down the yellow line on the Fifty-three.

"As long as he ain't runnin' up no tab, he can git far as he wants," Edith said.

I'd heard Hank say he'd seen Smalls begging beer at Nellie's. The guys there thought he made for a good party trick. I'm sure it especially warmed Hank's heart to see his competition in an advanced stage of decomp—gumming fries, or see if the loser with no lips could guzzle beer. Edith would come drag him out, which wasn't hard. Not like the old days.

To my mind, the upside for Edith was he couldn't beat her if he wanted to, and he needed her now more than she needed him. The downside, and this was big, was the nursing. I assumed that part sucked. He looked like he should be in the hospital for another year or two. His wounds ran pus and smelled foul, the scars zigzagging his face blazed angry and red. He wore diapers, which didn't stop him from soaking his pants with piss and crap. His chin flamed raw from the constant drool stream Edith wiped with whatever dirty rag she wore belted to her housedress. How he ate, well, that remained a mystery.

"Can you run up to the Cox's and get those damn wire cutters?" Fran snuck up behind me. "Hank's whined about them for weeks. In all the commotion Arthur forgot about them."

All the commotion.

"Smalls acted pissed off out there, don't you think?" I took the keys off the hook. It dawned on me that Fran was trying to get rid of me.

Fran wiped her hands with a tea towel. "Watch your mouth."

"He acts like he's mad at you, like he's trying to tell you something." I jingled the keys in my palm. Hoped she'd give me a clue about what she thought.

"I'm not losing any sleep over it and you shouldn't either." Fran patted down her pockets, like she was looking for something. "I'm gonna have a chat with Edith, nonetheless. If she wants to nurse him, she'd better get after it. Or call Doc Bates."

I knew she'd heard the Yous making an afternoon snack out of Smalls. She didn't try that hard to cover it up. I didn't think she'd broken any laws by ignoring it, other than maybe the laws of human decency. Everyone thought he deserved a good ass kicking, including me. But, dog mauling? That seemed especially cruel, even for Smalls. There was something. Fran knew something. I just didn't know what. You'd never know they'd had an outhouse romp, either.

I guess it's true what they say about a woman scorned.

I still couldn't think about it without bile rising in my throat. I changed the subject, not really wanting to know more. Let dead dogs lie.

"Gotta be tough for Edith," I said, stepping out. "It would've been better for her if he'd died. She's got to take care of him, chase him up and down the highway."

"She asked for it. She 'don't trust them town doctors. Doc Bates is right yonder, he'll fix Smalls up in no time.'" Fran stopped mocking Edith to flick her lighter, held it to the end of her Marlboro. "So don't feel too bad for Edith. We should all be so lucky." She sucked in her nicotine. "She's got the perfect husband. One with no tongue and permanent disability checks."

CHAPTER TWENTY-THREE

"You're telling me, Blanche," Margene twirled the phone cord around her wrist. "You know she had to hear those dogs getting after Smalls."

I stood at the Cox's screen door, fist raised to knock.

"I don't know about you, but I think something's up with those two," Margene said. "Did you see the way he looked at her at Hazel's memorial?"

I rapped on the screen, hard.

"Delilah. My goodness—you scared me." Margene turned guilt red. "Blanche, I'll call you later."

"Fran sent me up to get Hank's wire cutters." I didn't give her the chance to make explanations about whatever I might've overheard.

"Oh … yes … she called a bit ago. Let's round up Arthur." I followed her out.

"It's still alive. Getting bigger." Jefferson Davis housed his snake on the back porch. "See?" He lifted the lid with his name splashed across it. The snake inside lay inert, used to being the sideshow.

"Are you sure it's not dead?" I didn't think it looked at all well.

Jefferson Davis shook the box. His reptilian friend wound up quick, and like a sponge dropped in water, it grew to twice its size. I gasped.

Margene wrenched Jefferson Davis's nearest ear. "That snake's gonna bite you one a these days." Jefferson yowled while Margene wrenched harder. "But you're so rotten, the snake'd die. Now take that damn thing out to the barn."

Jefferson Davis hijacked his snake-in-a-box and bolted.

"I swear. I need to buckle down on that boy. We should do something about all the snakes," she talked to herself. "But they do eat the mice. Snakes and mice. Why'd I ever agree to move out here?" She looked at me like I knew the answer. "ARTHUR COX," Margene hollered, making me jump.

Arthur waved from the closest turkey pen, scuttling our way.

"Kind of a wasted trip, honey," Margene said. "I told your mama Hank could get those cutters tomorrow."

"Huh? Well, hmm, okay."

Oh, I got it. She couldn't have gotten rid of me today if Hank got them tomorrow.

"Why tomorrow?"

"Hank starts work up here tomorrow."

Arthur stopped to get stern with his snake-yielding son, hands flying in wild motions.

Margene nodded her husband's way. "Yep, he's really lookin' forward to the help."

"Help?" I stopped halfway down the steps. "Hank's gonna work?"

"Too much to do with all them birds, and the cattle, with Teddy Roosevelt headin' off to Wyoming to help my sister since her husband up and left her. We needed another hand to take his place till my sister finds her another man who can farm and turn a deaf ear to her naggin'. Might take a spell."

****

I'd gotten halfway home when I noticed a truck tailgating me. Close. Didn't take much more than a glance to know who drove. Willy Wally. He put on his blinker, veered to the side of the highway and parked. I should've kept going.

Should've. Didn't.

I pulled over onto the dirt shoulder. Willy Wally drove the few feet forward to catch up. I sat behind the wheel of Fran's station wagon, not moving. Oh, I wanted to jump out, make a complete ass of myself. But I managed to at least make him work for it—if you can call walking ten paces working for it. He knocked on the driver's side window that I hadn't rolled down. I could still drive away. I knew from his stupid air kiss what he wanted. I rolled down my window.

"Hey," Willy Wally said, all prom king confident. "Wanna go out sometime? Nice little theater over in Kearny. Dark too."

That implication pissed me off. As if he expected something untoward to go on under cover of darkness. The nerve.

"Sure," I said.

"Great. Tomorrow night?"

"Sure," I said again. My vocabulary took a dive when I felt flustered. "You break it off with Emily?" I knew the answer. She'd have told me first thing.

"Nope, but I might." He winked.

"What if she finds out?"

"Don't tell her. I know I won't."

If he thought I'd cheat with him behind my best friend's back, he didn't know me at all. Why I wouldn't consider it.

I turned an invisible key at my lips. "Lips are sealed. You know where I live."

CHAPTER TWENTY-FOUR

"Hank. Stop. Please."

"That goddamn freak show is still pawing around here. I—"

"He's not pawing around here on purpose. Our house is closest. He's not in his right mind."

After my too quick accidental rendezvous with Willy Wally I sailed past the beleaguered Smalls rooted at the fence. Hard to tell if he was giving me, or anyone, a menacing look considering the shape of what was left of his face. Soon as I walked in, I heard Hank, in a mood. He bitched, baited and insulted Fran all through the dinner she'd managed to throw together that no one ate. I'd given up and gone to moon over my secret... secret whatever Willy Wally could be called. Hank carried on, unimpeded.

I heard him jerk his recliner upright from my bed, my bedroom door cracked open just enough. "I ought to kick your ass over the fence, let him have you." Hank's words jumbled and slurred. Guess his booze addled brain didn't forget as much as I'd hoped. Since the house was so small, I could hear the ice in his glass tinkle, knew he swayed to and fro, too drunk to stay upright for long.

"Hank, you've got work tomorrow," Fran said. Her voice trembled just enough that I knew she was scared. "Let me help you to bed."

The sickening, raw sound of the back of Hank's hand slamming against my mother's skin shot me out of bed.

"Go help your boyfriend. He's sure as shit in tough shape."

I dodged by Hank's hulking form, headed toward Fran who cupped her cheek with one hand, the hand with her wedding ring on the third finger. For some reason that made the slapping all the worse in my mind. Why didn't I just keep my big mouth shut the night he passed out in the water bucket?

"Go back to bed, Delilah." Fran stood tall, nose up, like she was trying to get a better whiff of something in the air. "Hank's retiring for the evening, aren't you?" She met his stare with hard eyes, took a step toward him. I'd never seen her take any defensive stance toward him. Somehow that didn't encourage me. My gut clenched tight as my jaw.

Hank slammed his glass onto the dining table. "Keep your boyfriend away from the fence." He didn't acknowledge me, but lurched to their bedroom and slammed the door.

Fran pointed. "Delilah. Bed. Now."

****

"Mom?"

Fran's head snapped up, surprised. I'd called her Fran for quite a while, we'd both gotten used to it. "Dee. What's wrong?" The side of her face swelled blue, she touched it with feathery fingers. For once her t-shirt didn't bear a slogan—a serious clue that let me know the depth of Fran's despair.

"I ... I saw the light on under my door. Thought you might want some company."

Fran turned the TV down, pressed her eyelids down underneath her crooked wire rims. I thought she'd send me back to where I came from but no, she scooted over as far as she could in the big recliner. I nestled in beside her. We sat quiet. I could hear her even breathing.

"I'm sorry, Fran." A single tear weaved its way down my cheek and neck. I couldn't fight it, didn't try.

She searched my face. "What on earth for, Dee?"

"Hank. I'm sorry he didn't drown, that night. I'm sorry I didn't keep my big mouth shut. I shouldn't have interfered. You—"

"Delilah, what are you talking about?" Fran's face looked empty.

"Fran. That night. You know. The water bucket? He passed out in it?"

What was wrong with her? A little early for senility.

"Oh, honey," she pulled me in closer, tight, too tight. "I think you got scared, that's all. Hank says things he doesn't mean when he's had a few too many. You imagine things. Everything is fine. You don't have to worry about me or anyone."

Fran never believed confession improved the soul. Why I thought she'd changed, well, who knew?

Same old Fran but not the same old me.

Seeing her beaten face, knuckles scarred and glasses bent, felt like a punch to the throat. I could feel her defeat settle over both of us, but I rooted for her to get off the mat like Rocky Balboa, bruised, battered, but the winner. I leaned against her and let myself cry a little longer.

Her stomach rumbled. I said, "Want me to fix us something to eat? No one ate." I decided I'd ridden the hair of this horse already. Might as well move on to something useful.

She smiled. "Oh no, that's okay honey. It's late and dinner got shit canned." She sat quiet for a second then said, "Well, there is some thawed hamburger in there. Wouldn't want it to spoil."

I got all the fixings out for tacos. The house filled with the sizzling aroma of seasoned meat, and oily, frying taco shells. I filled Fran's with a scoop of meat, sharp orange cheddar cheese, crisp lettuce, cherry tomatoes and a thick, glorious glob of sour cream. I set her plate on the TV tray I'd slid in front of her.

For reasons I didn't understand, I blurted, "Willy Wally wants to date me."

Fran's eyebrows crept upward. "Oh? Well, date him if you want."

"He's still going with Emily. It wouldn't be right."

Taco half raised to her mouth, she looked at me straight on. "You listen to me. A girl's gotta take care of her own. No one else will. That I can promise you," she said, voice hardened with years of hands on experience. "Secret's safe with me."

She leaned over her plate, overflowing taco in hand, hovering over it, so any dripping wouldn't be lost. She took a big, scrunchy bite. Then another. She put her half-eaten taco on her plate and swallowed hard, wiping at her eyes with her taco-less hand.

"Delilah," she looked up, taco grease running down her chin. "You're the best cook in the world. You really are."

I wiped her chin with the napkin by her plate and went back to the kitchen where I worked like hell not to cry and loosen the grip around my chest.

2005

CHAPTER TWENTY-FIVE

I'd just finished my shift at Vi's, getting ready to close for the day. Mondays and Tuesdays the place closed at six. For a Tuesday, traffic on the highway seemed busier. For so many years hardly anyone who didn't live here came on purpose. Now it was, dare I say, getting a tad touristy. I'd even had a customer ask to see the napkin signed by Johnny Cash during one of his many drunken excursions through here back in the sixties. How word spread about that, I couldn't hazard a guess. Ole Johnny had gone out "to see a man about a horse" and ended up headfirst in a ditch across the Fifty-three. To show his gratitude for help patching up his scrapes (no one would've ever thought to alert the press) and a couch to sleep it off on, he signed the napkin. The low expectations on the highway were almost always met.

I'd been steadily busy—enough to keep my mind off Billy Dale and his revelations and Penelope and her accusations. Getting caught lying about Cordon Bleu was embarrassing but not illegal and I hadn't seen Matthew in eons. Just like I'd said. I didn't have a care in the world.

Well, that wasn't entirely true.

Before I could get my apron off or dwell Jefferson Davis burst through the front door I'd forgotten to lock.

"You gotta come home."

He looked like he'd just fled a crime scene—hat askew, out of breath, eyes popped.

Vi came in carrying bags of supplies. "More in the trunk."

"Sorry Vi, we can't stay." Not like Jefferson Davis to deny help to an elderly lady.

I said, "What the—"

"The pigs. Somethin's gone bad."

****

"Parvo?" I said, looking at one of at least half a dozen dead pigs.

"Nope." Jefferson Davis looked almost impressed that I knew anything about animal diseases even if I picked the wrong one.

We stood ankle deep in one of the muddy sties examining the pigs. Over half appeared normal, rolling around, doing their pig thing. Several others stumbled around, running into each other, and the sty, falling over.

"I told you about the dysentery, remember? Thought I got the sick ones outta there in time. But they're dead too." He jerked his head toward the sty that he'd quarantined the sick pigs in. "That's enough to kill 'em. E. coli." Jefferson Davis moved his hat around the top of his head. "They act stoned though. Kinda weird."

I watched a pig fall over, his legs kicking like crazy, uncontrollably, in the air. "Well, what next?"

"This is the only sty affected. The others are fine." He nudged a pig carcass with his boot. "Cost more for a vet than to get new pigs. Vet's over past Kearny."

I hadn't considered bringing in a vet. On the highway, back in the day, the shotgun served as the vet. Or in the case of chickens or turkeys, a good neck wringing cured every ailment. I'd guess Jefferson Davis thought the same. Old school as he was about a lot of things.

As if he could read my mind Jefferson Davis said, "I'm gonna put the rest of these down. Burn 'em all, muck out this sty, then get new pigs if you want 'em."

Before I could answer he went on, "Bigger ones. I told you last time piglets are cute," he said "cute" in a girly tone. "But they're not hearty enough. If you want to start breeding any time soon—"

"Whatever. Get bigger ones. Obviously, pig raising isn't my specialty. Yet."

Jefferson Davis started toward the barn to get his gun. "Well, look there. Your boyfriend."

Billy Dale cruised to a stop in front of the porch.

Oh, yippee.

CHAPTER TWENTY-SIX

"What do you want?" I hollered to Billy Dale's back as I got closer, my muddy rubber boots squishing and squashing the whole way.

"Howdy do to you too," he said.

Doc drove in, waved, kept driving toward the sties. Jefferson Davis must've called in reinforcements to deal with the hog disaster. The dumpy Doc had proven himself to be a good hand. He could dig a trench, clean a sty and wrangle pigs like a man born to farm. I'm sure he'd find no difficulty putting the stumbling, sickly porkers out of their misery. If he could drop Willy Wally like a sack of hammers, what're a few pigs between friends?

I traipsed past Billy Dale up the steps, through the porch, stopped to yank off my boots, then sailed into the house. He tailed me.

"Heard something happened with your pigs?"

"How do you know about that? I barely know about it."

He sat at the kitchen table while I made coffee. Why I didn't kick his weanie ass out, even I couldn't fathom. I had to admit there was something a little endearing about his weanieness. The anti-cool guy is cool because he's anti.

"I must've just missed you." Billy Dale ran his hand through his hair. "Had a couple beers with Vi. She told me you ran outta there 'cause your pigs got sick or something."

"Vi's Place is closed."

"She still sold me beer."

"I'm sure you're not here to talk about my pigs."

"No, no, not just about the pigs," he said. "I am interested though." He crossed one creased denim leg over the other.

What kind of sociopath irons his jeans?

"This place'll look real nice after all the trees and such go in." He motioned outside at the holes, tilled up dirt, endless pots of saplings, shrubs and general debris. "Looks like you're settling in, planning to stay awhile."

"Who knows? We'll see." The fixing up would be delayed until the pig situation was taken care of—just as it was getting started too, dammit. I ran water to do some stray dishes.

"How'd you get away with it?" he said, oh so nonchalant.

I worked at not blinking. Glad I was looking into the sink and not his face. He left the "it" open ended, like some kind of trick. I scrubbed at a plate with hardened egg yolk on it. Didn't talk.

"The Cordon Bleu thing. You know, the chef thing?" He filled in his own blank.

It was almost worth telling him exactly how just to see the look on his dumb face.

"No one ever looked into it." I shrugged. "Doesn't matter now." I put the dish in the drainer. "Coffee's ready. Help yourself."

He did.

"So Doc's out here a lot?"

"Not that it's your business, but no. Occasionally he helps Jefferson Davis. As you can see," I gestured toward the dug up, unfinished grounds, "there's a lot to do for one person. I'm not much help with any of that. Doc's an ass but he's our ass."

Billy Dale chuckled. "He does that free?"

I faced him. "You still don't get how things work here. We help each other without expecting anything in return. It all works out in the end."

"Tight knit crew out here, tightlipped."

I finished up my dishes tightlipped.

Thought about Doc yakking away about his Willy Wally cheating-with-the-unidentified- tramp-from-Kearny theory but I wasn't going to blab about that. Besides, I was more than a little curious about why Doc really was hanging around here with Jefferson Davis. They didn't seem too friendly with each other.

Didn't want this outsider jerk hauling Doc off any time soon. Maybe Jefferson Davis would make a move on the widow Watkins now. Doubtful. He'd turned shallow as any other guy. Whatever good looks Wanda possessed decreased at the same rate her size increased. Definitely not worth driving to Sun City for.

"I'm sure you'll keep your ear to the ground no matter how pointless," I said to break the lull in conversation.

"Well, it's a funny thing. The shit I hear," Billy Dale said. "What with my ear to the ground."

"What shit would that be?" my heart did jumping jacks.

"Penelope's pretty obsessed with you."

Duh.

"I'm so charming."

"She insists Karen changed her story. Said she's lying now about you and her husband."

"Why on earth would she do that?" I started putting my clean dishes away.

"I thought you might know."

"Even you're not that dense. Penelope's got an agenda. Karen doesn't. She's got no reason to lie."

"She and her pilot husband..." Out came his stupid pad. "Um, let's see it's in here somewhere. Oh, right. Philip—Philip the pilot. He and Karen are getting divorced."

I slammed a cupboard shut. "So?"

"You don't seem surprised."

"I didn't know them well enough to have an opinion of their marriage one way or the other." I wiped the counter down. "How do you know they're getting divorced? You're a divorce lawyer too?"

"Ear to the ground, remember?"

"Which airline did Philip fly for?" he said suddenly off on a bit of a tangent. "It's quite a haul to the nearest real airport. Hours."

"Ah, something Chief Ear to the Ground doesn't know?"

"Just thought of it."

"Philip wasn't that kind of pilot."

"How many kinds could there be?"

"Boy, you're not that bright are you? You've learned not much at all living in ranch country. Crop duster."

"Huh. Never dawned on me. Swank lifestyle for a crop duster."

"Philip's a trust funder. Jesus, you are asleep at the wheel. Half that valley lives on inherited money."

Billy Dale wrote for several minutes in his pad. Always with the damn pad.

I put the last of the silverware into the drawer, poured myself a cup of coffee and sat across from him. "Is there a crime here? Something I'm missing?"

"No idea. But I told you before—I don't like coincidences. Willy Wally gets killed days after you move back here. You and Matthew had an affair, now he's missing. You may or may not have had a fling with Karen's husband. Now they're getting divorced and trying to leave town. That spate of weird deaths right before you moved away, all at least acquaintances of yours. The common denominator is you."

1985

CHAPTER TWENTY-SEVEN

H ank at work, Fran had gone to do some good deed for some hapless victim who didn't want her to. Actually, I think Fran used any excuse to get away from Smalls clinging to our fence in what looked like his death throes. So I had the house to myself. Since my cheating with Willy Wally, I hibernated, too ashamed to see Emily. We weren't exactly cheating. Not all the way cheating. We'd make out in his truck, sure, but nothing else.

Yeah, still cheating. Even I couldn't justify it to myself. She'd call and I'd try to sound oh so "who gives a flying fuck" but I know she heard guilt in my voice. Didn't she?

A fuss from the open bedroom window interrupted my justifications. The house was so small you could hear what went on in the front yard from a back bedroom. I skipped out to the kitchen where meddling came easier.

Smalls hung on to the fence with his three fingers. Edith, who'd always cut a much bigger figure than he, didn't want him to. Old habits die hard and her attempts to dislodge him looked timid, even though the Yous left him a wasted, worthless shell. Smalls hung on to the chain-link like it held the antidote to all his ills, digging his foot and a half into the dirt and standing his ground three quarters of the way.

Edith tried to dislodge his fingers from behind. He reared the top of his hairless, disfigured head slamming it into Edith's cheek. Her potato shaped head snapped back and she let go, her hands going to her face.

I marched out the door with purpose. Edith might still be afraid of Smalls, but I wasn't, not anymore. What could he do? Mime me to death? I brushed right passed him.

"Edith, are you all right?"

"Oh ... well, it's just a nick." Edith reached into the pocket of her faded housedress and took out a Kleenex. "It's not bleedin' very much. The skin ain't barely broke."

Edith held the tissue over her wound with unexpected elegance, her pinky out like a Vanderbilt sipping tea. Smalls still gripped the fence, spittle running down his chin.

"What are you trying to get him to do?" I didn't know why Edith wanted him off the fence so bad, he clung to it most of the day and she didn't mind.

"He needs to eat a little somethin' and it takes a bit of doin' to get anything down him."

Smalls wandered off, bored enough by our conversation to give up his post.

"See?" Edith said.

I didn't know how to respond, so I didn't. Smalls walked in a circle, dragging his half foot, not making any headway, just circled.

"He ain't right in the head since—" Edith didn't have to finish her sentence. "But now he's gettin' some strength again, he's meaner'n all get out."

I watched the man of the hour totter round and round. "He still looks pretty harmless to me."

Edith pulled the rag away from her cheek to look at the blood in a silent, probably accidental, rebuke for my cluelessness.

"Can I help you with anything?" I felt bad for being such a putz. "I can hold him down while you shove some mush down his throat." Helpful was my middle name.

"No, no. He wouldn't like it none," Edith said. "You could do somethin' else though. Have yer ma stop over when she gets home."

"Oh. Okay. I—"

"She really is an angel, yer ma," Edith said, aglow with admiration. "She's always been so nice, helpful. She felt real bad about me being gone and all when—" her big head nodded toward Smalls. "Well, she took me to my sister's that day. You know she does that sometimes. Wouldn't get outta this house no other way. She felt mighty awful for it."

Smalls toppled over, landing on his back on the hard ground. Edith didn't miss a trick, just kept talking. "She called right quick soon as she saw the goin's on." She pointed over at the man in question, pants soaked, diaper loosened and down around his scabby ankles, still lying down.

"Probably nothing you could've done anyway," I said.

"I'd a heard if I'd been home," Edith started crying. "I coulda saved my dogs, got 'em off a him. They always listened to me."

A flash of Fran yelling at the Yous to shut up whizzed through my brain. They listened to Fran too. More than once.

Smalls stood up again, making his wobbly way toward the highway.

"I better see if I can get him in." Edith wiped her tears with what was left of her shredded tissue. "You won't forget to ask your ma to stop over?"

"No, I won't."

****

I lingered at the kitchen window watching Edith drag Smalls toward the house. Their earlier scrimmage must've tired him. He didn't protest much.

I looked out at Hank's usual parking spot, remembering Fran on her knees, like a beat down animal, Hank's boot swinging toward her bowed head. My thoughts skipped around like a rock on a still pond. I knew Fran got Smalls into the dog pen. Probably pretty easy, he wasn't hard to goad, and she held a surprisingly firm grip on the Yous behavior.

I knew she was mad as hell at his snitching to Hank, but I thought despite that she still felt something for him—as repulsive as that thought was—at least for a while. She looked so odd the day Smalls met his fate. I still couldn't nail down her real feelings. I'd admit that her attitude presently looked a lot like hate.

If she'd done what I suspected she'd come this close to being a murderer. Or maybe that was murder.

Just like with Hank.

Fran was a passive aggressive almost murderer who got a little more aggressive with every bite at the apple.

I missed Emily, my friend, keeper of my secrets. I wished my conscience were clearer so I could call her. I'd told her too much already but she'd never say anything to hurt me. She knew hurting Fran would hurt me. She'd never do that no matter what awful thing she thought Fran did.

That's what she thought about me too, yet there I was—before I could berate myself again about Willy Wally, Edith and Smalls's wrangle near the fence caught my attention. Edith waved what looked like a cookie or a cracker out toward her mutilated and toothless husband, luring him forward, away from his usual fence rattling, rubbing her sore cheek with the other hand.

It took chutzpah to live a thankless life.

****

Edith's request for Fran's presence piqued my interest—something in her voice. A cunning undertone that I didn't think Edith had in her. All this mess seemed to start the day I saw Smalls fall out his front door, drunk, stoned, whatever. Edith had called Fran over that day too.

Suspicious.

I didn't know what to look for, but Fran's bedroom was the obvious choice. The only room in the house she could hide anything. What I thought she'd hide I didn't know, well, I guess I'd find out. The wobbly old pine dresser, with its doubled-up piece of cardboard shoved under it to even it up, beckoned.

I dug through the top drawer, full of tube socks and white cotton underwear—men's stuff. Ack. I moved on, wiped my sweaty palms on my Mickey Mouse t-shirt. The second drawer held nothing any more alluring. Some undershirts, a worn wallet with ripped lining, key chains, a couple heavy, metal lighters with military insignias on them, and more men's stuff. I groped way in the back—nothing. It figured. Even in the darkest recesses Hank was dull.

I wrenched the third drawer open hard, almost off its rails. The clean, summery Woolite scent of a woman's underthings floated out around me. Putting both hands wrist deep into the silky, fragile depths, I lifted out a satiny slip, held its luxurious softness next to my cheek and closed my eyes, almost forgetting the job at hand. I fished around some more among the nightgowns, half-slips, and old lady bathing suits before shutting the drawer—nothing of note.

One last drawer to go.

It opened partway, with an ominous creak, like a warning I wouldn't like what it held. I wriggled the drawer from side to side to coax it open. On top were several bras, beige and white, the serviceable kind, nothing lacy or sensual. I reached farther back. Something hard and square blocked my path. I uncovered it. The Joy of Sex. I wrenched my hands back like Satan touching the church doors.

If ever there were two people who found no joy in anything it was Fran and Hank. "The Joy of Getting It Over With" I could believe. Curious, but not enough to forsake my mission, I made a mental note to paw through it at another time. I kept searching, brushing up against a rattling rustle.

I pulled out a clear plastic bag with pill bottles in it—one empty, the other with only a few blue pills in it. Same labels. Diazepam.

CHAPTER TWENTY-EIGHT

Fran rushed out of her bedroom, a flash of stretch denim and white Keds. "Well, if Edith needs me, I guess I'll go over."

Soon as Fran walked in the door, I relayed Edith's message, and she'd headed for her room. I stood close by. I heard her rocking that drawer back and forth trying to get it open—the one with the pills in it.

That was it.

I'd never heard of whatever those pills were. I'd already forgotten the weird name. Whatever they were she was giving them to Edith. Fran launched out the kitchen door, not even trying to conceal the pills. It occurred to me that Doc's visits here and his huddle with Fran at the Cox's barbecue were all about those pills.

I watched both Fran and Edith outside conspiring, next to Smalls whose agitation grew tenfold when he saw Fran. She gave Edith the near empty bottle. I could see their lips moving in an energetic conversation that came to an abrupt end.

I raced to the couch and threw myself on it like I'd been there the whole time when Fran came back home.

"I'll be back in a few," she said in her singsong voice that she thought disguised whatever misdeed she intended to partake in.

Just about to confirm the pills were gone, the knock on the door stopped me.

Willy Wally pushed himself through the door I barely cracked open. Before either of us said a word, he was all over me. Like he'd grown eight arms. Up my shirt, under my bra, when his fingers tugged at my zipper I jerked back.

"Um. Hello?" I said, red in the face and breathless.

He looked all around, over my shoulder, through to the living room.

"No one's home. Where's your bedroom?" He started to drag me.

As much as I only wanted to feel adoration for him, I could feel the pissed off coming on strong. Who did he think he was? I knew what he thought I was and it hurt. I knew I deserved it. Only a tramp would cheat with her best friend's boyfriend.

"None of your business," I said. "What are you doing?"

"What do you think? You know you want it."

Just about to tell him to jump in front of the nearest tractor, Edith's yell screeched through the kitchen window. "Get off that fence. I mean it."

We both looked out.

I'd never heard Edith tell her wretch of a husband what to do, much less scream demands. Maybe the pills were for Edith. Jacked her up, but good.

Smalls had climbed halfway up the fence separating their yard from ours. It wasn't that tall, maybe four feet, but getting up as far as he did must've taken some effort. Edith pulled him off with one good yank.

"Good Christ he looks horrible," Willy Wally said, libido on ice. "He looks pretty pissed or is that just his face now?"

"Yes and no."

"He really wants to get over here."

"Does it every day. Never makes it."

Edith lumbered to her house, leaving Smalls to throw his tantrum, but he'd slowed. I expected him to make another run, so to speak, at the fence as soon as he shook off Edith.

Smalls slid down to the brittle, yellowed grass and rocky dirt, only his bony back against the fence kept him up. Nope, the pills were for him.

"He's probably drunk," I lied.

"How can he drink? Holy fuck, where're his lips?"

"The dogs ate 'em."

He laughed. "Oh, sorry. I know it's not funny—"

"I don't know what it is, to tell you the truth."

"Uh oh. Here she comes," Willy Wally pointed.

We'd both scootched against the kitchen sink to get as close to the window as possible. Edith trudged across the yard toward her catatonic husband, who by now had toppled over. "Good god. What's she gonna do with that?" Willy Wally let out a low whistle. "No. She isn't."

Edith heaved a thick, metal chain behind her. The kind you could pull a truck out of a ditch with.

"Is that a dog collar too?"

"I think so. What the fuck?" I said. "Look, it's got "You" written on it."

Willy Wally scrunched up his face like someone farted. "That collar's huge. Those dogs were monsters. Eww—" He leaned even closer to see. "Is that dried blood all over the collar?"

I didn't need to look to know. "Yes."

Edith, moving faster than I thought possible, secured the collar around Smalls's neck. Smalls didn't look conscious. I wondered for a second if he'd died. Edith hooked the chain to the collar then reached into the torn pocket of her shabby housedress.

"Is that a lock?" Willy Wally said.

Definitely.

Edith hung the lock from the chain and fastened it to the fence. If my hair caught fire I couldn't have moved.

"She did not—"

"She did," I said.

"Should we do something?" Willy Wally said.

"Like what?"

"Call Rusty?"

"Forget it," we said in unison.

Edith cocked her head like one of her precious Yous would've, examined her handiwork for a couple seconds, turned on her dirty heel and plodded back toward the house.

Leaving her half dead, mutilated husband chained to the fence by a dead dog's collar.

CHAPTER TWENTY-NINE

That did it.

I called Emily to see if she'd spend the night. She seemed surprised to hear from me but happy. I knew she thought I'd been avoiding her because of my jealousy over Willy Wally. Hopefully it'd stay that way. I couldn't let what happened with Smalls go untold. Of course, I'd leave out the other witness.

Emily's dad dropped her off and we raced off to my room. She didn't even give me a chance to open my mouth.

"What, in the name of Friday the thirteenth is Smalls doing chained to the fence?"

"I told you. Lots happening around here," I said, then spilled my guts about the pills, Doc's visits, Smalls passing out from what I assumed were the drugs.

"You shoulda seen the look on my dad's face," Emily said.

"Do you think he'll call Rusty or … or something?"

"No way. Rusty might as well be chained to the bar. I think everyone thinks Smalls deserves whatever happens to him, even if they won't say it. Dad just looked away and drove off like the whole thing was normal."

"For the highway, it is."

We cracked up at that, dropped onto my bed. The wicker headboard scraped the wall in response. We sat cross-legged facing each other, whispering. I thought she'd read my dalliance with Willy Wally in my eyes, on my face, immediately. Didn't.

"Fran came home not an hour ago with more pills, went to Edith's first thing. She thinks I'm a complete moron. She stuffs a bottle in her front pocket and thinks no one can notice the shape."

Emily twirled a long piece of her hair. "What kind of pills?

"Diaza-something. Some kind of sedative I'm sure. They give them to him and he goes practically comatose."

"Wait," Emily said. "Did she come home with the pills or did she give Edith the pills?"

"Huh?" I stopped to think about it. I'd assumed she gave them to Edith.

"She brought one bottle home. In her pocket," I said. "I saw it. She went right to the bedroom to put them in that old drawer. I assume she left some with Edith."

"Why though? I mean if they're for Smalls why wouldn't she just give them all to her. Why was she keeping them here in the first place?"

I searched every recess of my brain. Again, I didn't like the direction this conversation was going. "Well, if they're sedatives of some kind, maybe she takes them too." Fran moved like a downed electrical wire. I'd never seen her sedate for one second.

To my relief, Emily said, "That makes sense. Probably needs them to live with Hank."

"You know it."

"Did you hear that?" Emily turned toward my closed bedroom door.

"Hank, don't. The last thing you need is another drink."

We hadn't heard him come in what with all our gossiping.

"Speaking of," I said.

"Don't tell me—" The crash drowned out his words. He must've fallen. Sounded like he took a couple barstools with him and his usual highball glass shattered when it hit the ground.

We both bolted to the living room.

Fran hadn't move out of the recliner. Hank's recliner.

Hank lay halfway across the living room rug and the kitchen floor, blocking the door, amid the fallen bar stools, his long legs tucked up, fetal like.

"Careful of the glass, girls," Fran cautioned.

"Um … is he passed out again or do you think he's had a stroke or something?

Like I should care.

"I dunno," Fran said, with a flick of her lighter. "Kick him and see what he does."

Emily and I looked at each other, then Fran.

She couldn't be serious, could she?

Her usual MO, especially in front of someone else, would've been hopping up to his aid, an implausible excuse for his plight spilling out of her mouth, while she cleaned up the mess. No one moved. Emily knew Fran well enough to know her eat-shit-and-die nonchalance wasn't normal.

"Can you see if Smalls's still chained to the fence?" Fran said like she wasn't concerned one bit what happened to Hank. "That Edith. What a flighty bird."

Emily crossed to the window. "Yeah. He's still there. Looks awake, but barely."

"What did she say when you went over there?" I said.

"What's to say?"

"Her husband's chained to the fence, Fran. That requires an explanation in my book."

"I gave her the chain," Fran said.

"What?" Emily and I chorused.

"Well, Hank's chain. But he won't notice," she cackled. "Obviously."

"Smalls looks drunk," Emily said, back at my side. "Or drugged."

I held my breath. A little surprised Emily'd gone there.

"She's gotta keep him off the highway somehow, doesn't she?" Fran smoked. "The bastard might get run over. Wouldn't want that, would we?" She smiled, cigarette pressed between her lips still. "Keeps him from climbing the fence too. He could get hurt, you know."

"What does? The chain or the drugs?" I said. Emily made me brave.

"Who cares?" Fran said. "It works."

Somehow I didn't think this new development had anything to do with Smalls turning into roadkill or scratching himself on the fence. I felt no kinship with the idiot, but he'd suffered a lot for his jerkwad ways. Plus, Fran had played her part in the whole mess.

Hank stirred, then quieted again.

"Maybe she should take him back to the hospital?" I said.

Emily chimed in, "Or one of those homes. My mom said—"

"Why?" Fran tapped ashes off the end of her Marlboro. "He's moron material for the rest of his days. Why waste the time or money?"

"Isn't there some law against chaining a human to a fence?"

"Not here there isn't," Fran said. "The only direction Rusty looks is the other way."

"Surely she'll take him in before it gets dark." Emily noted the lowering sun.

Fran shrugged. "What's the diff? I'm sure she's got a blanket." Fran smashed out her cigarette stub. "Besides, it's summer. Warm now." She arched her back in a cat-like stretch and got up. "Better clean up Hank's mess."

I walked to the window while Fran stepped over Hank, tiptoed through glass shards and plucked ice cubes off the floor. Emily helped. I studied Smalls—dropped over, his legs folded up near his chest. I looked over at Hank, lying still as death on his side, knees bent, then back at the spectacle tied to the fence.

Smalls and Hank looked a lot alike at the moment.

2005

CHAPTER THIRTY

"How'd you hear about the pigs so fast?" I felt under surveillance. I knew Fran's I don't want to know what you're doing oath wouldn't last.

"Vi," Fran huffed out the last vapor from her smoked down stub. She crushed it out on my front porch. I'd heard her pull in.

I didn't bother to ask how Vi knew. That's a question I needed to extinguish from my vocabulary. The highway knew it all.

Fran pulled her too short "Damn I'm Good" t-shirt down over her exposed stomach. She sniffed toward the front door. "Something smells good. I brought you these salt and pepper shakers." She produced a small ceramic stove and refrigerator from her bottomless purse, both with holes at the top. "Got these on that shopping network. We get that now since we put in that satellite."

"We?" I took the bribe.

"Me and Vi. In case you didn't know I spend most my time up there."

I didn't know. I did know they were pretty close, and if one knew something so did the other. With Blanche and Edith gone, that left Vi. Margene would've never been a contender. Vi lived up the road from me, but that main dirt road sat pretty far from my property, which was set back quite a way. Plus, I spent most of my time in the back. I never even parked in the front. All the action went on in the back. Everyone had already been trained to park in front of the screened in porch. Fran could've driven up and down that road twenty times a day and I'd never have seen her. A lot could happen on that road and I'd never know.

"That's nice for you, Fran," I said and meant it. "You're the Golden Girls." We both laughed. "Smart to share expenses."

Fran got Hank's monthly retirement stipend but I didn't think it amounted to much.

"Something like that," she said.

Fran sprang up to sit on the freezer. She weighed little to nothing. "Are you cooking something?" Fran asked, head up again.

"Yes. Stay for dinner."

The kitchen had always been my comfort zone. Cooking for Fran felt good. No matter how nuts she drove me, or how frustrating she was in general, watching her eat food I'd made with my own hands brought me great satisfaction. Food was one of the few things she'd say I did well.

"Sure," Fran fished out a Marlboro. We both watched the pig bonfire in the distance. "Who do you think would poison those poor pigs?" Genuine alarm flashed over her features.

"Poisoned?" I felt the blood leave my face. "What on earth? Jefferson Davis never mentioned anything about poison."

Fran stopped mid-light. "Doc told us."

"Us? How? He's been here the last few hours." As soon as I said that I noticed his truck was gone. How long ago, I didn't know. Jesus, had I slipped into some sort of coma? "You'd think he'd tell me, wouldn't you?"

Fran pulled out her lighter from her magic bra that apparently held everything she needed. "Probably figured Jefferson Davis would give you the skinny. You don't think Jefferson Da–"

"Heavens no. Do you?"

She flicked her lighter several times, thinking. "No. But he's changed, I'm sure you've noticed. Toughened up. But I don't think he's changed enough to do that. He's always loved animals. Plus, he's the smartest of that bunch of little presidents. Wouldn't put himself out of a job away from his dominatrix mother."

"Domineering."

"Right, well. You never know."

"Well, what about me?"

"What about you?"

"Putting himself out of a job is certainly a consideration, but what about his friendship with me? I don't think he'd do that to me."

She puffed out a mouth full of cancer, waved her hand through it as if that mattered before saying, "That too."

I hoisted myself up onto the freezer next to my mother. "Weird you thought of him at all, actually." I certainly hadn't.

"He's hard around the edges. Started around the time Emily—"

"Okay, whatever."

"You just didn't see him much then." She flicked her lighter several times, nervous. "Then you moved off. A few years later he ran off to Kearny with Wanda. When Wanda could still run without her ass flapping against her knees. You know how that turned out."

Everything stopped. I could hear Fran's blathering but the earth felt off its axis. No one talked about Emily. To hear Fran mention her like a common point of conversation sucked the oxygen out of the space I occupied.

I willed myself to come around. "Why would Willy Wally marry someone like Wanda anyway?"

"Not a lot of choices out here and he was always lazy. Too lazy to look elsewhere." She fiddled more with her lighter. "Until he found someone worth getting off his ass for out of town."

"This place is crazy. Everybody's crazy."

Fran said, "Probably kids. Pulling pranks."

"What?"

"Kids. Maybe they poisoned the pigs. Pulling pranks. You know someone lit a pile of dog shit on fire over—"

"How would Doc know they were poisoned anyway?"

"He's a doctor. Don't need to be a vet to recognize the symptoms, he said. Did some doctor shit. Tests and whatnot."

"How many times do I have to say, he's a diet doctor? That's, like, fake. And why would he bother? Tests where? In the lab in my barn? That's ridiculous."

"Who knows why Doc does what he does? Maybe Jefferson Davis wanted to know. He's in charge of those damn pigs isn't he?"

"Well, yes, but—"

"Maybe that crazy Hardy woman." Fran still held her un-lit Marlboro. "That wife of your last paramour."

"Doubt it. Let's go in. I need to stir my sauce."

****

"What's in this sauce?" Fran licked her lips. "It's delicious."

I got up to get her a second helping. "It's just my regular old spaghetti sauce. Some tomatoes, garlic, onions, a little sugar and balsamic vinegar, of course." I brushed against her back walking by. She felt skeletal. I paused in front of the bubbling saucepan to really look at her. She'd always been thin, but now her face went gaunt around the cheekbones. I could see her collarbone through her thin t-shirt.

"Fran, you need to eat." I plopped another heap of pasta on her plate. "You know you're welcome any time. Just give me a little notice. Bring Vi too."

"Ach … you're as bad as Vi." She waved my suggestion away with a bony hand.

Fran ate with zest. Like she wasn't already on her second helping.

"You don't think someone's trying to hurt you, do you?" she said, mouth full, eyes wide. She'd just thought of that, I could tell.

"I hope not," I said.

"Not even the spurned wife?"

"Penelope? No, not Penelope."

****

I convinced Fran to stay the night and sleep on the couch. She'd looked frail to me, which wasn't her usual state. I had to ask Jefferson Davis to run up and tell Vi she wouldn't be there until morning so she wouldn't worry. I settled Fran in with blankets, sheets and a pillow, then headed to bed myself.

I paused at the doorway of my bedroom to take a last peek at Fran. She'd fallen asleep immediately. Her glasses perched on the tiny end table and her faded t-shirt draped over the back of the couch—inside out—which is the way she'd wear it tomorrow since front and back got either spaghetti sauce or dirt on them. She'd pulled the blanket flush with her chin and burrowed into the fluffy pillow, looked no bigger than an undernourished child. My eyes filled seeing her unguarded, relaxed, and at the mercy of anyone who wanted to do her harm. The way she looked when Hank was still alive. When he'd hit her with his fists and his words. I knew he'd left damage that would never be undone. With a swipe at my eyelids, I turned away.

It'd been an endless day. I sat on the one rickety chair in the one bedroom to pull off my jeans. I unbuttoned the fly then stopped to think. Damn nosy Doc. Stirring up shit with Fran. He should know better than to worry an old woman. Even though I tried not to let my mind rest on things best left buried, I wondered if I should worry about being harmed, but not by Penelope. Oh sure, she'd whine and fuss but that'd be about it.

I squirmed and shimmied to get my 501s down my legs. I kicked my feet to get them all the way off. I let them lie on the floor, a puddle of denim, even though the hamper sat open and handy within reach. I fell into bed, exhausted and wired at the same time.

If I couldn't escape everything I'd done since I left home back on the Fifty-three, I couldn't escape it anywhere.

****

I felt hands caress my face. Light, soothing. Smoothing out my forehead, patting my hair. I didn't have to open my eyes to know it was Fran. I'd fallen asleep in fits and starts. Even with my eyes shut I could tell the night still filled my room. She weighed so little she could sit on my bedside and not wake me. Tears threatened to seep out behind my lids when she kissed my nose. They fluttered open in time to see her back as she stepped out of my room.

Fran could only demonstrate her love for me when I wasn't looking, in the dark.

CHAPTER THIRTY-ONE

I hadn't seen Rusty since forever ago. As always, he stayed out of any investigation, including the one into Willy Wally's death. At least that's what I assumed since Billy Dale elbowed in. He hadn't been at the memorial that I saw and as far as I knew he never questioned Fran and I knew he didn't question me. Doc? Maybe. So why did his staggering into Vi's during my shift throw me? I knew he came to drink.

Still. The pig catastrophe calmed down, Jefferson Davis got us bigger pigs that, by all accounts, were healthy and doing well. Billy Dale stopped coming by. Penelope was a distant memory and I'd gotten into the swing of things at Vi's. Fran only felt the need to pop in a couple times a week. My optimism crept up off the ground, somewhere around my calves.

Now Rusty. Couldn't be good.

His yellow face and eyes gave away the state of his liver, which I thought would've thrown in the towel a long time ago. When I was a kid living on the Fifty-three rumors flew all the time that Rusty was on his way out. About to be replaced any second. He was such a nonentity even the rumor mill didn't give a shit about him now. I guess since no tragedy had befallen anyone in any out of the ordinary way (the definition of out of the ordinary was generous out on the highway) till Willy Wally, no one needed the law so who cared?

"Heard you were cookin' here." He yanked out a stool, took off his hat and sat. "You got better lookin' thank the good Lord."

"You didn't." I pulled a beer, hoped he'd drink it and get out.

"Think I'll try one of them fancy weenies. No bun. Just the crispy potatoes," he said in his best snob tone, which came out more like he was trying to stifle gas. "Guess fried ain't a fancy enough word?"

Note to self: tone down the menu. The asshat had a point.

"Stopped out at your place. Lookin' good, all the new trees and plants. Looks like ya'll cleaned up a lot around there. Startin' to look like a real home again."

I pricked holes through a couple sausage casings and threw them on the grill, along with some diced potatoes and spring onions. "Still a lot to do," I said a little louder so he could hear over the sizzling. "Lots of holes to fill yet with shrubs and what not."

"Doc said he's been givin' ya'll a hand out there. Just don't piss him off if he's got a shotgun in his hand." Rusty slapped his leg and laughed so hard he started coughing.

I flipped the potatoes over, poured a little water over the sausages and covered them with a pot lid. "You've got your nerve. Billy Dale said it was for sure an accident." I didn't believe it, but he wasn't the first to get away with killing up here.

"Billy Dale?" Rusty set his beer down.

My skin went cold despite my stance in front of the hot grill.

"The detective from the San Ysidro sheriff's office who was brought in to investigate." I put Rusty's lunch on a plate. "How drunk are you already?"

How wouldn't he know that?

"Billy Dale isn't from the San Ysidro force. He quit last year."

"What are you talking about?" I thought fast. Had he ever said he was a detective? He did, I remember. He showed me his badge. I remembered that too.

Rusty chewed a couple seconds before answering. "Well, quit isn't exactly right. More like asked to retire, early. He'd been moved from LA to San Ysidro for bad behavior. Didn't last long in the Valley."

I poured myself a huge glass of wine. Not supposed to drink on the job, but so the fuck what?

"Some kinda ruckus about his time with the LAPD," he continued. "Scandals always make the rounds. Even up here and around Kearny."

"What scandals?"

"Lots of 'em. Where Billy Dale goes, scandals follow. He liked to troll the blotter for ass." Another annoying facet to Rusty's almost nonexistent personality. He wasn't a real cop so he spouted lingo that I thought he'd heard on a bad buddy cop movie from the seventies.

"Blotter?"

"Yeah, the recent arrests. Billy Dale liked the crazy chicks—thieves, stalkers, drug addicts, dealers, prostitutes. Never met a female criminal he didn't want to bang. Problem was, some of 'em had pissed off pimps, drug lords, or husbands. Billy Dale's a legend and not just in his own mind. We were all a little jealous. Who doesn't like some nutty nookie? He got away with it for a hell of a long time."

"That can't be true."

"How many times you see him here?" Rusty wiped his mouth with his sleeve.

"A few." I didn't define here.

"Why do you think that is? The case was closed less than a week after the shooting."

Rusty was one of those whose confidence rose in inverse proportion to his abilities. The stupider he got the more sure of himself he felt. After twenty-odd years on the job, he hovered near genius, if you asked him. I didn't believe him. Did I?

"He can't go around impersonating a detective, can he?"

Penelope went to his office he said. He questioned Karen for Chrissake.

"He's a private detective now. The PD probably hired him for the Willy Wally thing. I'm not anyone's favorite over there either."

"Why would they hire him if they pushed him out?"

"'Cause they know he won't follow the rules. They can't have those shenanigans on the force, but they know it works so they got convenient memory."

Penelope must've hired Billy Dale too. He kept stopping by with his endless questions. I remembered Doc saying the nosy parker knew a lot about my show. I kept those bits of trivia to myself.

"Still, if the case is closed there's no criminal—especially not a woman. Doc's a man in case you forgot."

Rusty chuckled, drank more beer. "You can bet he's hot on the tail of some gal he thinks did something bad. Mark my words. And Billy Dale's never wrong about women on the wrong side of the law."

CHAPTER THIRTY-TWO

I'd been gone from San Ysidro for only a few months but I'd already forgotten how beautiful the drive was, and long. Not beautiful or lengthy enough to divert my attention from the purpose of my trip, but gorgeous scenery nonetheless—the lake, the blue as dark and rich as brand-new jeans, the miles and miles of shamrock green grazing land and lush lavender farms lined both sides of the road. Idyllic was an understatement. My stomach felt like I'd swallowed burning coal. Going back stirred up all sorts of shit and Billy Dale held the mixer. The closer I got, the more the bitterness filled my mouth and wrenched my heart. I'd loved this place, my house, my career. Gone. Just like that.

Only had me to blame, which didn't make it easier to bear.

Since the Fifty-three as a hideout turned out to be a joke, I'd bought another phone. Apparently, anybody and their wife could find me so what the hell? The ten-mile drive to get service crawled up my ass but I needed stuff only Google could give me—like Billy Dale's address. There he was, hiding in plain sight too, "Dale's Detective Services"—I put the private in private eye, his ad read. What a dolt.

I screeched to a dusty halt in front of his office, an old sixties style eyesore of an office complex. The Valley itself resembled a travel brochure. Home to hundreds of wineries, gentleman type farms, the idle trust-funders who bought restored Victorians or sprawling ranches, and the working class who sold groceries to the inhabitant's housekeepers, pruned rose bushes, and offered all the necessary, but low-brow services. Billy Dale's dilapidated place was an anomaly in a town obsessed with its image, where getting a remodel permit took years, and stood out like Mormon parents with only one kid. My old neighborhood was several miles from his, further into the Valley, where the more genteel raised miniature horses or grew grapes.

Much as I missed the place I'd considered home for years—I didn't come to talk scenery with my nemesis. I pushed through the front door. A little tinkling bell announced my arrival. He sat right there, no receptionist, just him. The tinkling bell must've come with the place.

For once, I was the unwanted visitor. He looked like he'd been slapped in the back of the head with a board, eyes popped, mouth hung open. "What—"

"I'm asking the questions now. What bullshit are you selling, Mister Fake Cop?" I leaned across his desk, got right up in his astonished face.

"Calm down," Billy Dale said. "You're gonna give yourself a stroke or something."

He got up. Pointed to a small table with two chairs. "Sit," he said.

"Did you think I wouldn't find out that you're not really a cop?" I jerked a chair out, sat down hard.

He didn't answer for a few seconds. Probably trying to decide what all I knew.

"No, I knew you would."

He decided right.

"So what's up? No lies."

"I never lied. You assumed I was a cop." He sat across from me. Still within smacking distance if I got the urge. "But, you're right. I knew that's what you assumed and I let you. I apologize."

"You showed me a badge. That's lying."

"No, my badge identifies me as a private detective. You didn't look close enough."

"You went out of your way to make me think you were the law and you know it."

"Says the woman whose whole career was based on a lie."

Hit that on the head.

"Were you really investigating Willy Wally's death?"

"Yes. Rusty's dead weight, but no one else wants to go to that godforsaken highway so they leave him be. But I've heard they're gonna push him out. He's past retirement age. Can't find anyone to take his place though. Yet."

"Fascinating. Penelope hired you to investigate me." Not a question.

"Yes ... " he trailed off. "And Karen."

That shut my mouth for several seconds.

"Penelope makes sense, I'll admit," I said. "I might do it too if I were her, but Karen? What the—"

"I shouldn't tell you this, but it doesn't matter now." Billy Dale reached across to put his hand on mine. Still so surprised, I let it lie. "Karen came first. Before you moved back. She told me she thought you stole her wine and you were screwing Philip."

I jerked my hand out from under his. "What? You told me Karen said the opposite of that."

"She did. Later. Changed her story. Made a point of it."

"Her conscience must've gotten the better of her."

"Not for long. She called me yesterday."

This cat and mouse shit pissed me off.

"For what now?"

"Wanted to know how to get in touch with you."

"Certainly you—"

"No. I certainly didn't."

"Why Karen would want to find me is—"

"Look, it's moot now anyway. As far as I'm concerned anyway," Billy Dale said.

"Why?"

"I'm not interested in investigating you anymore."

"Finally, some sense."

"I'd rather date you."

After that toe-curling proposition brought on an awkward silence, I noticed a large framed photo hanging on the wall across from us, over Billy Dale's desk. Before I could let his invitation sink in, or turn him down flat with a stinging rebuke, I got up to look. Inside the oddly ornate frame a young boy stood next to a woman.

He looked sad, a little scared. She looked like she just came out the winner at the bar arm wrestling contest. Tattoo up one side of her neck and covering the arm around the boy's shoulders. Her bright orange top did nothing good for her sallow complexion.

I felt his breath at my neck. I stepped farther away.

"That's me," he said before I asked. "And my mom."

"How old were you?"

"Ten."

I couldn't think of anything polite to ask about his Roller Derby queen looking mama. I'd never given a rat whisker's thought about her existence, but if I had she wouldn't have looked like this.

I wracked my brain. "She … you … well—" I couldn't think of one thing to say. It'd been an afternoon of silence provoking revelations.

"This is us in Chino."

"You're from Chino?"

"No, the prison's there—my mother's in prison for life. She killed my father."

****

For once speechless, I mumbled something unintelligible to Billy Dale and left. After I got in my car, I realized I'd let his "dating" idea hang, unanswered. Hopefully he'd take that as my answer. But I also didn't get any more reassurances or information about his now ended assignments from both Penelope and Karen. If I didn't date him, would he revive them? Was dating that geek a prerequisite? Quid pro quo?

Not gonna happen. Billy Dale could turn over every rock from here to New York. He'd never find anything on me. Would he? I wasn't the only one signing those confidentiality contracts. Everyone had to keep their mouths shut.

Shocked by Karen's renewed interest in me I thought I'd stop in. Find out what the fuck was going through her thick head. As soon as I drove up, I knew she'd gone. The "For Sale" sign hung out front, the place looked pristine (with Philip's trust fund money the upkeep wouldn't have been a problem). Not a car,

Range Rover, or truck in sight. I hoofed it out to the hangar, which was farther than I'd remembered. Stood on my toes to see inside the tiny windows on the side. Plane gone. Hmm. Maybe the plane was for sale too.

Since my old house was so near, I thought I'd pull out all the stops. See what losers owned it now. I could see before I got all the way up the driveway that they took good care of the place. Stunning as ever. House immaculate, wraparound porch decorated just right with all the best outdoor furniture. Gardens in full bloom. No cars in sight. Could be one or two in the four-car garage. Maybe I'd knock on the door, pretend I got the wrong address or something, to get a quick look inside. I parked, got out of the car.

A thought nagged me as I meandered up the walkway, taking it all in.

Where could Karen have gone?

Did I care?

Yes.

1985

CHAPTER THIRTY-THREE

Emily and I had gone straight back to my room after Hank passed out. We wanted out of there. Fran could decide what she wanted to do about him, if anything at all. From what we could tell she chose to do nothing. She brought our Hamburger Helper to us so we wouldn't have to see him lying there. We gossiped about the Hank/Smalls/Fran triangle, then moved on to usual girl talk (we both avoided Willy Wally, mercifully) till we fell asleep. Seemed like we'd just drifted off when Hank and Fran's fight started up.

"Divorce?" Fran said.

"You heard me."

Emily poked me but didn't need to. I was wide-awake and listening.

"I guess he regained consciousness," she said.

"Obviously."

"Did he say he wants a divorce?"

"Think so." I'd have been surprised till Fran's fling with Smalls got thrown out into the open. Now I'd been halfway expecting it. Something had to give.

"Hank, I don't know why you'd even suggest that. I—"

"I'm a lot of things, but damn fool ain't one of 'em." He slurred like he still hadn't sobered up. Or maybe he'd gotten a concussion. Who could tell?

They sounded like they were standing right outside my bedroom door, then I peeked over and realized I'd left it open a crack.

"You've been, well, not yourself." Fran said, calm.

I held myself rigid, in a full body clench. Emily grabbed my arm to comfort me. "He's been his usual self to me," I said low.

"Let me fix you a drink and we can talk about this." I heard Fran's footsteps to the kitchen.

"She must be desperate if she's fixing him a drink," Emily said.

I nodded even though she couldn't see me. The knots in my stomach moved to my tongue.

"Jesus, Fran, you distilling that shit or what?"

"You'll get it when you get it, or you can do it yourself." I heard the liquor cabinet open then shut with a bang.

"Is she talking back?" Emily said. "She must not care if he divorces her then."

"I hope he doesn't hit—"

"We'll go out there if he does." Emily reached for my hand.

We heard Fran go back, I saw a glimpse of jeans and sweatshirt through the small opening of my door. She didn't hurry. Heard Hank throw his recliner back in its usual position, footrest up.

Then nothing. No one said anything.

Then Fran, "Hank, you're acting ridiculous," she said, her tone much less subservient. "If you think I'll let you embarrass me with another divorce you're mistaken."

"You're embarrassed?" We heard the ice clink in Hank's glass. Probably already empty.

"That is not true. How many times do I have to repeat it? Smalls lied," Fran said, a cross between a screech and a scream.

"Wow," Emily said. "She's fighting back for once."

"Too late for all your pathetic excuses and lies." Hank stumbled through the conversation. "But not too late to get me another drink."

"I am NOT lying." Considering her more aggressive tone we were both surprised to hear her jump up to fetch him another drink.

"'I'm sick of looking at your chained up, chewed up boyfriend."

We heard Fran come back again with his drink. Silence again while he drank. This time for more than several seconds. Minutes went by, then more minutes.

"By all means, drink up you good for nothing asshole," Fran said.

I sucked in, sat up and Emily followed, ready to charge. I hoped we'd gather the necessary courage to take on a giant drunk. Then silence again. We held our breath for what seemed like an hour.

Emily turned her ear toward the door. "Listen, I think he's sleeping."

I listened hard. "I think you're right. I can hear him snoring."

We both heaved sighs of relief and lay back down. In a few minutes we were in dreamland.

****

I sprang up.

I never did know what woke me. Later, I wished to god I'd been a heavier sleeper.

I looked over at Emily, still asleep. I thought about shaking her awake but didn't. Maybe I'd had a bad dream I didn't remember—nothing to worry about, probably. Why were the hairs on the back of my neck standing up?

A possum surrounded by prey couldn't have stayed as still as I did, listening, wondering.

My curiosity overruled caution. I got out of bed quiet as I could. Padded to my bedroom door, looked out. The house was still and dark. No, what was that sound? Wait. I thought I heard a...something...I couldn't tell. The door to Fran and Hank's room stood wide open and they weren't in it. I crept out to the living room. Empty.

Shit.

Something bad was going down. I knew it.

I heard that sound again. A splash?

Oh no.

I ran to the kitchen window.

The full moon's light shone, sky full of bright, twinkling stars, making it pretty easy to see the horror going on.

Fran held Hank's face down in the water-filled plastic tub, dragged out from under the spigot.

"Oh my god." So terrorized I hadn't heard Emily come up behind me. "She's killing him."

****

I dragged a stunned Emily away from the window back to my room. Hysteria loomed. I hoped she wouldn't do anything that would force me to slap her, like screaming.

"I want to go home," she said, pacing my small room. "Hank's dead. Hank's dead. I want to go home."

"You can't, Emily," I said. "Please."

Her head fell forward. She covered her mouth and cried into it. I let her cry a while then she dropped her hand away from her lips. "She murdered Hank," Emily said, hissing like a pissed off cobra. "Oh. My. God."

I put my arms around her, held her close. "Come on." I led her back to bed in the dark. "You've got to follow my lead, Emily." What that meant I didn't have a fucking clue. But I hoped it sounded reasonable and nonnegotiable. "Let's get back under the covers. We don't want Fran to know we … we … well, anything."

We no more than pulled the blankets up to our chins when we heard Fran's quiet footsteps. I felt both our bodies stiffen. I squeezed Emily's arm, hard. Fran paused in front of my bedroom for several seconds, then went on to hers. Her door closed with a soft click.

I lay in the dark next to Emily, neither of us talking. The enormity of what we'd seen hadn't eaten its way through my fear, my need for self-preservation, my duty to protect my mother. That would come later, in spades.

"What now?" Emily said in my ear. I could tell she'd started bawling.

I turned to her. Our eyes had adjusted so I knew she could see me at least a little. "This is fucked up, I know. But Fran is my mother. My mother," I said as if she didn't get it. "I can't let anything happen to her. You know that." I didn't say Hank had it coming. He probably did, but I didn't say it. Still wasn't sure I believed it. "What would you want me to do it if it were your mother?"

"My mother would never—"

"You have no idea what your mother would do if she were in Fran's place," I said, snippier than I should've.

Emily didn't say anything for a few seconds. "Yes, I know, you're right. I think," she said, but not like she meant it.

What would happen now? My thoughts raced like a bullet train. Fran would, I felt sure, get up, pretend she didn't know Hank drowned, "find him," and then put on an Academy Award winning performance. She'd call Rusty. Then she'd—what? I realized Emily and I would need to react to whatever Fran said.

"What are we supposed to do?" Emily said, still crying.

I couldn't save Hank. But I could save Fran, couldn't I?

I gave Emily strict instructions for weathering the shitstorm coming our way.

CHAPTER THIRTY-FOUR

Emily and I didn't sleep the rest of the night. I pondered going outside to see Hank for myself but decided, probably wisely, not to. As the sun rose Emily said, "Should we get up?"

"No. We'll wait for Fran's scream."

"What if she doesn't scream?"

"She will for the effect," I said. "Besides, we never get up before her when you stay the night. We usually don't leave my room till lunch. We have to act normal, remember? Please tell me you remember everything I told you last night."

She started to cry. "Yes, I do."

"And stop crying. At least wait until it looks like you have something to cry about."

She sucked it up.

Then we heard Fran explode out of her bedroom. I think we both stopped breathing. As much as I'd tried to prepare us both, I was leaning too far out over my skis. My skin turned icy. Fran raced around the house, which didn't take long.

"Hank," she said, yelling it loud.

We jumped.

Not quite a scream, but close enough. Our prompt.

We jumped out of bed. I hugged Emily, a quick but sincere gesture of faith. Before we could get out of my room Fran threw the door open.

"Have you seen Hank? His truck is out front."

We shook our heads.

This was already not playing out right. How could we have seen Hank from my room where we were supposedly still asleep?

Fran wouldn't have thought much about not seeing Hank first thing, even though his truck was where it was supposed to be. He often hit his shed early to start his day with a beer or putter around doing who knew what. I hoped Fran would rethink her strategy. If she even had one.

"Probably in his shed," I said.

A scream stopped all of us in our tracks.

"Fran! Fran!"

Shit. Edith. Not the screamer I imagined.

Fran ran out the kitchen door. We followed, dread leading us by the noses.

Edith shuffled over fast as she could move, "Hank," was all she could croak out, pointing. Fran raced to the side yard where the first thing we saw was Hank's long legs straight out, on the lawn, Emily clenched my hand. Fran let out a yelp, raced over and yanked Hank's head out of the tub.

A sight I won't forget.

Dead men, whose heads have been submerged in water for hours, didn't look good. His skin looked like mush. Like if you touched it some would ooze off. Edith screamed again. Fran shoved the tub out of the way, dropped Hank's head to the ground. Emily cried in earnest.

"Oh my god, oh my god," she repeated over and over till I poked her.

"Call Rusty," Fran said to me.

So, I did, taking Emily along. I couldn't trust her alone out there.

We trudged back outside to let Fran know that useless Rusty said he'd be there in a sec. Fran, like she just realized I was there, ran to me, threw her arms around my neck.

"Oh, no," she said into my neck. "What have I done?"

That broke me.

The cryfest began. I didn't think anyone, even Emily, heard what Fran said, mercifully. I barely did. But that was enough to set me off on a jag.

My mother murdered her husband.

I saw her do it. Emily saw her do it.

Here he was, at our feet, a corpse.

Whatever shock had been holding me together turned tail. Reality felt like a punch in the face. All of us, except Fran, couldn't control the waterworks. Fran held on to me, dry-eyed. I don't think she knew what to do with herself, or how to arrange her face, how to not look like a killer. I scanned her expression, felt her breathing. Did she feel sorry? Guilty? Horrified? I'd probably never know.

Smalls came lurching out of the house—both hands around his mangled neck. Making choking sounds, I thought. He made gross sounds all the time. He struggled to stand, much less walk. His already twisted face twisted differently. Like he was trying to smile. Hard to tell. His hands squeezed his neck like he was trying to kill himself.

If only.

"Oh, lord a mercy," Edith said. "He's been doin' that since last night. Dang fool." Then at the top of her lungs, "Goddammit get back in the fucking house."

He stopped, dropped his hands in what I could only surmise was surprise, then he turned and trudged back in. If it weren't for the dead man in our yard, we all would've been stunned at Edith's unusually foul outburst, and that it worked.

For once true to his word, Rusty roared up in a matter of minutes, siren screaming.

"What in the world?" he said, kneeling down near Hank. "What happened?"

"He drowned," Fran said, calm and collected.

"I came out this mornin' and I saw him lyin' there, head in that there tub," Edith said, tears flowing. "Looked like he was bobbin' for apples. But he weren't, a course."

Then Fran, "I heard Edith scream, ran out and saw … saw what Edith said." She hugged me to her harder. "I yanked his head out, but, well, he was obviously gone long before Edith saw him."

"How'd his head get in that tub?"

I chimed in. "He's done that before. You know how much he drinks. He's passed out, fell into the tub, and stayed there. He was lucky we were there last time, Fran saved him."

"He's done it at Vi's too," Emily said, to my happy surprise. "Not in a tub of water, but face first into a bowl of peanuts. Once he shattered a glass his face hit it so hard."

Rusty stood up, steady, of all days for him to be sober. "You weren't aware he'd done it this time? Nothing amiss?"

Jesus. Rusty acting like a cop. What next? Locusts?

"Of course not," Fran said. "I got up this morning and couldn't find him. He wasn't in the house. He does that too. He goes out and stays all night in Vi's parking lot, or in his shed. I saw his truck so unless he walked, I figured he had to be around somewhere close. I no more than got my shoes on when Edith hollered, and I ran out." Fran had used the time between Edith's scream and Rusty's arrival to get her story together. A sensible one.

Rusty put his hand on Fran's shoulder. "I'm sorry Fran. We all figured Hank's drinkin' would kill him one of these days. Maybe not like this, but in some way."

Nervy bastard. He should talk.

"I'll call the ambulance," he said. "They'll take Hank to the hospital so they can—"

He stopped. Probably didn't want to say, "declare him dead."

Fran said, "Okay, fine."

I hoped Rusty chalked up Fran's creepy stoicism to shock.

"Emily, you better call your dad. He'll be pretty upset. He and Hank were best friends." Fran walked into the house without a word to anyone else.

Rusty shook his head, mumbled a few words, got on his radio to call the ambulance. "You girls can go on in. I'll stay with Hank."

Edith crushed both Emily and me to her generous and heaving bosom. Sobbed out her condolences, then went to deal with her own corpse-like husband. Emily and I went back to the house, she to the phone to call her parents, me to Fran's bedroom where I was met by the closed door.

I pressed my ear to the door and listened to her cry.

****

Blanche and Earl came to see Hank and to console Fran but Fran wouldn't come out of her room. That, I didn't expect.

"Don't push her, honey," Blanche said. "She's lost her husband today, that's a big shock."

Earl, wiping his wet eyes with a handkerchief said, "I'm sorry you girls had to see Hank that way. I'm sorry I did."

Emily and I looked at each other, panicky. "It was bad, but not as bad for us as it was for Fran," Emily said. I relaxed. Emily wouldn't tell what she saw. I knew it.

I followed them out the door. There Smalls was again, chained to the fence. Edith chained him up in front of the law, God and the neighbors. No one gave one shit. And he was at it again, hands around his collar making choking sounds. At least that made some sense. But he looked straight at me with that weird almost smile again. I looked away.

The paramedic loaded Hank into the ambulance covered up with a sheet. Some neighbors started dwindling over. Earl and Emily loaded up into Earl's truck, Blanche stayed behind to say a few words to Rusty. I turned to go but not before I saw Rusty's hand resting oh so comfortably on Blanche's ass.

CHAPTER THIRTY-FIVE

I'd been in the kitchen trying to put something together for dinner. By tomorrow the house would be full of food brought from miles around. But not tonight. Reaching for the skillet, I noticed the liquor cabinet door open, I went to shut it, then saw the bottle. I yanked it up. The same bottle that used to be in her drawer. Empty. Next to the Seagram's. Well, that's how she got his head into the tub. I put the empty bottle back, shut the cabinet door, shut off the part of my brain that knew what Fran had done was wrong.

But thinking of her, I realized it wasn't like Fran to not check on me. Even though she'd suffered the tragedy, if killing counted as a tragedy—for the killer. She'd still want to know I was okay. The later it got, the more I worried.

Forget this.

I went in her room without preamble.

She rushed to close her robe but not soon enough. I saw the dark bruises up and down her torso and around her neck. I started toward her.

"Don't," she said. "I'm fine."

"You're not fine. What happened? Did Hank try to strangle—"

"Doesn't matter anymore."

"Fran, at least let me call Doc to come take a—"

"Please, Dee. I've had worse."

I bit my lip till it bled so I wouldn't make things worse by blubbering.

I sat beside her on the big bed, wondering how Emily and I didn't hear anything. Then I realized how Hank ended up with his head in the tub. They were already outside when he wailed on her. The one thing Hank had never been too drunk to do was pummel Fran. He'd hit her before, then passed out. That's what he did the night Fran had second thoughts and pulled him out of the water.

I tried to remember what she had on earlier today that we wouldn't have seen the bruising around her neck. Must've been a button up or high-necked t-shirt. Hank's situation got all the attention. I hadn't noticed a thing. No one else had either. A woman with a dead husband and choke marks around her neck would garner interest even from a shithead like Rusty—the same shithead who was apparently either sleeping with Blanche, or about to. Ack.

I'd planned to confront Fran about what I saw, tell her Emily saw too. But seeing her deflated, bruised and beaten, I couldn't do it. Not yet. Maybe not ever.

"You should eat, Fran. I'm making patty melts. You love those."

"Oh, no. You go on without me."

"Everything's gonna be fine, isn't it?" I realized that sounded insensitive. Not what I would've said had I not known what really happened. "I'm really sorry, Fran. I never understood what you ... why you—"

"That's okay. I know you won't miss him."

There was that brief moment, at the beginning of summer, when I let myself hope he could change. I knew somewhere underneath the man he was, there was the man he wanted to be, but couldn't.

"No." I said. "Will you?"

"No," she said right away, but didn't look at me. "Not for a second."

CHAPTER THIRTY-SIX

The sirens startled me.

After not convincing Fran to eat or say much, I went to bed. Worries that Emily wouldn't keep her trap shut kept me awake for quite a while. Blanche had called to check on us, to offer food, or whatever we needed. But Emily hadn't asked to speak to me. That didn't feel right, considering the circumstances. I'd listened to Blanche's quick conversation with a critical ear. Did I catch suspicion in her voice? Did she really call to see if I sounded weird? Did she hope to talk to Fran to weigh her guilt? I realized my paranoia would take me over if I weren't careful.

I must've fallen into a pretty deep sleep, a miracle if you ask me. When the sirens stirred me, it took a few seconds to realize what they were, and a few more seconds to remember Hank wouldn't be joining us in the yard to say, "What in hellfire was going on?"

Three times in one summer, sirens blared on the Fifty-three. Unheard of.

I pulled my dirty jeans on and flew out the door. The sirens got closer. I hadn't even checked Fran's room certain she'd beat me out. She hadn't. I rushed back in, threw her door open. She'd just pulled on her "It's Not Nice to Fool Mother Nature" t-shirt, not in any particular hurry.

"Fran, come on," I said. "Sounds like they're right out front now."

I jammed. Fran might still be in some kind of trance from the last twenty-four hours. She'd come out eventually. I wasn't going to wait.

An ambulance and Rusty in his patrol car slammed to a stop in front of Edith's. My eyes went immediately to the fence. The chain with the padlock hung from its usual place, only Smalls was missing.

I heard our screen door fwap shut. Fran moseyed over. Edith lumbered out wringing her dimpled hands. She looked over at the fence too.

"Edith, we've got some bad news."

"Where is he?" Edith said, her voice higher pitched than normal. "In there?" she jutted her head toward the ambulance.

"'Fraid so," Rusty said, his hat in one hand, his other patting Edith's big shoulder.

I headed toward Edith, expecting she'd need comfort or something. Fran stayed put. I cocked my head in Edith's direction trying to get Fran to come with me. No way Jose.

"Dead?" Edith said.

"Yes. I'm so sorry, Edith. Run over by—"

"Does she need the gory details right now?" I said.

"Go on," Edith said to Rusty.

"Run over by a truck. A semi. Driver said he didn't see him. He thinks Smalls was lying at least partway on the highway when he, well, you get the picture."

Edith started toward the ambulance. Rusty put an arm out to stop her. "You don't want to see him this way. You can come down to the coroner's later." For the first time he looked in Fran's direction. "Maybe Fran can drive you."

"If it's just a matter of identification how hard can that be?" Fran said, snippy. "He looked like he'd been run over by a truck since the Yous—" She didn't need to fill in the blank. "I'll ID him."

Rusty's mouth opened like he was going to dissuade her but he nodded at the paramedic standing like a statue by the ambulance. He opened the doors. Fran marched over, hoisted herself in, poked her head out, "It's him all right," then jumped down.

She stood next to Edith who hadn't shed a tear.

Of course, this was her husband, not her dogs. The Yous croaking was a real loss.

Rusty spied the chain dangling from the fence. "How'd he get loose?"

"Darned if he didn't have his ways of gettin' whatever in tarnation he wanted," Edith said. "He wanted loose."

Rusty closed the book on the investigation right then. Didn't even examine the chain and lock.

I stayed over in our yard to better observe the scene in its entirety. Rusty said a few words to the paramedic who got back into the ambulance and drove off, then he patted Edith some more and said stuff I couldn't make out. Probably about claiming the body, or whatever. I still didn't know what Fran would do about collecting Hank.

Two dead husbands in twenty-four hours. The Fifty-three had outdone itself this time.

Rusty drove off, waved at me on his way by. About to go over to Edith's yard I saw her and Fran exchange smug looks that kept me from taking one more step in their direction.

Fran whispered to Edith then seized the chain off the fence. I saw the open lock. Did Fran set him loose or did Edith? I refused to worry about it. I knew more than I ever wanted to already. The pills Fran gave Edith to dole out to Smalls made him pliable enough to be led anywhere. And Edith could carry him, if need be.

"Edith, come on over for supper tonight," Fran said. "Dee can make that Coca-Cola cake you like."

"Be over 'bout six then," Edith said.

Edith turned toward her house, smiling.

Fran plunked the chain in the trash.

"Let's go in, Delilah. Nothing more to be done."

I remembered Smalls with his hands around his throat and his morbid half smile. He'd seen Fran and Hank's altercation outside. He'd been chained to the fence. He'd seen Fran drown Hank. But Smalls was no threat. No one paid any attention to his garbled noises, or him in general, unless he pissed on their leg. No way of understanding anything he tried to say.

So why risk a murder rap on him? Because there'd be no murder rap.

The highway served as its own judge and jury. No one interfered from the real world. Two men, deemed deserving, died in ways the Fifty-three thought fair.

That was that.

2005

CHAPTER THIRTY-SEVEN

On the drive home the photo of Billy Dale and his convict mother crossed my mind. Imagine having something so horrible in common. What were the odds?

Did he know about Fran?

I swerved off the road, overcorrected and almost flipped my car at the thought. He couldn't know. No one knew. Not anymore. I couldn't worry about that. It was so long ago, no point in it.

I pulled into Vi's for lack of something to do. I could use a drink, actually. I could've gone home but I didn't feel like it yet. I'd have a beer and one of Vi's nearly inedible burgers.

Margene lingered at the bar, alone. I looked at my watch. Too late for lunch, too early for dinner, so the bar was quiet. I sat next to Margene, actually anxious to hear some good gossip to take my mind off everything else.

"So what's new?" I asked.

"Other than your pig poisoning, nothing," she said. "What a damn shame. Who'd do that?"

"You know what? I'm not worried about it anymore. Jefferson Davis burned the dead ones, got me new ones, and we're moving forward. It'll be fine."

I tapped my fingertips on the bar. "Where's Vi?"

"Oh, she and Fran had to run up to their place. A leak or something."

I got up to get my own beer. "Their place?"

Margene flushed. "Oh, I thought you knew. I—"

"Well, I knew Fran and Vi were sharing expenses, but I didn't think of it as their place." I sat at the bar with my cold brew. "Silly,

I guess. But Fran does still have her own house, still spends time there, sometimes."

Did she though? That house had nothing in it but lawn furniture and a coffeepot.

"Yes, well, she did keep her—"

"So you're saying they're a couple. Like a couple? More than roomies?"

"Yeah, reckon I am." She stared at me for some reaction.

My talent for storing and retrieving trivia brought the conversation I'd had with Jefferson Davis about gays on the highway. He'd said I wouldn't believe him if I knew. Everyone knew but me. I thought about Fran and Vi as lovers. Well, that didn't sit well, but picturing Fran as anyone's lover made me squirmy. Other than that normal mother/child/sex reaction, I felt fine. I tossed the idea around some more to be sure. Yep, I was more than fine.

"Good for them," I said. "My mother never knew a man who didn't treat her like shit. I'm happy for her and Vi."

I couldn't imagine the romance part, but who could blame Fran? It had been right under my nose the whole time I'd been back, but I never thought much about it. If Margene thought I'd disapprove, she'd need to rethink. I'd been through hell and back with Fran. I wouldn't begrudge her happiness no matter how it came.

"Not long after you left, she moved in up there. Then Edith got the Alzheimer's so your mama spent some time at her own house to help Edith out. Then Edith fell out the window and it plumb near killed her. So Fran took her to live with her sister up to Portland," Margene said, like she was telling me about her bunions. Nothing weird ever seemed weird to anyone who lived on the Fifty-three. And falling out a window was as odd as catching a cold on the highway.

"Um hmm." I took a too healthy gulp of my brew.

Margene put her clammy hand on mine. "You know, your mom was never the same after the rape."

"What?" I slammed my beer mug on the bar so hard it splashed over the sides.

"You didn't know that either?" Margene got up, poured herself a coffee refill. "I'm tellin' all kinds of tales out of school today. I'm awful sorry, honey."

"Raped? That can't be true. How would I not know that?"

"'Cause you was just a young'un. Not long before Hank died is what I heard." Margene tore a bright pink packet of Sweet'N Low open over her coffee.

The truth crashed and rolled over me like a tsunami. How could I have been so blind? I felt the blood leave my face. Another thing right under my fucking nose and I missed it completely.

"It happened here, at Vi's." She pointed toward the back. "In the outhouse."

I knew that didn't I? I'd been right there outside, while Smalls raped my mother. And I thought she—I couldn't bear to finish the thought. The beer I gulped swooshed up the back of my throat. All these years I thought—

"How did you know?"

Fran never told anyone anything, ever. She never even told Hank. Not even when he beat the shit out of her.

"Edith told me."

"What? How would Edith know?"

"'Cause Smalls did it and he told her."

"Why would he tell Edith he'd raped his own neighbor? Edith's good friend?"

"Braggin'" she said, her voice lowered so no one could overhear. "The ass actually bragged to his own wife."

"No one went to the police, like usual," I murmured.

"Oh, honey, we all knew your mama wouldn't a wanted that. If she had, she'd a made the call her own self. Besides, by the time we knew, it was too late. It'd already been taken care of."

Already been taken care of needed no explanation.

"Did Fran know her rape was common knowledge?"

"Oh, honey. Who's to say?"

"Did she know Edith knew?"

"That's not something Edith would tell Fran, now is it?" Margene sipped her coffee. "But who knows? Got a lot of pride, your mama. If she knew, she never told."

"That's Fran all right. Bolted down like a submarine porthole."

"Soon after, Smalls got mauled by Edith's dogs." Margene's lips stayed close to her cup. "And I'll tell you something else I probably shouldn't. We all thought Fran and Smalls had something going on till Edith told us all about the rape—"

Get in line.

"Us? Who is us?"

"Me and Vi, right after the dogs chewed him up. Justice served, as far as the highway was concerned. Smalls lived like a dog, died like a dog."

"Yes, I'd say the scales were balanced that day."

"Gettin' run over by that semi…too merciful if you ask me." Margene sipped her coffee.

I could only murmur agreement.

"I can tell you, not one soul 'round the highway looked down on Fran. We're small town folk with old ways, but we don't cotton with 'she musta been askin' for it' neither." Margene wouldn't shut up when she got going. "And I know you don't either. Fran is the most selfless person ever to set foot on the Fifty-Three. Why, I can't even count how many times she took Blanche to town, or Edith, and look how she drove her all the way to Portland so she'd have a safe place to live, or how many beautiful things she's given me and just 'bout everyone else. No, siree. Your mama's 'bout the best person on this highway."

CHAPTER THIRTY-EIGHT

After I left the bar, I thought I'd go up to Vi's Place, well, Vi and Fran's place, to see if they got the leak fixed. And to quench my curiosity, to see how they lived together, if I could tell just by looking that they were happy. Fran's Impala was parked under the carport, Vi's truck gone. I'd never been to Vi's trailer. I'd never even driven this far up my own road. And I thought my place was way up it.

Fran met me at the door.

"Delilah, what on earth?" Her face shifted, paled. "What's happened? What did you do?"

"Jesus, Fran. Nothing. Can't I drop by to say hello? You do."

She blinked a few times. For a second I thought she'd hug me, but like gas, it passed. It'd never occurred to her I might stop in. I felt bad about that. Fran opened the door wider so I could get in. The rickety floor creaked and moaned as I made my way to the expensive sofa I'd given her. I barely walked in but it felt homey right away. The paneled walls, tacky by any standards, felt like a warm embrace. Crocheted pillows and blankets were tossed about. Even the nose burning cigarette smoke smell comforted me. I could picture Fran here. Despite my nouveau riche (now poor) ways, I could picture me here. Curling up on the sofa under a handmade blanket, a place I could lick my wounds. Fran stopped in front of the TV for a couple seconds then turned it off.

"Fire somewhere in San Ysidro," she said. Fran was a news junkie since satellites made their way to the Fifty-three.

"Fire season," I said. "Dry as Hades this time of year."

She scurried to the kitchen area, came out with an Italian mug, one of the four-piece set I'd sent her from Florence, hot coffee steaming out the top.

"The place looks nice, Fran. You and Vi have made it cozy and warm. I like it."

All the furniture I'd given to her filled the space, mixed with some tattered ones that must've been Vi's. The walls were covered with the pictures from Fran's house and some I didn't recognize. A framed photograph of me, a toddler, sitting on Fran's lap sat on the end table nearest me. Fran was looking at me and not the camera. She looked joyful, carefree. She'd once been young, in love, a person who hoped, had dreams, felt happy. I'd never known that woman and I grieved for her. I felt my eyes water and took a drink of my weak coffee.

"It's my favorite place in the world," Fran said, after a minute or two. "My home."

I knew she'd make no explanations about her relationship with Vi. She didn't owe me, or anyone, that. I planned to respect what I knew she wanted and not ask. Fran wasn't the sort of woman who explained. She'd learned over the rocky and tragic years of her life that knowledge was power. And she'd never let anyone have that kind of power over her again.

What about the rape?

What was the appropriate rape conversation segue? I wrestled with myself over it as we sipped. Fran kept quiet, which was unusual for her. I'd guess she was sorting some things out in her head too. I knew she never expected to see me at her door despite the fact I lived a mile away. I hoped she wasn't uncomfortable that I'd invaded her space, though god knows she never minded invading mine.

Was my motive for bringing up the rape clean? Did I want to remind her of such a painful act to ease my conscience, to apologize for not knowing, not helping, or understanding? I'd about talked myself out of it when I blurted, "Fran, why didn't you tell me what happened with Smalls? The rape?"

The only outward sign she was distressed by the question was she started rubbing her thigh with her free hand—back and forth, back and forth. "I would ask who told you that, but I guess I know, and I guess it doesn't matter," Fran said.

I wouldn't insult her by asking if was true. I knew the truth.

Always hard to read, she held her features still, her face a stony blank. Fran could've made a killing at poker. A barely noticeable pink climbed up her neck, but no big show of emotion. I felt like crying. For the first time in, I don't know how many years, I wanted to break down and have a good tantrum.

"Why didn't you tell me?" I said.

"What kind of mother would tell a child she'd been raped?" Fran said, her tone even.

I got that.

"What about later? I haven't been a child in a very long time."

"What would've changed?"

"Everything."

"For who?"

"Us."

It only explained everything about that summer.

Fran's eyes shut tight, her mouth pressed to a thin, sharp line. She breathed out through her nose. I didn't know what to expect if I brought the subject up, but I didn't expect anger. Now I thought she might yell at me, if she spoke at all.

"It wouldn't have changed a damn thing, for anyone," she finally said. "You girls these days assume your own importance, take it as a birthright. You take for granted that somebody's gonna give a shit." She pushed her glasses up her nose. "That has never been my life."

She got up, grabbed her mug, and went to the kitchen.

I shouldn't have blurted that out. But for all our differences, I wanted Fran to know that I knew, that I would've cared about it then, that I cared about it now. I would've wanted to help her in whatever way a sixteen-year-old kid could.

"Let's not bring up the past, Delilah," Fran said. "It's never done a damn thing for either of us." She organized herself in that way she had, that let me know the subject at hand was closed. She lit a cigarette, studied the paneling, held her neck and back stiff. Her whole body warded off any further conversation about rape. I knew she didn't want me to say another thing about it, ever. I wanted to take her in my arms, show her love, let her know I finally saw her as a real person, not a cartoon or a mother, but as a woman who'd known pain, been hurt, scarred. I knew she wouldn't have it, so I stayed in my seat.

I had to let it go.

She picked up my mug, refilled it, and gave it back to me. I took that as a sign that she at least didn't want me to leave.

"Where's Vi?"

"Town. Gotta get some stuff to fix the leak. Reminds me, don't use the toilet. All the water's shut off."

"Oh, you didn't go with her?" Duh. Now I was blathering about nothing.

"She's not my unborn twin, Dee."

"Do you think you'll sell your house?" Blurting was my thing today.

"I dunno. I've thought about it over the years. But, it's the only thing I own in my name. Hard to give that up."

"I know the feeling."

"Yes, I suppose you do," she said without much sympathy.

I got up to go. As usual, our potential heart-to-heart died on the vine.

"I'm glad you're happy here, Fran, with Vi."

Then she said something I never thought I'd hear this side of the second coming. "I am. Vi makes me feel like I matter."

CHAPTER THIRTY-NINE

"Where you been all day?" Jefferson Davis said.

"Funny, you don't look like my dad," I said. As if I remembered what he looked like. Something about his tone stopped me though. He looked tense, worried. It'd been a strange day. Add that to the list.

"Just not like you to take off without a word in my direction."

"I think we need a dog," I said.

"What? Where'd that come from?"

"Listen, my old neighbor in San Ysidro might be a little unhinged."

"What neighbor?" He leaned on the shovel he'd been digging holes with for plants around the fence he'd built surrounding my house.

"The winemaker."

"The one who gave you all that pricey wine? That's weird. What's her problem all of a sudden?"

"What makes you think it's a 'her'"?

"Ain't it?" He spit a brown stream of chew onto the ground. "Thought you said a girly name one time."

"Well, yes. She thinks I slept with her husband."

"How many husbands you sleep with?"

"As a matter of fact, I didn't sleep with Karen's husband. She's just convinced I did."

"What's that got to do with a dog?"

"A dog would make some noise if a stranger came on the property."

"What's that got to do with your neighbor, ah, Karen?"

"I think she poisoned my pigs," I said. "And thanks a lot for telling me. I had to hear it from Fran. You DO work for me don't you?"

"I didn't tell you because I'm not sure it's right so don't go blowin' your asshole out."

"Nope. You should've told me what Doc said."

He looked at me without expression. "You're right. Should've. Didn't. Sorry."

Worst apology ever. "Anyway, my old neighbor's off the deep end."

"What? I think you're off the deep end."

He stepped down hard on the shovel, drove it deep into the dirt. I guess feeling sorry didn't staunch the snippiness on any other topic.

"Where'd you get that fruit loop idea?" he said. "Rich people who own wineries don't get close enough to live pigs to do anything to 'em."

"You don't know Karen. Billy Dale told me she's trying to find me. He's not a cop you know, he's a private investigator."

"Same difference to me. Crawls up my ass either way."

"Let the church say amen."

Jefferson Davis dug dirt. "I thought no one knew you'd moved here. She'd have to know a lot about you to know about the pigs."

I picked up a few pots of flowers to arrange them where I wanted them planted.

"My wishful thinking. I think everybody I ever met knows where I am."

"Well, that one gal does. The one whose husband you did sleep with—that fella from your show. You know, the one who fell off the face of the earth apparently."

Like I forgot? He might as well have said, "The one you got rid of."

"Penelope? What do you know about her?"

"I live right over there," he pointed to his little cottage. "Think I'm blind and deaf?"

Jefferson Davis didn't miss a lick. Like mother like son.

"Never mind Penelope." I picked up a gorgeous bubble gum pink hydrangea. Set it aside to plant up against the house. "Can you just get a dog?"

"Your wish is my command." He spat again. "I'll bring one from the turkey farm. We keep lots of dogs up there. Ranch dogs. Smart and loyal."

"Perfect."

"Supposing Karen didn't mind slopping through the mud to mingle with the pigs, what would she know about poison or how to get it?" Jefferson Davis worked steadily down the fence. I followed with pots.

"Her husband's a crop duster. He's got all sorts of poisons. You know farmers keep poisons, for rats, vermin, whatever. Especially around here and the Valley where you can still get the illegal stuff."

"True enough. Still, don't set right with me—a winemaker from one of the richest areas in the state sneaking around in the dead of night to poison pigs. On foot? We'd have heard her drive up."

"Stop overthinking this Jefferson Davis, and get the damn dog."

****

After a dinner of barbecued steaks (Jefferson Davis manned the grill) we sat out on my porch to survey our handiwork. I'd bought some cheap, plastic chairs and a small table so we didn't have to sit on the freezer anymore. The sun had started its slow descent. Daylight still lasted till nearly seven every evening but would come earlier and earlier as fall swept in.

"It's starting to look like a real farm now," I said. "Your cottage is adorable. You've really fixed it up. I love the white paint with the bright red shutters and door. You're quite the decorator."

"Same color as my mom's place. Habit." He popped the top off a can of beer. I kept the kind he liked stocked. "I'm gonna do yours the same."

"Fine with me." I poured myself a hefty glass of a nice, chilled white wine, set the bottle on the table. Matchy-matchy houses. How Ozzie and Harriet.

I realized we'd started behaving like an old married couple. I studied him while he looked straight ahead. He looked more like a man since he'd been here, away from his nagging mother. He'd filled out some. Already handsome, he looked rugged and handsome. Like the Marlboro Man. I cooked for him almost every day. So he ate well. I'd noticed he'd started drinking more. He drank only beer, but that'd put weight on him, but not like most men, no gut. I wondered idly why he drank more. Oh well, didn't we all? I drank more out here too. For oh so many reasons.

He didn't notice me taking his measure so I kept staring at him. I'd have to say his unsettling good looks, straight talk and straighter shot, and his ability to not give a shit about being liked, transfixed me. I liked him more and more every day. No game player, this one. I could smell the Ivory soap that hugged his skin and the Tide detergent on his clothes. No girly-man cologne for him.

I was definitely attracted to Jefferson Davis.

Now that'd be a fine mess, Ollie.

Shake it off, Delilah. You're a man hound. Leave the poor guy alone.

"Are you ever gonna leave this highway, Jefferson Davis? Get married? Have a family?"

"Are you?" He set his beer on the table.

"I left for a long time."

"Yet here you are. Again."

"Well, yes, but I'm moving forward." I did a game show hostess sweep of the hand across the span of land in front of me, pigs everywhere.

"Moving back isn't moving forward."

Why was he always so sensibly, annoyingly, simplistically right?

"What about that TV show guy?" he fiddled with his beer can.

"Matthew? What about him?"

"Well, he's obviously not interested in that irritating, clingy wife. I could hear that shrew carrying on when she snuck up to your place. If he's not six feet under somewhere, why not hook back up with him?"

"I have no idea where he is, for one," I said, pouring the last of the wine into my glass. "And for another—that's done. Over."

"What about you? You ever been in love?"

Didn't expect that question. I swallowed my Chardonnay.

"Are you crying?" he said.

"Heavens no." I wiped at my eyes. Then to even my surprise, I broke like a hammer hit cantaloupe. I turned away—once the sadness escaped, I couldn't stop it. I could feel Jefferson Davis's discomfort. I thought he might run, but once I got the ball rolling, I kept on.

"Hey, hey," he said. "Get a hold of yourself girl. One of the things I like about you is you're dead inside. So stop it."

He took out a handkerchief (who in the twentieth century carried one of those?). I grabbed it.

"So I take it the answer is yes," he said. "You loved that Hardy guy."

I gathered myself. Dried my never more useless tears, drank more wine. Kept my eyes firmly on the beauty of my surroundings. I let several minutes pass.

"Who cares who I loved or didn't? Doesn't matter now." I kept looking straight ahead, watched the sun skulk lower, the sky darken.

"I didn't think you had a heart, now the damn thing's broke," he said.

I had to laugh at that. "Yeah, it's broke. I just wish it had broken slower."

We both got quiet. Me, letting myself wallow in self-pity and Jefferson Davis … who knew what Jefferson Davis wallowed in?

"Don't you want a wife and kids?" I finally said, tears gone.

"Not on my mind. I need to see this through."

"See what through?"

"This place. Still lots of work to do and you can't pig farm by yourself. Not with as many pigs as you want."

Jefferson Davis came in behind Fran by a flea's length in deadpan. He didn't know I'd been a CIA worthy decoder my whole life. His face didn't change, his tone stayed even, but something made his one eye a little twitchy. Deciphering twitchy was my jam.

"Besides," he said. "I'm not the marrying kind. Give me my handkerchief back. Better not have boogers on it." He looked it over for an offending booger, finding none, he shoved it back into his jeans pocket.

"What about the dating kind?" I said.

"That'd lead a girl on, wouldn't it?"

"In the fifties."

"I'll pass."

"You were engaged once, to Wanda. So you must've been the marrying kind then."

"I know now I never woulda married Wanda. I was just trying her on for size. When her size was manageable."

I cracked up at that. He didn't.

"Jefferson Davis, don't you ever laugh?"

"On the inside."

Out of the blue, Billy Dale roared up out front in his sedan, skidded to a too quick stop, like he'd driven hell to leather to get here to tell me something urgent.

"That guy doesn't know when to quit, does he?"

Neither of us got up to meet the unwanted Billy Dale. He hopped up the steps, opened the porch screen door, and there he was, again. I almost said, "you miss me?" but then I remembered his distasteful suggestion that we date. So I kept that gem to myself. Turned out I didn't need to spark the conversation.

"I suppose you heard," Billy Dale said, still standing.

"About?" I said.

"The fire."

"End of summer in a drought?" Jefferson Davis snorted. "What's next? Pie's round? Cornbread's square?"

Billy Dale kept both eyes on me.

"Fran mentioned something earlier," I said. "Didn't pay much attention."

"Your old house and your neighbor Karen's place," he said. "Burnt to the ground."

1985

CHAPTER FORTY

B lanche and Earl wheedled Fran into going through with the time honored, Highway Fifty-three memorial ritual. Two for one, they thought was a grand plan, since Smalls's roadkill situation had run neck and neck with Hank's drowning. Had Hank died of his own accord, Fran would've been hard pressed to disguise her glee at the thought of a memorial. All that attention and the opportunity to play the widow would've been right up her martyr alley.

She would've been in her element. Clucking, tittering, waving off all the "you're awfully brave" and "no one could've tried harder with a man like him," with Muhammad Ali-esque humility. But now she went along to get along—somber, not caring about the arrangements. Blanche and Earl handled all of it. As usual, no one saw a body in either Hank or Smalls's case. I'd overheard "cremation" mentioned so I assumed that's how it went down somewhere over in Kearny.

Edith did what Fran told her to do. The memorial duet was settled.

Vi's Place burst at the seams with all the revelers.

I wondered, to keep my mind off wondering about other worrisome things, what they'd do if so many locals didn't die. Their social lives would hit the skids, quick. The late summer sun broiled down on the gathered. A few of the hometown women stood by the bulging food tables waving flies away. Sweat ran down cowboy hat covered heads, and almost everyone held on to a brew. Had to drink fast while they still held their chill. A steady stream flowed in and out, hands clapped shoulders, necks got hugged, "Haven't seen ya'll in a coon's age," rang out a few times, even though they'd seen each other at every memorial these past few months, and that accounted for quite a few social interactions. Still, the highway came out in full force.

A two for one memorial was not to be missed. Ding, dong, the pricks were dead.

Fran and Edith sat side by side at the bar making it easy for everyone to pay their condolences, which they took as graciously and seriously as they could. Fran ordered a beer, which she never did. Edith tried to keep her toothless smile from giving away her real feelings, succeeding about half the time.

I hung back to examine Fran's face. Sometimes, when I woke up in the mornings, it took me several seconds to remember what she'd done. Then it'd shower me like Niagara Falls over an idiot in a barrel. I knew I wore Fran's guilt on my face but no one seemed to notice it and Fran, well, she went about it cool as a superhero who can deflect all manner of harm with her forearms. No matter what came her way—boulders, bullets, speeding trains, drunken men, they'd bounce off her with just a flex of an elbow.

I admired it.

"Jefferson Davis," Margene yelled. "That better not be that damn snake box."

Jefferson Davis flipped open the box he carried to show Margene the napkins inside. "Vi told me to bring these out," he yelled back in protest. Arthur cuffed his goofball kid on the head in anticipation of a future transgression.

I didn't see Emily until she came to hug me but I could tell she didn't mean it. She dropped her arms to her sides after a couple seconds around my neck.

"Are you all right?" I said, like I thought she'd say yes.

"No, are you?"

"No point in being otherwise. It's done. Over. We have to forget about it."

Please, please, please, forget about it.

"Well, I can't and I can't believe you can either. You're good, Delilah. No matter how many awful things have happened to you, and all around you, you're still good. Loving. I know you."

My skin turned hot with shame. Hard to say which felt worse, my willful ignorance where Fran's crimes were concerned or my trying to steal Willy Wally. Emily's lamenting kept me from deciding.

"I can't believe I helped cement Fran's story to Rusty. First Hank, then Smalls. Did Fran do both of—"

I pulled her outside where more of the crowd milled. But they were rowdier outside, noisier. Less chance Emily would be overheard.

"No, she absolutely didn't," I said. "Smalls got loose. You know how he wandered around. It's a miracle it hadn't happened before now."

"I don't know. Too coincidental." She chewed at her already bloody fingertips. "Your mom is out of control. She needs help. She'd probably go to some psychiatric facility where—"

I shook her. "Stop it. It's not like Fran's some crazed serial killer. She does need help, but not in some loony bin." If ever I was going to plead like my life, and Fran's, depended on it, it'd be now. "Emily, my mom needs a life without a man in it who belittles her and beats her. Please. I'm begging you. Don't say a word."

Emily didn't say anything, but I could tell by her face she heard me and took what I said to heart. She just sighed, resigned. I hoped.

It hadn't escaped me that Edith was immediately off the hook. She'd chained Smalls to the fence for fuck's sake but Emily thought Fran did the deed anyway. Well, she halfway did, I supposed.

When I thought we were out of the woods Emily dropped this, "Hank wanted a divorce. He treated her like shit, but she tramped around. What did she expect? She could've gone along with the divorce instead of—"

"You think tramping around is worse than being a wife beater? Seriously? I thought you had a much bigger heart, Emily."

Emily'd started up with the tears. "No, but two wrongs don't make—"

"Maybe you should worry about your own mother," I said, pissed off now, frantic really. Fran was all I had in the world. No way I'd let her get carted off to the pokey or the asylum.

"My mom?"

As serendipity would have it, at that exact moment Blanche and Rusty were standing oh so close together near the casserole table. I pointed in their direction.

"She's tramping around with Rusty."

Emily peered over my shoulder. "What are you talking about? They're just talking, big deal."

"They do more than that. I saw them."

"When?" Emily swiped at her wet face.

This whole convo wasn't giving me the satisfaction I thought it would but I couldn't put the brakes on it.

"When they were all at my house, after Hank ... I saw Rusty squeeze your mom's ass and she liked it."

"You're lying."

Exaggerating, yes. Lying, not exactly.

"Look at them."

Blanche rested her hand on Rusty's shoulder, laughing a goofy, teenager like giggle—both of them oblivious to their surroundings. Earl was off on a toot, as he had been since Hank's death, so they didn't need to worry about him. I couldn't have asked for better backup for my story, although it didn't feel good to skewer Blanche to save Fran. But I'd do what I needed to do.

"I'll keep your mom's secret if you keep Fran's. Your dad wouldn't be thrilled to know."

Emily's obvious pain crushed me. Yet I couldn't stop myself. Fran was the only family I had, my mother for Chrissake.

"Like they're even close to the same kinds of secrets," Emily said, then took off in the opposite direction.

"What's her deal?" Willy Wally popped up out of nowhere.

"Nothing. Girl stuff." I wondered if he already knew. I searched his face for a hint, but he looked like he always did. Too good looking for his own good and on the make.

"Come on." He led me away from the potluck tables, toward the highway.

"Where are we going?"

He pulled me across the highway. No traffic. Everyone was at Vi's.

"My truck."

"I shouldn't. This is Hank's memorial in case you forgot."

It should've annoyed me that this is the first I'd seen of him since Hank drowned. Not a call or visit to see how I fared. What did I expect from a cheater?

He opened the passenger side door, I got in. "And what about Emily?"

"You haven't been that worried about Emily before."

"Well, she's here, you imbecile."

He shut the door. Walked around the truck bed to the driver's side, then slid in beside me on the bench seat. His lack of sensitivity should've been a detriment to this whole scene, but my only requirements in a boyfriend were looks and his position on the football team, not his capacity for empathy. Though I could hardly call him my boyfriend. I don't know what I'd call him. But studly quarterback Willy Wally checked both boxes.

Before I knew it, we were in serious make out mode.

Before he could get my bra undone the truck shook like an earthquake hit.

An earthquake named Emily.

She threw the driver's side door open. "What are you doing?" she said, her yell dropped the libido level to negative numbers. Willy Wally and I scrambled to put ourselves together.

"Emily, it's—"

"Shut up, Willy Wally. I hate you both." She slammed the door closed then raced across the highway. Before we could close our mouths, opened in shock, Emily screeched out onto the road in her dad's truck.

I sat, unmoving. "What have I done?"

CHAPTER FORTY-ONE

After the shock and guilt wore off (took about a week) nothing filled Fran with more glee than widowhood. Who could blame her? The absence of violence and conflict in our house felt like a living force. Fran reveled in it. She shimmered with an incandescence normally earmarked for those answering the door to find Ed McMahon on the other side with balloons and one of those giant checks. Not drawing attention to her happy relief by skipping around singing "Que Sera, Sera" was her greatest difficulty.

I hid her "Another One Bites the Dust" sweatshirt under my bed.

She obviously didn't know Emily held her fate in her pissed as fuck hands.

I considered it a good sign that Rusty hadn't shown up at the door to slap the cuffs on Fran and force her to do the perp walk. Emily must still be contemplating options. If she ratted on Fran, she'd blow up her family as well as mine, if I made good on my promise to sing like a bitter bird about Blanche and Rusty. That would give her pause.

I didn't know what to do next. School started next week. What then? How could I face her? I tried to call to apologize but she hung up as soon as she heard my voice. I hadn't heard word one from the coward Willy Wally. It still stung to remember him jumping out of the truck to chase after a fleeing Emily. Before I could work myself up into a dither Fran said, "Go see if Edith wants to come to dinner. She's been locked up in that house since Smalls got creamed by that truck."

"Maybe she wants time alone," I said. Not caring what she did over there. I had my own shit to worry about.

"Well, we had that memorial. Aren't those for whatchacallit? Closure?"

"Some people need more than a week for closure, Fran," I said. "Besides, you go over there five times a day. It's like a hostage situation." I'm sure Fran feared Edith wasn't cut out for the life of a hardened criminal and she'd break, confess to her part in Smalls's demise, and Fran's.

I picked over the cascade of homemade offerings laid out on the breakfast bar, dropped off over the past several days by just about every woman still alive on the Fifty-three. I tried to disguise my inappropriate, at a time like this, gluttony when anyone stopped in to pay respects, tortilla pie or cherry strudel in hand, but could usually only muster a periodic long face between mouthfuls.

"I'm sure Edith's not starving to death. Her place looks like this too," I said, mouth full of cold fried chicken and Oriental salad with broken bits of Top Ramen, mandarin oranges and a smattering of almonds—almost enough to make me forget the doom I lived under.

The ringing phone cut off whatever Fran was about to say. "Probably Margene. She's after me to go get all Hank's tools from their place." She answered, but held it out to me. "Emily."

I almost fell off the stool. Why would she call? Couldn't be good.

"She hasn't called in a while, come to think of it," Fran murmured. "Odd, considering."

I took the receiver. Bit the bullet. "Hello," I said, in a squeaky tone.

With no niceties she went right for the jugular. "It will interest you to know that my dad found out about Rusty all on his own."

"Oh?" That was all I could think to say. "Well, I'm sorry about that, Emily. Really. I'm so sorry about all—"

"And Willy Wally and I are engaged."

"Engaged?"

That got Fran's attention.

"Yes, he said after you threw yourself at him, he realized what a find I really am. So he wants to marry me."

I bypassed the insult. "You're only sixteen. Are you going to drop out of school?"

Fran's mouth popped open. "What the hell?" she mouthed.

"No. Since he graduated, he's going to get a good job and save some money and—this is none of your business. I just thought you might want to know. In case."

"In case what?"

She'd hung up.

I stared at the phone for a few seconds, then put it back in its cradle. Feeling every emotion under a merciless sun.

"Emily and Willy Wally engaged? That's sheer nonsense. No way Blanche and Earl would let Emily get out of school early to marry that jack-of-no-trades, master-of-none."

"You thought he was good enough for me."

"What's good enough for a high school girl crush and good enough for a husband are two different things. And that was before this. That bottom feeder will come to a bad end, you take my word." Fran dropped down into Hank's old recliner. She never sat anywhere else now. "I swear, sometimes this place is like the Ozarks. Girls still get married before they're out of puberty. No wonder half the locals act inbred. Probably are."

Reeling with unwanted information, I propelled myself back to the food heaped bar. I peeled the golden brown, flaky crescent roll away from the shriveled, pink hot dog nestled inside. "Blanche probably has enough on her plate, what with Rusty and all the fallout."

Till I die I won't know why I said that.

Fran pitched forward. "What about Rusty?"

Overwrought with fear about what might happen since Emily now had nothing to lose, I blabbed like my fingernails were being peeled off at Guantanamo Bay. I told her everything. From Emily witnessing her drowning Hank, Smalls's sedatives, Earl finding out about Blanche and Rusty, the whole kit and caboodle.

Fran looked like the coalmine canary that just got a beak full of gas, suspended on the edge of Hank's sacred chair. "Do you think she'll tell?"

"To be honest, I don't know. But I'm leaning toward yes."

"Oh my god," Fran turned to me. "You saw it too, didn't you? You must've. You saw me … when I—" She couldn't finish.

Shit. I'd never wanted her to know I'd seen even more than I didn't want her to know Emily had seen. Of course, she'd put two and two together.

"Yes."

Fran pursed her lips so tight it looked as if her pursed lips were pulling every muscle taut, the only things keeping her upright. I counted a full, ten slow seconds before she spoke.

"Well, now you know what I am. What I've become."

She didn't cry. She didn't yell. Her face lost all its animation. The first time I saw the mask she would wear off and on for the rest of her life.

"Fran, Hank drove you to … to … that. It's not your fault."

"I should've let him divorce me," she said.

"You don't know that he really would've. How much were you supposed to take?"

And that cemented my lifetime habit of fending off anything that threatened Fran. She didn't live alone in this life. I lived it too. I saw every smack, heard every slap, picked her up from every kick down. Waited on tenterhooks for my turn, which thankfully never came. Yes, she was wrong to have drowned Hank, but I understood it. I understood her thinking on this. It was the one thing about her I did understand.

"Doesn't matter. I crossed the line I can't come back from."

If we'd been different people, I would've thrown my arms around her, but we weren't that kind of people.

"What are we going to do now?" I said.

"Nothing. As far as I'm concerned Hank's death was an unfortunate consequence of his drunken habit of passing out. I've got nothing to worry about."

"But, Rusty's the law, and if he finds out, then what?" Panic leapt up my chest like a jackrabbit. "Fran—"

She turned on the TV. I knew Fran would never speak of this again, come hell or Emily's high water.

Edith's banging entrance startled both of us.

"No point in hanging around the house with my head pulled in like a scared turtle." I handed her a paper plate. She took it. Must've eaten through her stash already. Fran turned the TV down, but not off.

"I just can't believe it," she said, in her breathy voice, fat weighing down her air supply, piling several tiny sandwiches on homemade rolls, and a hunk of pecan pie onto her plate. "With my Smalls gone, and Hank, why we're just a couple of single ladies." She crammed a whole roast beef roll into her mouth, lips unencumbered by teeth, with a satisfied smile.

CHAPTER FORTY-TWO

With no word from Willy Wally, which I didn't expect, considering, and no more semi-threatening phone calls from Emily, I forced myself to think about school, which was starting in two days. I'd waited till the last minute to think about new clothes, which wasn't like me at all. Usually, Emily and I went together.

Not this year.

I couldn't imagine that Emily hadn't spilled her guts to Willy Wally. Maybe she'd manage, for old time's sake, to not say anything to Blanche or Earl. But Willy Wally? No way.

"If you're going to go you better get on." Fran brushed donut stick crumbs off her "Save a Tree Eat a Beaver" t-shirt. "You've waited till the last minute as it is."

I sighed really loud so she'd know how put out I was by her completely unreasonable request. "If I have to," I said. Didn't take me long to stop feeling so bad for Fran. Well, I'd always feel for her pain, mistreatment, and her actions, but you'd be surprised how little dent that put in my teenage annoyance with her. I didn't own up to my anger toward her for years. That would come later, when I determined two contrary emotions could exist side by side. And I felt divided about Fran for a long time.

"Yes, you have to." Fran mimicked my snotty tone. "You know I won't allow you to drive on that windy road in the dark."

"Whatever."

I figured I'd better quit with the snark before she decided to not let me drive alone to Kearny. She'd let me before, for food, but it wasn't her favorite.

The crackling sound of tires pulling around the gravel corner stopped us both.

"Rusty," I said. So stunned and scared, I went numb.

"Good heavens, what could he want?"

Fran's face twisted around like it couldn't find a comfortable spot, but by the time she opened the door, she looked blameless as a fawn. "Rusty," she said, like the man of her dreams just swooped in. "What brings you by?" She pushed her hair up at the sides, primping.

Rusty picked his hat off his head from the top, nodded, then dropped it back down, covering up his bald spot and ever more sparse reddish hair. "Mornin' Fran ... Delilah." I could tell he tried to act official, serious. He didn't show a hint of a smile with his greeting, but he wouldn't meet Fran's eyes—a bad, bad, sign. I thought I might pass out, wondered if we had any money for a lawyer.

"Sit down, won't you? Delilah, cut Rusty a piece of that apple pie you made yesterday, and put a nice slice of cheddar on it like you do for me."

Too dumbfounded by Fran's nonchalance, I cut the pie.

Rusty softened right away, sat on the sofa across from Fran.

"I think I will, Delilah," he said, his freckly face stretching into a sideways smile. "Pie sounds perfect, right about now. I'd be grateful for some coffee to go along, if you've got it."

I nearly cried with relief. He wouldn't eat pie, drink coffee, then arrest Fran for murder, would he?

"Of course," Fran said, settling into Hank's recliner for a comfy chat. "In fact, why don't you just wrap up whatever's left of that pie and some of that meatloaf, Delilah, for Rusty to take home?" Her voice clear and smooth, a lilting melody. "We can't eat all that food and it's so hard for a man ... alone." She turned to Rusty, her mouth in a downcast, perfect sympathetic pose.

I almost broke into song while I laid a thick, orange piece of aged cheddar over the flaky, golden crust, poured strong, hot coffee. I delivered both, then busied myself back in the kitchen rustling for Tupperware and spooning out food to go. For the umpteenth time, I admired Fran's art form—she was a racehorse, at the top of her game when challenged.

"I hate to bring this up, Frannie," Rusty said.

Frannie? Brother. Fran would worm out of this one with hardly a wiggle.

"Hank's autopsy—"

"Autopsy?" Fran and I chorused. I froze midair, macaroni and cheese half on the spoon, half in the container.

"Yes, well when someone dies like that, you know, so unusually, and at their own home, it's the law," Rusty said, mouth full.

Fran, the stricken, wounded widow leaned forward, looking anxious to hear any news about her soul mate's unfortunate demise that might help make sense of her almost unspeakable tragedy. I felt a pinprick of worry. An autopsy wouldn't show his head had been held down in the water, would it? I mean he wasn't struggling or anything. Too drunk. Rethinking that terrible scene, Hank's inability to fight for his life, brought me to unexpected tears.

"Rusty," Fran said, her voice low. "This is awfully upsetting for Delilah, could you—"

He looked my way, blushed. "Oh, of course. I'll get to it. Don't you worry honey," he said to me. "Everything's fine, I'm almost sure."

Almost?

He set down his plate and cup on the coffee table. "Hank had a high dose of—" he took a crumpled piece of paper out of his shirt pocket. Held it out at arm's-length, squinting to see. "Let's see ... diaz ... diaze ... diazepam. Yes, that's it. Along with a blood alcohol level of—well a real overload, let's just say."

"Oh, no," Fran said, reaching for the Kleenex box. "I worried he'd take too many, but you know how he could be, Rusty." She reached across to rest her hand on his leg. "He wouldn't let me monitor him."

"Doc said the same thing," Rusty said.

The consummate performer, Fran didn't wince once. Kept right on as if she'd expected this information all along. "Yes,

Doctor Bates and I did discuss this very topic. But Doc felt sure the medicine would help calm Hank down, make him less anxious. You know, Hank did so want to stop drinking."

I barked out a laugh that I somehow managed to make into a sob. Jesus, Fran and I were turning into the Barrymores. Fran's devotion to Doc, and his blank page of a daughter, turned crystal clear.

He picked at his pie. "You know, word was Edith gave Smalls the same pills. She's at her sister's so I haven't confirmed. No proof since an autopsy—um, you saw what was left—well, no need for one."

"If anyone needed to calm down, it was Smalls," Fran said, dabbing at her eyes with a tissue. "You know how Edith tried to keep that poor man from harm's way. Doc tried to help. What else could he do? First, do no harm, you know."

Rusty cleared his throat. "Yes, well, I do Fran. I do. But, that's kind of the problem."

The room felt smaller, closing in on all of us. I think Fran felt it too, but the show must go on, and her wide-eyed innocence never dropped.

He continued. "I know he's your good friend, mine too. I'd hate to have to turn him over to the DEA, but do you think Doc's overprescribing dangerous drugs?"

CHAPTER FORTY-THREE

After Fran's master class in getting away with murder, I finally started for Kearny. I left home while Fran explained away Doc's generous prescription writing while Rusty lapped up any excuse to not have to seriously look into anything. So worried about Fran, I forgot to look for any telltale signs that Earl had beat the shit out of Rusty for diddling his wife. Would've been obvious, wouldn't it?

Maybe Emily lied about Earl knowing, to shake me up. If so, it worked.

On a whim, I flipped a U to go past Emily's. What I expected to find I didn't know. I drove past her trailer at what I thought was a normally cautious speed. Slow enough to check it out but not stalker slow. Looked like no one was home. No truck outside anyway.

Just the thought of the damage Emily could do to Fran made me sweat. I gripped the wheel so hard my knuckles and palms ached. I hadn't realized till being near her turf how frightened I really was. And under Fran's cool remove she had to be quaking every hour of every day too. Fran did not like limbo. When Fran acted calm in calamitous situations, it was Michael Corleone calm.

I remembered Fran mentioning a few days before Hank's stuff still at Margene and Arthur's. I couldn't believe Fran hadn't made the trip to get a read on Margene. She had to be dying to know if anything malicious had been spread around the Fifty-three. If there had been, Margene would be at the center of it. I'd come this far up the road, might as well see for myself.

After I parked along the side of the house, I did a quick search of the yard to see if I'd see her out in her garden or doing some kind of ranch wife work, as she often did. Not finding her, I knocked on the back screen, leaned in when I heard her voice.

"Edith cried harder when them damn dogs died," Margene said, disapproving, into the phone. "It ain't seemly the way she's a laughin' and carryin' on. I mean, I can completely understand she'd be glad to be rid of the bastard, but not everyone is as understanding as we are."

The only thing passed faster on the Fifty-three than Margene's coconut cake at a potluck was judgment. Margene spoke in that quasi quiet kind of church voice that let you know she could bark at a carnival in the next sentence. I leaned in closer, spellbound, hoped she wouldn't notice and might talk a blue streak about crap I needed to know.

"Oh, right. You're kidding. Fran's—" Margene must've seen me loitering. "I gotta git on now." She plunked down the phone. "Delilah," she said like her prodigal daughter had walked through the door after twenty years gone. She held both arms held aloft. "Come in you poor child." Margene crushed me against her bulbous bosoms.

I tried to pay careful attention to her attitude and actions toward me. I didn't like the way she said "Fran" right before she hung up to whoever was on the other end of the phone. Who was it I wondered? Blanche? I didn't think she was home from the looks of their trailer. But after the tedious small talk about how we were all managing, and no suspicious questions or weird looks, I felt confident she hadn't heard anything about Fran's dirty deeds.

She poured me a glass of homemade lemonade. "What can I do ya for, honey?"

"Oh," I almost forgot my excuse for showing up. "I came to pick up Hank's stuff."

She shut the refrigerator door. "Oh, sure thing, honey. I plumb forgot about it."

She took off in search of Arthur. I followed her out but only as far as one of the picnic tables out on the grass. Margene kept a beautiful yard. Even in my irritation I could appreciate a good flowerbed and herb garden. About to relax a little in the sun,

Jefferson Davis swaggered over, kicking dirt up with his boot toes as he made his way over, then slumped on to the picnic bench across from me, his pimply chin cradled in both his dirty hands.

"Why so glum, butthead?" I said.

"What's it to you?" Jefferson Davis said, peevish, which wasn't like him. He usually got nicer when I got nastier—ingratiating little bastard—or ran.

"Not a thing," I took a big gulp of the cold, crisp lemonade. Made a loud smacking sound just to further annoy him. The little asshole looked like he'd lost his best friend. How you could lose an imaginary friend, I didn't know, but I almost felt a little sorry for the jackwad.

"Okay, I'm falling for it. What's wrong?" I said.

He got up from the table and ran toward the barns, my bitchy laughter chasing him onward. What a dumbo. I'd decided to follow him, for shits and giggles, but Margene met me halfway.

"Honey, Arthur said your mom came by early this morning to get Hank's things."

"Huh?"

"How I missed her, I don't know. Arthur said she came out to the pens herself, thought she might find Hank's tools without botherin' us."

"Oh, right. Um. Okay, then."

"You know, poor thing, she might not want to see a soul right yet. Can't say I blame her, what with all the grievin' goin' on at your place and Edith's so close. I'll take a look around though to make sure she got everything. Coulda swore I saw his thermos not an hour ago. If you can wait just a few."

After forever and a day, with no thermos, I sped back down the road, flummoxed. Maybe the stress of it all had finally gotten to Fran. I mean, it wasn't a big deal she didn't tell me she'd gone up to Margene's. I hadn't been sleeping well, usually not drifting off till near morning, so I tended to sleep a bit later. So she must've gone early, before I got up. Or maybe she'd had some kind of psychotic break finally, and lost it. Soon she'd be wandering the highway like Smalls. Then I remembered her pitch perfect conversation with Rusty. No, the old girl still had her wits about her. No doubt.

When I got close to Emily's I slowed down. Habit more than anything. I wanted to stop, grovel another apology. Make another heartfelt plea for Fran's life. Earl's truck was still gone, but that didn't mean Emily wasn't home. Willy Wally's truck wasn't there either.

Emily was probably gone. Planning her stupid, child-bride, redneck fucking wedding.

CHAPTER FORTY-FOUR

S irens. Again.

My eyes flickered open from a restless slumber. By the time half a thought formed, I pulled my jeans on and ran into Fran on my race to the living room, my feet sticking to the wood floor. The wailing screech was getting to be an everyday occurrence.

"Mother of god, what now?" Fran said, snapping her robe closed, her footsteps heavy.

We both hustled outside, to see if we could tell anything by standing in the yard.

"Were they coming or going?" Fran said.

All ambulances and fire trucks came from Kearny. If the sound came from our left, they were coming, from the right, leaving.

"I think coming." They'd passed our house.

"Maybe a fire. Haven't had one of those all summer."

No fires were a rarity. "Maybe," I said.

Edith lugged herself out too, "How many do ya think?" she hollered, hauling her girth through our gate.

"At least two," Fran said. "I thought I heard two, or maybe three."

"Me too," I said.

"Used to be sirens meant a fire or a car accident out here," Edith said. "Now you just don't know what all's gonna go wrong with folks," she said like Smalls and Hank's deaths were a complete mystery to her.

The three of us lined up in a row like bowling pins waiting for the ball to knock us over. None came, so we kept standing there. Me in my Guns N' Roses nightshirt and jeans, Fran in a cotton robe so thin I could see she didn't have on underwear, and Edith in a food stained, XXXL housedress with a pair of men's corduroy slippers, ripped out at the toes. I knew we weren't the only ones keeping watch on the highway. Everyone on the Fifty-three knew sirens meant something bad happened. I didn't know for sure what time it was. The sun already felt hot, the last of the cool night air evaporated under its rays. I could smell the dirt, baking.

"No point in chasing ambulances," Fran said. "We'll find out soon enough."

****

I cracked another egg into the hissing cast iron to fry with its friends, spooned hot grease over the bright yolks to cook them just enough to make them safe to eat, the way Fran and I liked them, sopped up with a thick slice of bread, charred just so.

"Edith, how do you like your eggs?" I said.

"Out of the shell," she said.

I don't know why I bothered to ask. I'd learned most of her food preferences since Smalls's death—anything on offer. Edith always made a big deal about my culinary skills, so I didn't mind. Plus, cooking gave me something to do other than worry.

All About Eve played out across the TV screen, in panto-mime, since the sound wasn't turned up, while Edith and Fran debated the pros and cons of widowhood. So far, the pros beat the cons ten to one. Fran had put on some underwear (I assumed), stretch pants, and a "Black Is Beautiful" tank top.

I'd just turned the toasting bread over on the griddle pan when the jangling phone gave us all a scare. I turned toward the living room. The high octave ring volleyed off the paneling.

"Answer it," I said, louder than I needed to. "I'm a little busy here."

"Hello," Fran said. Her ass hit the recliner fast, like a wreck-ing ball had hit her. "What?"

I turned the flame under the eggs off to pay attention. Fran's bottom jaw dangled open, the skin around her mouth hung slack.

"Oh no," she said before covering the bottom half of her face with her free hand, for once not holding a cigarette. Fran never uttered another word, just listened. Edith watched Fran too, still and quiet. Fran placed the receiver back with the lightest touch, like it might break.

"Emily's dead."

2005

CHAPTER FORTY-FIVE

"Jesus, both places?" Jefferson Davis said. "Wow. That's a damn shame." Although he didn't sound like he thought that in the least.

"Up in smoke," Billy Dale said. "Listen, do you mind if I have a word with Delilah—"

Jefferson Davis didn't make him finish his sentence. He grabbed his beer, opened the porch door, said, "You know where I am if you need me, Dee," then went on his way giving Billy Dale the stink eye the whole way down the stairs.

"He hates me." Billy Dale took his seat. "How many porkers you got out there now?"

I noticed he'd changed his clothes since I'd seen him earlier. Must not've been in too big a hurry to get here. He'd donned his faux cowpoke outfit again.

"Five hundred or so," I said. Night had settled. The flies buzzed around the porch lights I'd turned on and everywhere else. I waved them away.

"Thought you wanted a few. Got a lot more than a few."

"Yeah, well, Jefferson Davis and Doc hooked us up with an organic grocery chain," I said, not sure why we were talking about pigs. "We're still scaling up."

"Might as well have a glass of wine," I said to me, but he thought it included him.

"Sure, might as well."

I dodged into the house, brought another bottle of expensive Chardonnay and a glass for Billy Dale. Why drink on the cheap if I had to put up with this fuck face? I poured two generous helpings.

"Still the bounty from Karen?" he said, daring me to get riled up.

"Matter of fact, yes. Great gift giver, that Karen."

"You didn't seem surprised to hear about your house. Or Karen's."

"How should surprise look?"

"Well, surprised. An, 'oh my god,' or 'you're kidding,' kind of surprised," he said, opening his eyes wide, putting both palms on either side of his face.

"Sorry to disappoint."

Even under duress I could enjoy a buttery glass of Chard. We drank awhile in merciful silence.

"You know your mommy issues might be getting in the way of your judgment," I said.

"Definitely."

Didn't expect that.

"Well, sorry to break your streak, but I'm not your mama or a criminal."

He polished off his wine. I poured both of us more. "Why don't you just spit it out, Delilah. You know what happened to Matthew Hardy."

"Where'd that come from? And what does it have to do with the houses burning down?"

"I'm no drunk, lazy, Rusty," he said. "I've actually got a theory and maybe some evidence."

"Go ahead, impress me."

"I think you killed Matthew Hardy in your house. Penelope and Karen poking around got you scared, so you burnt down the crime scene."

That actually did impress me.

"If that were the case, why would I burn down Karen's house too? Did I kill Matthew, then drag his corpse to Karen's so there'd be two crime scenes? I'm two times as stupid?"

"It's fire season. You didn't mean to burn them both down. Smart as you are, even you can't control fire."

"Evidence?"

"Penelope called. Said she saw you at your house this afternoon. About forty-five minutes after you left my office."

"Penelope. What a twat. Her word is hardly evidence. And she's following me now?" Isn't that what she hired you to do?"

"Yes, but I told you, I'd dropped her as a client."

"Unbeknownst to her apparently."

"No, she knows. But her new information got her back in."

"Penelope's whining isn't evidence."

"No, but this is."

He held out his phone with a photo on its screen. "She emailed me this."

I stared at the blurred image, and not a straight on view, from the side. Not clear, but maybe clear enough for a positive identification. The woman in the photo was tossing gas out of a can.

"Holy shit."

"Yeah, thought so. Anything you want to explain?"

"Not really."

I leaned back in my chair, drank half a glass of wine in one swallow. Refilled. Bits of intel gathering together in my head like storm clouds.

"I can make this go away," he said, scooting closer to me.

"I've got an idea. You go away."

Billy Dale wasn't the only one who could put his ear to the ground.

CHAPTER FORTY-SIX

"I can't get over how gorgeous it is out here. Hard to remember how awful it was when I first moved in," I yelled out, sitting on my porch steps, wine glass in hand, watching Jefferson Davis mend fence. Jefferson Davis walked my way, took off his Stetson, wiped the wet off his brow with his handkerchief, picked his beer up off the ground. I'd noticed both Jefferson Davis and I drank earlier and earlier in the day. I'd need to stay reasonably sober so I could man the grill at Vi's tonight. Soon I wouldn't need the job with the pig deal, but I didn't plan to quit. I loved cooking for people, even in Bumfuck.

My life would be almost sublime if it weren't for Billy Dale and his evidence hanging over my head. No idea what hung over Jefferson Davis's head. I asked once. "You're my boss, not my shrink. Butt out," he'd said. So I gladly did. He could solve his own shit. I could barely handle my own. I'd slept my way from job to job, but never out of trouble. Not that I wouldn't, I guess. I wanted those days to stay behind me. The thought of blowing Billy Dale so he'd leave me alone—between a rock and a limp place—I'd need to go another way. What way, I didn't yet know.

I chased those unpleasant thoughts aside to ogle my place. Things had really shaped up, thanks to Jefferson Davis—the almost drunk. It looked like a different place altogether. Trees, shrubs, a few varieties of flowers for the occasional pop of color, most of the debris had been cleaned up and hauled off to the dump. The big barn still needed some repairs and paint, as did the remaining cottages. My house, Jefferson Davis's cottage, and the grounds got most of the attention so far.

"Getting it done bit by bit," Jefferson Davis said between swigs. "Lots left to do, still." He pointed to my meager yard, several holes, and the dirt still surrounding my house. "Your place looks like shit."

"I said I'd do it and I will."

"We'll both be dead by then. Just let me do it," he said. "Those holes don't fill themselves. Plus, those saplings are too big for you to plant yourself." He slapped at a buzzing bee.

"That's all you know," I corrected him. "I planted a couple in the back plus a few shrubs. Doc helped me, if you're interested."

"Saw 'em," he said, not impressed. "Stick to cooking. Doc? I thought you didn't like the old codger."

"He's all right. Been good to Fran over the years." I didn't elaborate. "Although Doc and Fran don't seem tight anymore."

"What makes you say that? Only women notice that kind of shit."

"I dunno. They were kind of snarky with each other a while back. Seemed odd for them."

"She's got Vi. What's she need Doc for anyway?"

True. Her sedative giving days were over. Fingers crossed.

"Right, well I'm off to check on our snorting livelihood. Care to join?"

We walked in tandem toward the pigs. At first glance, it looked as if the pigs roamed free, their area spanned over so much of the property. You needed to take a close look to see the fences. Several snorted their way in and out of the barn. They ran the place as they pleased. A wiry ball of fur dashed past. I tripped, caught off guard.

"Just the dog," Jefferson Davis said, but didn't try to steady me. I straightened myself out, surprised Jefferson Chivalrous Davis watched me stumble around without so much as a by your leave.

I kept forgetting about that damn dog. A beautiful Australian Shepherd, or some sort of shepherd, I'd been told. I couldn't remember its name—just that it was a girl dog ... or a boy. I didn't care.

"Reminds me," Jefferson Davis kept on course toward the pigs and barns. "Keep your gate shut."

"Um, okay. Why?"

"Leeann likes to dig around in your yard."

"Leeann?"

"The dog."

"The dog's name is Leeann?"

"Yep," Jefferson Davis repositioned his ten-gallon hat. "Even the dog's embarrassed by your yard. Keeps trying to dig it up."

"Fine, whatever."

"Got the hogs separated from the sows for now," Jefferson Davis pointed, apparently finished with gardening tips. "They're in the back ten. It's getting cooler, they'll all need access to the barns in a couple months for warmth."

I nodded. I knew a lot about pork—live pigs not so much. But I was learning.

"Got a handful of sucklings next to my place," he said. "They're ready for slaughter."

"Best pork in the world, tender, succulent. If you haven't eaten—"

"Jumpin' Jesus, him again?" Jefferson Davis shifted his attention. Billy Dale's car inched toward my house in a dusty whirligig. "Thought you told him everything he needed to know."

****

Jefferson Davis went on wading through pigs while I waded toward the pig who waited for me on my porch.

"I thought you'd come to your senses and gave up this charade," I kicked the dirt off my boots and jumped up the few steps to the old faithful porch. Billy Dale sniffing behind me.

"Delilah, I've given you a couple weeks to come to your senses."

My shadow PI followed me into the house. We both sat on the sofa at the same time. If I had been in my right mind, I'd have taken the chair, a single seat, away from him.

"Nothing's changed for me," I said. "I didn't kill Matthew Hardy. I didn't set fire to my or Karen's house, despite that stupid picture."

"Why don't you tell me what you think happened? Where do you think Matthew is and who is that woman in the picture if it's not you?"

"Those are easy ones. I think Matthew doesn't want to be found. When he turns up it'll only be to divorce his purebred, but hysterical wife. The woman in that picture could be any dark-haired woman. It's just not this dark-haired woman. I don't suppose it's occurred to you that Karen might've set the place on fire to collect the insurance. It's been known to happen."

"Yes, of course I thought of that. The fire was obviously set on purpose, with gas probably stored in the airplane hangar. Insurance won't cover an intentional fire. Karen must be smart enough to know that."

"Don't bet on it."

"At any rate, I can't track her down all of a sudden either."

"I don't know what to tell you."

He leaned on his knees with both elbows, chin in hand. Finally quiet after his onslaught of questions and accusations. Not for long.

"No one knows better than me that sometimes things happen," he said. "Bad things. People get pushed to the edge. Sometimes they go over. Is that what happened? Did Matthew promise to leave his wife? Then you got fired, lost your house, your income. That must've been a lot to swallow. No one could blame you if—"

"If I killed him over it?"

"Yes, exactly." He got closer to me, I got as far as the couch length would let me. "I can help you, Delilah. I'm not the enemy. I'm on your side."

"As much as I appreciate that thrilling proposition, I'm still gonna take a hard pass."

His face turned red.

"Billy Dale, surely you don't need to get laid that badly."

"No matter what smut Rusty's been peddling, that's not the way it is." Billy Dale ran both hands through his thick, wavy hair. "I just know that not everyone deserves to go to prison, even for killing."

I felt the same way. I did everything for Fran that Billy Dale would've done for his own mother, to keep her from the prison sentence I felt sure would come her way, if I hadn't protected her. I sympathized a little for Billy Dale, whose mother had been taken from him at such a young age, his father killed. No parents. His life couldn't have been a walk through a daisy covered field either.

"Look, I appreciate what you're saying, I do," I said.

"And?"

"I didn't do what you think I did."

He let out a snort of air through his nose. Closed his eyes for a second.

"Why did you tell me you hadn't been here for more than twenty years at Willy Wally's wake or whatever that was? You've been up here several times."

I laughed, now Billy Dale's tone wasn't so mild. "I never said I hadn't been here. I said I hadn't lived here in more than twenty years."

"Why'd you come back?"

Billy Dale was starting to feel like a bad tooth—a constant, nagging, pain.

"My mother lives here. Jesus, your mother's in prison and you visit her, don't you?"

"Visiting is not the same as moving here. I was under the impression you two don't get along."

"Wrong impression."

Not exactly.

"It's weird that in all the conversations I've had, with so many people here, over all the months since Willy Wally died, not one person straightened me out on that."

"You're still wondering about this place? You're not welcome here. You never will be. No one will ever cooperate with you."

"Believe it or not, you keep digging, you find one or two who aren't so tight lipped."

I tried to keep my face from giving away my sudden panic. Who knew anything?

"Years ago, there was a spate of weird deaths here all in a row—weird even for the highway. Your neighbor's husband, your mother's husband, your best friend, in a four-month span. A year later you dropped out of school and left town. You turn up to live here again then, pow! Willy Wally gets a bullet in the throat."

I noticed Billy Dale hadn't taken his pad out. He didn't need to consult notes anymore he'd been at it so long.

"You know what happened with Willy Wally. That was Doc's doing. Why you'd think I was connected to that in any way is just plain asinine."

"All those still unexplained calls between him and Fran. It smells. Bad."

I was going to point out that those calls made Fran look suspect, not me. But, I didn't.

"They were explained," I said. "You just didn't like the explanation."

"Stupid explanation, that's why."

"All right. You got me. I'm a serial killer."

That shut him up for a few seconds.

"Then your pigs. Poisoned. Who would do that? Why?"

"That's out of the blue."

"I don't think it is. Somehow, it's a piece of the puzzle. You ever find out what kind of poison?"

"No. To be honest, I'm not sure they were poisoned. That was Doc's opinion. He's not a vet and did no toxicology report. Most likely a disease killed them. They're vulnerable to all kinds of crap. Ask Jefferson Davis. He's not sure either."

"My good and cooperative friend Jefferson Davis? No thanks. Either way, a bunch died. And poison isn't definitely ruled out. Since they've all been cremated, no way to know. But it's another thing that doesn't mesh."

"Don't know what to tell you."

"I'm surprised. You've got an answer for everything."

"Isn't that what you want? Answers?"

"Guilty people do that very thing. An answer for everything."

"This is getting old Billy Dale. I'm humoring you for reasons I don't know. I felt sorry for you because you got the boot from the force and your mother's in prison, and you can't get a woman. Now I'm tired of you and this whole ridiculous line of questioning. If you're going to arrest me, do it. If not, you know where the door is."

"I'm not a cop. So no, I'm not going to arrest you. Although I could certainly give you up." He got up. Stretched his arms. "Like it or not, I'm on to something. Only a matter of time before it all comes together. Then it'll be too late for you."

CHAPTER FORTY-SEVEN

"Why doesn't Billy Dale move in?" Jefferson Davis pulled a kitchen chair out. "Smells good. I'm starved."

"Brisket. You'll like it."

"Every time you say he's gone for good, he's not."

"Boomerang Billy."

Feeding Jefferson Davis calmed me. Like my purpose in life was being fulfilled. It wasn't to cover for Fran, or to dwell on my life as a teenager, my catalog of bad decisions and horrible mistakes. It was this. Feeding people. Caring for them through a meal well cooked. I hadn't seen Jefferson Davis since yesterday, since Billy Dale showed up ringing his alarm bell. Which was a little odd since we almost always ate dinner together. I pulled my brisket out of the oven where it'd been braising six hours. The smell transported me to heaven, if one existed. I covered it with foil to rest a while. The mashed potato casserole had a few minutes to go. I got Jefferson Davis a beer and poured myself a fruity Pinot, then sat. Pooped.

"Where'd you run off to yesterday? Don't tell me Billy Dale scared you off?"

"Town. Somebody needs to keep this place stocked. Far as I can tell, it's not you."

I could've asked him to elaborate but I preferred not to go catatonic before dinner. I enjoyed my wine instead. Jefferson Davis made short work of his Coors, helped himself to another.

"Something wrong?" I pointed to the beer.

"No, it's plenty cold."

"That's not what I meant. I think you drink a lot more than you used to."

"I thought I didn't live with my mother anymore." He opened the beer with a loud pop as an exclamation point. "Nothin' wrong. I like beer."

I dropped it.

"How long did the hapless, hopeless Billy Dale root around yesterday?" Jefferson Davis said.

"Forever? I don't know—an hour maybe. Felt longer."

"Still singing the same song?"

"Never tires of it."

No point in passing on all the new shit I had to worry about with Billy Dale. Plus, I didn't want him to know. Less is more. I drank my wine in baby sips in case Jefferson Davis started in on my drinking habits.

"Gotta wonder why," Jefferson Davis said. "He must be hangin' his hat on something or he wouldn't keep coming around, would he?"

"Is there something you want to ask me, Jefferson Davis?"

I'm sure he thought I killed Matthew Hardy too. Knowing Jefferson Davis, he'd come out with it. Not one to pull punches or play coy.

"Yeah, who was that lady the other night?"

"Penelope? That was months ago, not the other night."

"Not her. The other one."

"What are you talking about?"

"The lady in the Range Rover. Penelope's blonde, this one's darker haired. Come on, you're not that senile yet, are you?"

"And I thought I didn't live with my mother anymore."

"Dog barked like crazy when she pulled in. You think I'm deaf to that too? That's why you wanted the damn dog."

That damn dog all right.

He scraped the chair backwards, got up. "Want me to cut this meat before it gets cold?"

"Sure. Pull the potatoes out of the oven." And talk about something else while you're at it. Did Jefferson Davis watch my house 24/7? Christ crucified. He saw everything. Heard everything.

He cut the brisket like I'd taught him, not too thin, not too thick. "You're not gonna tell me who she was, are you?"

"Is Doc prescribing you something for your hallucinations?"

"I'll take that as a no."

Fran letting herself in put a muzzle on Jefferson Davis's nosiness.

****

Fran helped herself to my coffeepot and the can of Folgers I kept for her. "You want to tell me what the devil is going on?"

How Fran could talk with a cigarette jutting out from the corner of her lips was beyond me.

"Nothing's going on except Billy Dale can't take no for an answer. And before you ask, no, I didn't set my house or my neighbor's house on fire."

"Want me to get another plate?" Jefferson Davis stood.

"I'll help myself," Fran said.

Of course she would. She and Jefferson Davis fixed themselves plates, sat down, and dug in. I did the same.

"Your neighbor find you the other night?"

Jefferson Davis glared at me. I looked away.

"Fran, what—"

"Don't yell at me. I thought it'd be good for you to see a friend, so excuse me. Stopped at the bar, looking for you. She's the one who gave you all that wine, said she brought you the a . . . the a . . . something harvest." She snapped her fingers. "New harvest. Late harvest? That's it. Thought you'd be out of the other stuff by now."

"I'll say. Months—"

I kicked Jefferson Davis under the table.

"She's a real nice lady. You could use friends, Delilah. Try it. You'll like it."

Leave it to Fran.

"Speaking of dogs," I said to Jefferson Davis. "She didn't make a peep when Fran came in. Great watch dog."

"Oh, she was busy digging in your yard," Fran said, mouth full.

"Where? Again? That dog will not stay out of my yard. Always pawing around."

"Out front. Smart dog. She knows you never look out front."

Jefferson Davis wiped his mouth, picked up his beer. "I'll go get her outta there. Put her in the barn for a while."

"No, I'll do—"

"Halfway there." He walked a few paces to the front door. We heard it slam.

"Fran, I told you when I moved here, I didn't want anyone to know where I'd gone. I need a breather from … from … everyone. Everyone from my past."

Fran belched. "That's a compliment to an Eskimo."

"We're not Eskimos and don't change the subject."

"Oh honey, you've been out here for months. Your farm is going gangbusters. You're settled in real nice. I just thought—okay, I'm sorry. I promise I won't do it again."

"Oh, Fran. You don't understand. I—"

"She doesn't mean you harm, does she?" Fran sat up straight. "She didn't do anything bad, did she?"

"Why do you think everyone wants to do something bad to me?"

"I don't. You do. You're the one trying to hide."

"Well, in case you forgot, there's plenty to hide."

"Oh my god." She clutched the front of her "Stayin' Alive, Stayin' Alive" t-shirt. "You've done something to that Hardy guy, haven't you? I knew it."

"For the last time, no. How many times do I need to say it to you and everyone else in this godforsaken place? No! And you know that's not what I'm talking about."

She had the good grace to blush. "That's all done. Isn't it?"

Where to start? Before I could decide if I even wanted to go there, Fran piped up, "How's Jefferson Davis working out?"

She didn't want to go anywhere near there.

"He looks pretty comfortable here."

"I hope he is. He's good. Works like a slave every day. Couldn't ask for better."

"Oh, lord. You don't have a crush on him, do you?"

"First you tell me he's gay, now you think I've got a crush on him? No, I don't."

"Gay or not, you could do worse." She got up to put her plate in the sink. "You know, he's lived with his mother his entire life," she said like I didn't already know. "If you can believe what you see on CSI, a grown man living with his mother is never right in the head. They're up to no good."

I got up, while she sat back down, to start the dishes. I hoped the running water would shut her up. No such luck.

"What about that dog?" she said, louder, to be sure I heard.

"What about it?"

"You like it?"

"She's fine. I don't really need her now since it's a fucking thoroughfare here now."

"Your mouth hasn't improved since you've been home." She ate the last bite of potatoes in the casserole dish with her fingers. "Does 'it' have a name?"

I thought a few seconds. "Um, yeah. It's a ... kind of a weird name for a dog." I scanned my memory. "Leeann. That's it. Her name is Leeann."

Fran lit a smoke even though I'd asked a million times that she not smoke in the house. She took a few puffs, sipped her coffee oh so leisurely, like she hadn't asked the question, then, "That's a weird name, don't you think?"

"Well, unusual sort of. I dunno."

"You don't remember, do you?"

Now what? I shut the near to overflowing water off. Leaned against the counter and thought. "No, I guess I don't remember."

"Your memory's bad as Vi's. Leeann was Emily's middle name. Emily Leeann."

1985

CHAPTER FORTY-EIGHT

I don't remember much about the days, weeks or months following Emily's death. I might've blacked out after Fran delivered the news that morning, whole thing's all a blur. Everything moved as fast as sound and glacier slow at the same time. I don't think I said a word for days. What I would remember, forever, was Blanche's soul stripping, primal, grief. There's no other sound like the one a mother makes when she's lost her child. The animal rawness of it slams you hard, like a boulder to the throat.

I don't remember driving to their trailer or getting out of the car. I know Edith came along. I don't know if we stayed five minutes or five hours. I don't think I said anything at all. I don't remember if Earl was there, but he must've been. For the rest of my life, the year I spent on the Fifty-three after Emily died is on semi-permanent lockdown in my head.

Every once in a while, it'll hit me, out of nowhere, what happened. Details, breathtaking anxiety, panic. Then it's gone, quick as it came, back under the rock in my brain.

But I can remember the sound of Blanche's suffering like it was yesterday, and Fran, after delivering the initial news to Edith and me, staring at her hands like she'd never seen them before and saying so quietly we could barely hear, "Snakebite. Emily died of a snakebite." Then a lame, "Hank always said, 'it's the season.'"

Much later, I wondered if Blanche knew anything about Fran's murderous summer and if Emily'd said anything to her or Rusty, or both. Blanche might put it all together and suspect Fran had a hand in the snake business. The relief I thought I might feel that Emily couldn't tell anything now gave way to more fear, which I didn't expect. Fear that once again, I'd lose my mother.

The strikes against her kept piling up. Her benefit of the doubt card was filled.

How could I have let this happen?

Why didn't I keep my big trap shut? It was my fault entirely.

I didn't go to school those first weeks. I stayed in my room, away from Fran. She avoided me too. Willy Wally came by a few times, I refused to see him. My heart felt full—past its capacity for every feeling under the sun, mostly bad feelings. I put one foot in front of the other, slow and deliberate, a tightrope walker without a balance bar, just to get around the house.

I wished I could remember more about those first days, if Blanche gave Fran the cold shoulder, as if that'd be the right response, or any other sign that she thought something was amiss. But, I couldn't. And as it turned out, I needn't have worried.

To my surprise, and horror, Blanche showed up at our door. They'd decided, for the first time in the highway's history not to have a memorial. It was too much, even for the Fifty-three. The thought of the Caligula style banquet and scores of drunks didn't sit right with anyone, much less Blanche and Earl. When she showed up, I thought she'd either changed her mind about the memorial or come to kill Fran with her bare hands.

It was neither.

"It's my fault," Blanche said, falling into Fran's arm with a wrenching sob.

Fran purred soothing words, nothing I could make out. I crept back. I couldn't take the grieving. I felt my palms sweat. My heart leapt like a rabbit under my shirt. I covered my mouth to keep from screaming.

Fran led the still wailing Blanche to the couch. I ran for my room, but didn't shut the door. From my bed I could still see and hear everything. I wanted more than anything to close my bedroom door but more than that, I didn't want to draw any attention to myself.

"I left her alone." Blanche pulled away to face the window. "I … I … was with … Rusty." She fell sideways and would've landed on the floor but for Fran's quick reflexes.

"I can't believe I would spend the night with that loser, while my daughter—" She collapsed in a heap again. Fran brought the Kleenex box over, patted and soothed until Blanche could finish her sentence. "While Emily—" Blanche stopped, not able to say the words.

"Blanche," Fran said, in a creepy calm, almost stern tone, steering clear of the Rusty topic. "It's not your fault at all. It's nature. A fluke. You couldn't have stopped it if you'd been home, could you?"

Blanche soaked up Fran's words like they could save her, save her family, her eyes huge, swollen. She looked almost unrecognizable. Face red and puffy, from crying, drinking, sleepless nights, aged twenty years. Then she broke down again.

"You're wrong." She beat the couch with her fist. "Wrong, wrong, wrong."

Fran grabbed her by the shoulders. "Blanche, stop. What are you saying?"

"They said at the hospital that Emily was allergic." She pressed the tissue to her lips, tried to keep the crying to a dull roar. After several minutes she pulled herself together enough to say her piece. "She … she was allergic to the venom."

"Isn't everyone?"

"No. Listen to me." Now it was Blanche's turn for shoulder grabbing. "Even with that, if she'd have gotten help sooner, she could've lived." She looked Fran full on in the face. "And you know folks up here know what to do for a goddamn snakebite." She yelled at Fran, "I know what to do! Almost every year some dumbass hunter from the city gets bit. No one's died. No one EVER DIES." She really yelled that bit.

"Blanche, don't torture yourself this way," Fran said.

I realized I'd never seen Fran so empathetic, so gentle. She knew my door was open, she could see me with barely a turn of her head, but she avoided it. She never once looked my way.

Blanche wouldn't be convinced. "From the bite marks they could tell the snake was a small one, a baby. If I'd been home Emily would still be alive."

CHAPTER FORTY-NINE

I agreed to see Willy Wally only because I needed to hear the scuttle, if there was any. I sat with him at our rickety table on the old, cracked concrete patio.

"I'm surprised you'd show your face here," I said. "You're a liar and a cheater."

"Hello, pot? Kettle calling," he said.

Asshole.

No point in rehashing all that bullshit. I got sidetracked easy. My head was constantly filled with Emily. I couldn't stop seeing her in my dreams, haunting me, filling most of even my waking hours.

"Look, let's not fight," he said. "Emily's gone. Nothing else matters."

We both cried over that. After a few minutes of floundering in our memories we sucked up our respective guilt and sorrow to get on with it.

"Emily told me about Rusty and her mom," he said.

I held my breath.

"She told me Earl found out. Told her mom to get out."

He stopped talking when Fran came out bearing sodas. I knew she kept the door open so she could hear through the screen. She stood near it the whole time. I hoped that wasn't as obvious to Willy Wally.

"And?" I said.

"Did you know?" he said.

Ah. Emily didn't tell him that I delivered that nasty bit of news to her myself. Maybe she didn't tell him anything else either, about Fran and her, well, her proclivities. He'd have mentioned that before now, wouldn't he? Like to Rusty or a real cop in Kearny?

"Yes," I said. "I don't think those kinds of things are as secret as anyone hopes. As you should know."

I remembered Rusty and Blanche frolicking at Hank and Smalls's memorial. Before Emily caught Willy Wally and me in the—I couldn't finish the thought.

"I guess the only upside to Emily dy—" His eyes filled again. He couldn't say the word. "—is Earl and Blanche patched things up."

"How do you know?"

"I heard Blanche talking to Margene about it over at Vi's."

"Blanche spends a lot of time at Vi's I heard. Drunk."

"Blanche and Earl both. Shitfaced most of the time now."

"You hanging out at Margene's now?" It just dawned on me what he'd said about being there.

"Working up there. Since I'm out of school now, and Hank's—"

"Dead."

"Um, yeah. Anyway, they need the help." He laughed.

"What's so funny?"

"I never noticed how weird that Jefferson Davis is."

I laughed too. It felt wrong, but I couldn't help it.

"He's a lot younger than you. You wouldn't have noticed him at all probably. He's a first-class dork, always has been."

He nodded, didn't say anything for a while. The air between us shifted, felt heavy, uncomfortable. I could feel Willy Wally's uneasiness. The last person I felt like talking about was Jefferson Davis, or Emily for that matter. Before I could think of a suitable, different topic, Willy Wally went onward.

"He jumped off the roof of one of the barns, broke his leg."

I almost choked on my Dr Pepper. "What? When?"

"Yesterday. You didn't hear?"

"No."

Our house had been entombed for weeks. The whole highway had ceased its normal functions, including lightning rounds of gossip—all still reeling from the shock of Emily's terrible death.

"If he hadn't hurt himself, I think Arthur would've strangled him."

"He's a little old to play airplane, isn't he? I don't blame Arthur. What an idiot kid."

"That's what Margene said. Something similar. Boys will be boys, whatever."

Willy Wally fidgeted in his chair. Grabbed at his soda can, took a long drink. Wiped at his eyes.

"What's wrong?" I said.

"Every day I've been out there he acted, well, I don't know how to explain it. Just off. Really off."

"Sounds about right to me. What about all those turkeys?" All I could think of to switch topics.

"I don't think Jefferson Davis was just fooling around, doing stupid kid stuff."

"What was he doing then?"

"I think he tried to kill himself."

****

Too dumbfounded to say much about Willy Wally's observation, I mumbled something moronic about teenage angst, or feeling like an outcast, or both. At any rate, Willy Wally finally put me out of my misery. He hugged me, apologized for everything, then took off.

Surprised Fran hadn't broken down the screen door to get the details as soon as Willy Wally drove off, I saw she'd moved away from the door. Even the best of snoops had to pee, I guess. I got up to go in the house to tell Fran what I'd heard when Edith called me over to the fence. Which was odd since she came over at least three times a day.

"What's wrong, Edith?"

Looked like plenty. Her breathing was heavier than normal, she twisted the dirty rag at her waist with a clenched fist.

"I don't wanna rock no boats, but I gotta ask. Even if it makes ya madder than a hornet kicked out of its nest."

"What are you talking about? What could possibly make me mad at you?" I leaned closer, she was whispering, kept looking over my shoulder toward our kitchen window.

"Don't want yer ma to know a thing, you hear?"

"Of course."

Now she started crying.

"Edith, what the—"

"You don't think yer ma killed that little gal, do ya?"

I froze. I knew it'd come up sooner or later from someone. I wondered who else thought it, considered asking Edith if she'd heard it anywhere else but she kept talking.

"Weren't her fault what she saw ... Hank ... yer ma. Oh, that poor little gal."

I struggled to find my voice, or words, or air. I held onto the fence, tight.

"Do you think Fran's a snake handler now? Really, Edith?"

"Hey you two," Fran said, more of a yodel. "About time for dinner, don't you think, ladies?"

2005

CHAPTER FIFTY

"You seen Leeann?" Jefferson Davis appeared, hatless, at my porch door before I'd even poured coffee. I'd slept in. Late night at the bar.

"Um ... yeah, couple days ago, I guess." I moved aside, an invitation to Jefferson Davis to come in. He didn't.

"She's gone," he said in a way I didn't like.

I suspected Jefferson Davis had been avoiding me the last couple of weeks, since the dinner we'd had when Fran dropped by. He turned down so many dinner invitations after that I stopped asking. He and Doc spent a lot of time on pigs and landscaping. They both stopped pestering me about finishing my yard. Their presence rubbed me every which kind of wrong. Billy Dale and his constant questions had worn me down, though I hadn't heard from him either. But his unseen presence hung over my every move. Talk about loose ends. He felt like a giant one. My mood sank to an all-time low. I was in no mood for Jefferson Davis and his stupid dog problems.

I leaned against the door jamb. "She's a dog. Don't they wander off, run with the wolves, or whatever the hell? Maybe she found herself a man dog." I laughed. He didn't, not on the outside or the inside, I'd bet.

"She's a ranch dog. She knows her job and wouldn't leave it." He looked over my shoulder like he thought I'd hidden her behind my sofa. Between Penelope and Jefferson Davis behind the sofa was getting pretty crowded.

"Have you checked up at your mom's place? Maybe she went back home, animals do that sometimes, right? Why don't you come in. At least I can drink coffee even if you don't."

"First place I went was Mom's place," Jefferson Davis said, not moving.

"Well, I'm sorry, Jefferson Davis, I can't help you, I'm not the keeper of all things lost. Christ. Get another dog. Or not."

Like bad magic, Billy Dale drove in. As if the mere thought of him conjured him up.

"I'll leave you to your boyfriend," Jefferson Davis huffed off.

****

"I'm not saying another word to you, Billy Dale," I said. "If you're here to arrest me for whatever bogus bullshit you think I've done, have at it. If not, get back in your car and don't come back."

"Big talk from someone who knows I've got pictures of her setting her own house on fire."

As promised, I didn't say a word. He stood at the bottom of the steps, me at the top in the doorway. I turned to go back into the house.

"You don't have to talk, Delilah, but you might want to listen. And look."

Goddammit. I wished I didn't want to know. I wished I had the backbone to slam the door in his face. But no, he got me. Curiosity had always been my downfall.

"Are you gonna come down here or am I coming up there? Or am I leaving? Up to you."

I strolled down the steps, parked myself in front of him, still silent.

"I talked to your old TV crew," he said.

I barely blinked.

He held out a photo. A different one this time—not of me, or anyone who might've been me, a man this time. A man I definitely knew.

"Recognize him?"

Still good on my word, I didn't answer.

He didn't say anything else, just stared at me. I stared back. I thanked God right then for my training at Fran's knee. If he thought I'd crumple he'd be sorely disappointed. Amateur. Maybe surprised I didn't take the bait, he held out yet one more picture. Was this jerkoff a walking photo album or what?

"What about this one?" He held the second photo closer.

Held my tongue.

"Let me help you. This is Matthew Hardy. As I know you know, whether you say so or not. Penelope was kind enough to supply the photo. He held the two photos side by side."

No fucking duh. If she'd hired this asswad to find him, she would've given him a picture. It was all I could to keep my eyes from rolling. I was getting tired of standing though. So I sat on the bottom step. Uninvited, Billy Dale sat next to me.

"So, I showed Matthew's picture to a guy on the crew. As an aside, not mentioning any names, but I think you might've thrown him over for Matthew so he was inclined to blab."

And they say hell hath no fury like a woman scorned. Don't even start me on men.

"We had a nice long chat. He told me he knew you had another boyfriend. The whole time you were seeing Matthew, you were seeing another guy too. You busy girl, you."

I didn't confirm or deny.

"If you're wondering how he knew, which I assume you are, he was a stalker sort of guy, till he got another job and had to leave your bushes and your parade of men. He was kind enough to give me a surprisingly detailed description. My sketch guy drew him up and I thought, 'I've seen that guy. I know it. But where?'"

He didn't actually think I'd volunteer that, did he?

"Then I remembered. That whatchacallit. When I first met you. The wake or whatever you call those things. That's where I'd seen him. I kindly asked his mother for this photo. Karen and Penelope were both right. You did have a man visiting at all hours after Matthew served you with a restraining order. They were wrong about the 'who.' Your other man was Willy Wally Watkins. His picture was in a nice big frame at his memorial."

1985

CHAPTER FIFTY-ONE

After that day at the fence, Edith never mentioned her suspicions to me again. For a while I thought she might break down and ask Fran, but she never did—at least not in my hearing. For a few weeks she didn't come over as often but Fran seemed too preoccupied herself to notice. Then it all went back to normal—at least between Edith and Fran. Edith took her normal spot at the dinner table every night. I cooked sometimes, and went to school, albeit reluctant and sullen.

For the first time since the brief interval of peaceful relief between Hank and Emily's deaths, our house felt shrouded in darkness again, like something was moving in for the kill. Fran and I might've been strangers. I avoided her so often that it took me a while to notice she avoided me too.

The yearbook that year was dedicated to Emily, but other than that brief remembrance, Emily faded into legend. Her name would always be followed by "oh that poor girl" or "you remember her—the one that died of a rattlesnake bite." But self-involved teenagers love the drama of death, but not more than they love themselves, so everyone went back to worrying about prom queens, clothes, boyfriends, girlfriends, sports, and their weight.

Jefferson Davis entered his freshman year with a cast up to his thigh.

"What kind of idiot would throw himself off the roof of a barn?" I said the first time I saw him at school. If looks could've killed, I wouldn't be telling this story. He hustled away from me as fast as his crutches would let him. We didn't speak again before I left town.

Willy Wally stopped by occasionally, hoping to start up with me again. Turned off by my challenged hygiene and my newly dyed pitch-black hair, he finally gave up.

My own depression nearly buried me. I turned into that Goth girl who smoked behind the school and snuck booze out of Fran's liquor cabinet, slim pickings since Hank died. My grades torpedoed. I skipped class more than I attended. If the school ever contacted Fran, she never brought it up.

The weeks turned into months. Just like that, the temperature rose and summer snuck in. I'd be out for the summer in a matter of days.

The last weekend before summer break, I followed my same routine. I'd stay in my room for a few hours, stare off into the abyss, examine the paint on the walls, or the planks on the floor, then I'd trudge out to the living room, cheerful as a death row inmate, where I'd spend the rest of the day in front of the TV. I even stopped cooking. Fran would toss a hot dog or grilled cheese at me, I'd nibble a few bites, Edith would finish it and I'd count the minutes till I could slog back to my bedroom and start the cycle over again.

Fran's exasperation with my routine was the only highpoint.

"Delilah, you've got to get out of this...this...funk or whatever it is you're in. I've been patient with you all year."

Too tired to take issue with Fran's needling, I craned my neck around her so I could see the TV better. Fran adapted, moving sideways to block my view.

"Delilah." She grabbed my chin and forced me to face her. "Is there something you want to ask me? Or say to me?" She closed her eyes and stiffened her spine waiting for whatever blow I'd land on her.

"No," I said, and meant it.

"Do you have any plans for the summer? You know Margene—"

"No." I eyed the dried cornflake stuck to her "Here Come da Judge" sweatshirt, idly wondering if I should reach over and flick it off.

Fran fumbled for her lighter on the coffee table. "Delilah, this can't go on. Doc said—"

I held my hand up, a classic Fran move. "Don't talk to me about Doc."

Fran hesitated long enough to set the end of her cigarette on fire.

"It's bad enough Blanche and Earl are the town drunks now. Is that where you're headed?"

I didn't bother with that one.

"Senior prom is tonight. Why don't you go? You know Willy Wally—"

"I'm not a senior and no one who's graduated goes to prom. Not even in this backward hellhole."

"You know the prom is open to everyone. The school's too small to get picky. Plus, you're almost a senior. If you somehow manage to pass this year."

I fished out the remote from under my ass and turned up the volume.

"Delilah, I'm serious." Fran abducted the remote and pushed mute.

"I don't have anything to wear," I said, as if that would've mattered.

Fran sighed as loud as she could, jumped off the couch and stormed into my room, her house slippers flapping at her heels. "You've got clothes you haven't even worn yet," she hollered. "And shoes. How can a kid have so many pairs of shoes?" I could see her mom jean covered ass protruding from my closet as she kneeled on the floor, in the recesses, pitching shoes out. Out flung a Nike running shoe and a pair of high-topped Reeboks.

"Where are those darling sandals you HAD to have but never wear?"

Like anyone who wasn't a psycho wore sandals.

Shit. Fuck all.

Like a possessed person, I sprang off the couch, raced toward my room, tripped on my own feet before I took three steps. "Fran, get out of my closet. Can I have at least some private space?" I picked myself up off the floor.

Fran's voice stopped me dead. "Holy Mother of Jesus, Delilah. What did you do? I knew it, I knew it."

The enormity of what was about to happen almost dropped me back to the ground. All I could do was stay still. There was nothing else. This was it.

Fran staggered out, carrying a smashed in, empty, cardboard box with Jefferson Davis's name scrawled all over it in red ink.

You know the one.

2005

CHAPTER FIFTY-TWO

"You might as well come in," I said to a triumphant Billy Dale.

Forever the feeder, I poured us both coffee and popped bread in the toaster.

"Delilah, you've gotta come clean now." So far, I'm the only one who knows any of this. I'm still willing to help you."

"In exchange for a date? You can't be serious."

"No, not that. I told you, I don't think you deserve prison. Everyone else would, I don't."

I buttered the toast, dropped two more slices of homemade bread in.

"Billy Dale." I put his toast in front of him, got in his face. "You have no idea what I deserve, or what I've done, or haven't done."

"Then tell me." He didn't back his head away or even flinch.

"Ask away," I slathered butter on my own toast, then sat to get the third degree.

"Were you having an affair with Willy Wally?"

"Yes."

"What went wrong?"

"Nothing. Unless you count the bullet that killed him."

"Did you ask Doc to kill him?"

"Absolutely not." I chewed toast. Billy Dale left his to get cold.

"Did you know he would get killed?"

"No."

"Did Fran ask Doc to kill him?"

"I doubt it. Why? She didn't know anything about my relationship with Willy Wally."

"How do you know?"

This guy was quite the jokester. "Because she'd have never let me hear the end of it. She woulda mentioned it, trust me."

I almost let on about the suspected affair with the waitress from Kearny but didn't. No point in blowing up Doc's life by handing Billy Dale a motive.

"Did you move here to be with him?"

"No. I told you why about twenty times."

"Did you kill Matthew Hardy?"

"Now you're annoying the shit outta me more than you usually do. NO."

"Did you—"

"No, I set fire to NOTHING."

I ate the last of my toast while the realization he was back to square one hit Billy Dale. Other than the fact I had a fling with Willy Wally, he got nothing new, nothing to implicate me in anything except that picture. And that was iffy. Not a very clear pic. He knew he'd lost, again.

"Did you love him?"

I wasn't ready for that, at all.

"What a weird question."

"Your eyes are welling up. I hit a nerve, didn't I? You were in love with Willy Wally, weren't you?'

"Are you done with your toast?"

CHAPTER FIFTY-THREE

"You pigs are snort happy today, noisy as hell." I talked to the pigs a lot. They were the only ones around without an agenda apparently. Got rid of Billy Dale, but with a real bee in his bonnet. Inadvertently, I'd let my guard down about Willy Wally, which worked in my favor. Unintended consequences. But good ones—he left feeling bad for me.

Rounding the corner, in search of Jefferson Davis, I'd spied his truck bed peeking out from behind the barn, the one nearest the back of the property. I'd schlepped all the way out there, plowing through the sludge, the pigs in symphony all around me. It occurred to me while I tromped, I didn't notice the gamey odor so much anymore. I'd gone nose blind. Jefferson Davis and I stumbled into one another. He'd traipsed out of the barn bearing pig cargo.

"Lover boy gone already?"

"Obvious, isn't it?"

Not crazy about the tenor he'd adopted lately. He often asked snarky shit, but the past couple of weeks, there was a definite edge. I'd always known Jefferson Davis didn't hold much affection for me, which I didn't mind in the least. Made work easier, made him more attractive, if I'm admitting. But this new tone I didn't like.

He sidestepped around, but kept going, not acknowledging me. I followed his denim shirt covered back.

"What are you doing?"

He pushed open the gate with his shoulder and plopped the small pig into a small, empty pen. "Butchering," he said, spitting on the mud at his feet.

"Right," I said, crossing my arms on my chest. So engrossed in my recent saga, I'd forgotten we'd agreed to butcher several young pigs.

"Good thing you're here," he said. "You can help for once."

"You can jack down the hostility," I said. "I pay you so I don't have to help."

He spit a stream of tobacco, barely missing my feet. "You helping, or not?"

"No, I'm out here because you're so fucking pleasant to be around."

He reached for the twenty-two rifle I hadn't noticed, leaning against the barn, easy peasy, no big deal. The pigs still in the barn squealed like they knew what came next. "They're hungry," he said, answering my question before I asked. "Gotta stop feeding 'em a day before."

"Yeah, I know." Chefs knew more about butchering and its details than Jefferson Davis realized.

"Get in the pen and talk to the pig."

"Pigs can't talk, why would I—"

"You talk to the damn things all the time."

I did what he wanted. "We need to get this done before I leave for my shift at Vi's."

"Stand over there." He pointed, not concerned in the slightest with my schedule.

I got in position, a few feet from the pig. "Hey guy," I said. It trotted closer, I stepped back.

"Don't," Jefferson Davis said from somewhere behind me. "Stay still and talk."

I'd never looked so hard at a pig's face. It really was darling, all pink and pug nosed, floppy eared. I made some noises I thought it might appreciate. It rewarded me by paying attention, standing stock-still, its precious little head held up to gaze lovingly into my eyes. Before I could take a breath, Jefferson Davis dropped the gun barrel onto my shoulder, inches away from my neck. A sharp crack about blew my ear out, dropped the pig, a neat hole between its eyes. I didn't even have time to jump. My ear rang like a telephone climbed inside it. I rubbed it, hard.

He stepped around me, jerked the pig by its hind legs to drag it out of the pen.

"Won't take long to bleed out a pig this young, then we can cut out the innards and hang it in the walk-in," he pulled the pig along, cloven hooves up.

"Leeann never turned up," he said, like we'd been talking about her all along.

"Huh?" Before he could remind me, I said, "Oh, right."

He stared—unblinking—dead pig at his feet, the high-pitched, keening pigs waiting their turn provided a running soundtrack.

I softened a tad. I knew he loved that dog. "I'm sorry about that Jefferson Davis, really. Maybe she'll still turn up."

He spit again, not taking his eyes off me.

"You hadn't planned on me doing this with you, right?" I broke the uncomfortable silence. "Young pigs or not, this'll take all day, at least. I do have to work today."

Jefferson Davis's head did the pointing again, this time back toward my house where a red truck careened around the edge of the property, toward us. "Doc's coming."

"Doc?" I said, surprised.

"Since when do you care if Doc comes and helps? He's free—your favorite kind of labor. He's here all the time."

"I know, just didn't think he knew much about butchering, so don't let him fuck it up. If he does, that's on you. I really don't give a shit how you get it done. Just do it." Jefferson Davis wasn't the only one who could bitch slap with words.

Jefferson Davis stood firm, face expressionless, not saying anything else, wisely, for once. Shaking my head, I turned on my slop-covered heel and tramped back where I'd come from.

I stomped on my steps to shake off some of the dirt before moving onto my porch. It dawned on me that Jefferson Davis never asked me about what Billy Dale wanted. He hated the hapless rent-a-cop but always wanted to know what he'd said. All that concerned Jefferson Davis today were the pigs and the dogs.

Still convinced Doc was an odd choice to do any butchering. But he was a real doctor, as he liked to remind everyone, maybe he did know a thing or two about anatomy, even a pig's. Plus, you'd be hard pressed to find an able-bodied man, willing to work, still living on the highway. All Jefferson Davis's presidential brothers still worked the Cox ranch, but they'd have their own work to do. As far as anyone knew none ever left the property. Jefferson Davis didn't have a plethora of choices for ranch help. Doc would do.

I tugged off my boots and went in to change my grime spattered clothes so I could go to work. My ear still rang a little. Damn Jefferson Davis and his drama. I'd just dropped my filthy pants, about to pull on the clean ones when I stood up straight, dropping the jeans I was about to step into on the floor, stomach burning. Jefferson Davis had planted himself so close behind me with his gun—he might as well have been me. He could've easily sweet-talked that pig himself. He didn't have to go all Wild Bill Hickok and shoot over my shoulder, on my shoulder, the gun barrel so close to my head I could've turned and kissed it.

He wanted to.

****

Vi's, early in the day, was tough to take. Unlocking the door, stepping in, took a strong constitution. It smelled bad. No matter how often Margene mopped the whole place down, or used how much bleach, the piss-beer-grease aroma never abated. The concrete floors, dark paneled walls, and only one window made it nighttime all the time. So entering the building assaulted, and confused, the senses first thing.

I left the screen door open to welcome in some fresh air and parted the sullied, ripped up curtains on the one window to let in the light, made a mental note to have Margene make some new ones. I'd worked there long enough to develop an opening (and closing) routine. Going to the same place, performing the same rituals, offered me a reassuring stability, which is what drew me to the kitchen so many years before. Cooking provided the perfect mix of rule following and breaking. If I colored too far outside the lines by changing up a recipe, or a cooking technique, I could step right back in and follow the directions, saving the food and myself. The world stayed on its axis when I cooked. I could forget, for a few precious hours, the trouble that followed me for most of my life, a lot of it trouble I invited.

Even though I'd closed the night before, I wiped down the bar and futzed around behind it, arranging steins, coasters, fiddling with the taps. With an old dust rag, I swiped at Johnny Cash's napkin, Bush Senior's tie. I'd just turned the knob on the fryer and cranked up the griddle when I heard the front door slam. The closed sign still hung on it so I knew it had to be my mother.

"All right. Spill it," Fran said. "Why is that nosy parker Billy Dale, after all these months, still poking in?"

I tied my apron and slid from the kitchen like a breakdancer to behind the bar.

"I think that's for you to answer, Fran." I could tell she knew what I meant. After all these years I knew when she wasn't forthcoming—just as she did about me.

Fran produced her usual Marlboro, the lighter flame fizzling up the cigarette paper, then surprised me by telling the truth, right up front.

"I tried to talk Doc outta shooting Willy Wally." She pointed at her regular coffee mug. I loaded up the machine to get some started. "Wouldn't listen to a lick of sense."

I filled the filter with grounds, smacked the top down, then flipped the on switch, thinking the whole time. The calls. All those calls.

"That's why you made so many calls? To try to talk Doc out of it?"

"Yes."

"But what about the calls to Willy Wally?"

"When I couldn't get Doc to listen to sense, I tried Willy Wally. I told him he ought to stay home, not hunt, spend time with Wanda or some such bullshit. When that didn't work, I made up some dumb excuses, like I needed help moving some furniture or a doohickey needed fixing. He didn't bite. Went on anyway, damn fool."

"Fran, I know how terrible the whole Hank and Smalls thing was, and then all that with—well, Blanche and Earl." I still couldn't bear to think about Emily.

"Nothing to do with any of them."

"Well then, not to sound like a complete snatch, but why would you interfere? You knew Doc would get away with it, and he did. Why bother?"

I poured a steaming cup of coffee, pulled a coaster close to Fran, then put the hot mug down. "How dumb do you really think I am, Delilah?"

"I don't. That's my point," I said.

"I knew about you and Willy Wally. I knew it was you he was, as Doc said, messin' with."

"How on earth did—"

"You loved him, Delilah." Fran drank her coffee but I saw the wet on her lashes. "You always have. When you decided to move back home, I figured he was the reason. I knew the two of you dingbats might do something stupid, like run off, or make the whole thing obvious. He never deserved you, couldn't trust him far as you could throw him, but that doesn't matter, does it? Not when it comes to loving."

I dropped my head. Held both sets of fingers against my eyelids, tight, to stem the onslaught.

"Willy Wally wasn't worth your heartache then, isn't now, Dee. You know it," she said so gently it made me cry harder.

That was Fran's version of a loving embrace. I understood that and appreciated her intentions more than I could ever say. She let me cry a good while. After several minutes I looked at my watch, wiped my running nose with a towel.

"You've still got time before you open. Pat your hair and pinch your cheeks."

"Oh no," I said. "Does Doc know it was me?"

"That would be a definite no. Never will. Only you and I know that one."

"Vi?"

"Some things between a mother and her daughter are sacred. Not up for grabs."

I almost started crying again.

"Now you tell me, Delilah."

"Tell you what?"

"I don't know. Why don't you start with Matthew?"

I repeated, again, the same refrain about him and the house fire.

"Don't you wonder what in hellfire is going on then?"

She believed me. Surprised me a little, but she did.

"Not really. I don't care. I want to live my life away from all of it. I'm done with my past and everyone in it."

Fran picked at some imaginary food in her teeth with a toothpick she'd plucked from the shot glass full of them on the bar, resting her burning Marlboro in the plastic ashtray, in no hurry to rebut me. I headed toward the door to turn the closed sign to open. Her voice stopped me.

"You lie to your friends, Delilah, and I'll lie to mine," she said, calm as a funeral director. "But, let's not lie to each other."

1986

CHAPTER FIFTY-FOUR

Things at home were never the same again. Never good between Fran and me.

Already tense, the atmosphere after Fran found the snake box nearly choked us both. Fran blamed herself for what I'd done because she couldn't stand to blame me. I didn't know if I wanted to, or could, live with it myself. I knew my only prayer would be to leave.

As was her way, Fran never spoke about the events of that summer last year, or even danced around them. It was like they'd never happened. Some days, I almost forgot they really did. But not for long, then it'd rush over me like a tidal wave of guilt and self-hatred. Going forward was the only way we knew to go, mute, leaving the dead alone with the secrets they could never tell.

Blanche and Earl stopped talking to everyone but Vi and then only to order booze at the bar. What was left to talk about? Edith, as far as anyone knew, never brought up her suspicions about Emily's death to anyone and she certainly kept her mouth shut about Hank and Smalls. Soon all unpleasant events were forgotten. More than forgotten. The highway protected its own, no matter how many sins they committed against each other.

Fran and Edith cozied up to each other and Fran was back in the zone, filling her station wagon with household goods, groceries, my clothes, hers, whatever she could give away, in no time flat. Hospital, doctor's office, and grocery store runs for all comers kept Fran and me out of each other's hair most of the time. The rhythm of the highway carried us and everyone else along like it always had.

Before we knew it, those gone from the Fifty-three that year were elevated to a position of honor that the dead always seem to achieve, no matter how much of a bastard asshole they were in life. At every potluck, BBQ, or memorial (they never stopped) reminiscing about Hank and Smalls brought fond smiles to everyone's faces, and little laugh lines around their eyes. "Remember when he kicked you into the dirt?" morphed into "Remember what a gentleman he always was?" The highway buried their dead along with their bad dispositions with great cheer, and they always would.

No one ever talked about Emily.

When the last of my junior year was over, Fran and I had run out of steam. We decided it was best for all if I got my GED and moved to Louisiana, with my dad, only he didn't realize he'd have to let me live there, which didn't exactly give his new wife the giggles. So there I found myself alone, far from home, in an old Chevy Vega bought with some of Hank's insurance money, with no one but the ghosts of the past to ride shotgun.

You know the rest of the story. Or you will.

2005

CHAPTER FIFTY-FIVE

My eyes flew open.

It took a few seconds to get my bearings, to remember I was home, in my own bed. It'd been a mercifully busy day, then night, at the bar. Kept my mind off Willy Wally, his fate and my role in it. Fran assured me, with what I knew to be true. If not me, it'd been someone else. Willy Wally's early demise in a violent way was practically predetermined by his own actions.

Still. I couldn't duck all guilt.

Fortunately, or unfortunately, I still had other unpleasant things on my mind.

Even so, I started to drift again when I heard the sound that must've woke me in the first place—a thud and a scrape, followed by another thud and a scrape.

I sped to the window.

I could see Jefferson Davis digging up the shrubs in my back yard. His shovel hitting the dirt, then scooping it up made the thud and scrape noise.

Holy shit. Well, I only had myself to blame. Again. He'd given me plenty of warning. Him and that damn dog, but Billy Dale kept turning up to monopolize my time. I ran out the front door still buttoning my jeans, barefoot, wearing the thin, raggedy t-shirt I'd slept in.

"What do you think you're doing?"

Jefferson Davis stopped just long enough to lift his head. The night sky on the highway had always blazed, alight with stars and a moon that seemed bigger there than anywhere else. Emily and I hadn't had any problem seeing Fran drown Hank and I could see Jefferson Davis clear as could be.

"I'm a little slow sometimes," Jefferson Davis said, back to digging. "I knew you'd gotten rid of Leeann, but I couldn't figure out why, at first."

My bare feet gripped the dewy grass. "I didn't do anything to Leeann," I said, annoyed more than afraid.

"Shut it," Jefferson Davis said, tossing dirt from his shovel to one side. "She found something here." His shovel rammed into the grassy, hardened ground. "In your yard."

I stepped forward, and just like the day he shot the snake in my barn, he whipped out his gun and cocked it. "You're gonna stay right there while I dig it up. Whatever it is, and however long it takes."

Any ice I thought I had in my veins, melted. I felt fear, real fear, for the first time in a long while. "Can I sit?" I thought I'd fall if I didn't.

"Suit yourself." He jammed the gun into his waistband and dug.

They say your life flashes before you right before you die. Mine didn't, which gave me hope I might live. I did mull over where I might've gone so terribly wrong. But, where would I even start down that winding, treacherous road? I considered my options long enough to realize I didn't have any. He'd kill me, I knew. He'd been thinking about it for a while, maybe the whole time he'd lived here. All he needed now was an excuse, which I'm sure he thought he'd find buried, as I did too.

Suddenly, he stopped. He pushed against the shovel, which had gone down about three feet and seemed stuck. He got on his belly to use his hands, flinging dirt out the top of the hole in a fury. I didn't move. No point in it. "Jesus, you're unbelievable," he held a head up to the moonlight, by his once blond, now dirty blond hair, like an Indian with his first scalp. "So here's what's left of the mysterious Matthew Hardy," he said.

"That's not Matthew Hardy."

****

We sat, the three of us, or two and a fourth of us, on the wet grass like we'd brought a picnic. Our asses soaked through, under the clear, dark sky, so beautiful you'd have never thought any bad deed could take place under it. We'd moved so we could lean against the house. He kept a firm grip on Philip's head. After we sat, it dawned on him he was holding a severed head and he dropped it like it was made of porcupine quills. But not the gun. He kept a clutch on that. I could tell Jefferson Davis was bugged about not knowing, almost as much as he was bugged at me in general. He pondered whose head sat between us. So convinced, like everyone else, that I'd offed Matthew he had a hard time making room in his brain that it'd be someone else.

"Who is it I hate to ask?"

"Philip Bond."

"The winemaker pilot?" His face wrinkled up like an old apple. I couldn't decide if it was disgust or disbelief or any other of the dis words.

"The very same." I rocked side to side to get circulation to my wet ass.

"I don't believe it," he said. "How many guys you kill?"

So sick of saying I didn't kill Matthew I refused to say it again. I left that to Jefferson Davis's imagination. Let him think whatever he wanted.

"What'd this poor sap do? Catch you with Willy Wally?"

I leaned forward, away from the house to see his face better. I couldn't believe it. Fran wouldn't tell. She told me she wouldn't, didn't, and I believed her, for once. "How do you know about Willy Wally?"

"Never mind. We're talking about you right now."

The guy with the gun got his way.

"It was an accident."

"Original."

"Look, I don't have any reason now to lie and frankly, I don't give one fuck if you believe me or not."

He fondled his gun a second or two. "Go on then."

"He fell, hit his head on the corner of that big freezer. I thought he'd just knocked himself out. Turns out it killed him."

"If it was an accident, why didn't you call the cops? An ambulance? Accidents do happen."

"Because Karen didn't want me to."

"His wife? What?" Now it was his turn to lean forward to see me better.

"Look, Philip was a skirt chaser and worse. He tried his damnedest to get up mine. I wasn't interested. But Karen knew him. She knew what he was up to. Right after he fell, she barged in and there he was, on my floor, dead."

"She believed the accident story?"

"Didn't care."

"Women. And you wonder why I don't get married." He poked at pilot Philip's head.

"Well, unless you've got a zillion dollar trust fund, I think you're safe."

"Sex or money. Almost always a motive to kill."

"Oh, there're a few others, but yeah, pretty common."

Our congenial conversation belied our current circumstances. He still held that damn gun. Could he really be that pissed about his missing dog? I stole a glance at him. His held his back straight, his jaw tight. I think he might've been afraid of me. I hadn't taken that into consideration. After all, he did find a head in my yard. Most often not a good character reference.

"Why'd she come here the other night?" He pointed the gun at me again. "And don't lie this time."

"She'd asked Billy Dale to find me. He already had, but wouldn't tell her. As soon as I heard that, I got nervous. Well, that, and she burned down both our houses."

"Karen did that? What for?"

"She knew Penelope was hot on my trail too. For all Karen knew I'd offed Matthew. Everyone else thinks so. She worried they'd search my house, find Philip's DNA. So far, no one's reported him missing. She wanted to keep it that way. Her house was an accident. I called her here to find out what the hell was going on with her, and if she meant to implicate me. After all, I'm the only other person who knew Philip was dead. And I was the idiot who carried his body around in the freezer."

"What'd ya do that for? Her husband, her problem."

"I don't know. Philip was a prick. He knocked her around. I didn't blame her. Seemed like the thing to do at the time since I was the only one of us with the giant freezer."

"Mighty neighborly of you." Jefferson Davis wiped at his nose. "So now where is she?"

"Karen? No idea. I doubt anyone'll ever find her. Money can help a person disappear. I imagine Karen's on some tropical island sipping mai tais."

"Where's the rest of him?"

I took a good look at Philip's face. He looked bad. The stump of his neck was cut clean, a surgeon's slice. I knew my way around a dead animal, as I'd said before, chefs usually do. He looked asleep, other than the decomp and the sickening pea soup color of his skin. I brushed the dirt out of his thick, longer hair. I guess it really did keep growing.

"Is there more of him still down there?" He'd taken out the gun again, so I prattled on like a fool with nothing to lose.

"Yeah," I said, resting my elbows on my knees. "Probably half."

"What'd you do with the other half?"

"Fed him to the pigs, sometimes in sausage form."

"No shit?" Jefferson Davis said, surprised or impressed, maybe both.

Cutting up a body isn't for the faint of heart. As much as I tried to think of Philip as any other animal, I couldn't. Wife beating cheater he was, but even that didn't make me blasé about the Hannibal Lecter routine. I tried with all my will, but half was all I could manage.

He considered that fascinating, horrifying factoid for a bit.

"So she poisoned the pigs?" he said.

"No, no," I said. "I thought Karen did that. That's why I called her, told her we needed to talk. She didn't do anything other than set the fires."

Fast as the wind, he'd put the gun in my face.

"Then who did. Someone did."

"I thought you said you didn't believe they were poisoned. Doc didn't know anything, remember?"

"He took a dead pig with him to run some mumbo jumbo doctor tests. The pigs were definitely poisoned. Arsenic."

"Must've been kids."

Before he could say it, I said, "Why on earth would I poison my own pigs?"

"You're daft?"

"I think it was you."

There he went with the damn gun again, waving it close to my face. "Why would I do that?"

"You're pissed about something Jefferson Davis. You really want to kill me over a dog?"

"You really are clueless, aren't you?" he said.

"Enlighten me."

"Didn't you think I'd figure it out?" He banged his head against the house. I thought he might cry. For a few seconds he looked like the old Jefferson Davis, guileless and scared. I felt sorry for him, despite the gun.

"Figure what out?"

"You killed Emily with my snake," he said, just like that.

The simplicity of it sliced through me. My hands leapt to my face to keep the waterworks in, but to no avail. I tried to cry quietly.

"I had to protect Fran. It was desperation and dumb youth," I said, sniffling. "I know, I know, not an acceptable excuse. But Emily scared me like I'd never been scared before. I could not let anything happen to Fran."

"Why would Fran need protection?"

Shit. Now I'd let that cat out of the bag. I'd forgotten how young Jefferson Davis was that summer. He didn't know what went on outside his own ass.

"Never mind. Just shoot me already."

He went radio silent. I cried more.

Finally, "Nothing would've happened to your mother. Rusty would've dropped the ball like he always did, and still does. Hell, he wouldn't have picked up the ball to begin with." He cocked his pistol and pointed at my face.

So he did know—enough anyway. Or suspect.

"I couldn't take that chance," I said.

"Didn't you think I'd notice my snake was gone and figure it out?"

Before I could confess that it'd never entered my mind, he said, "No, you didn't." He spit out a long stream of saliva. "Nope, nobody ever thought dorky, doofus, Jefferson Davis had a brain in his big, faggot head." He pressed the gun's nose to my cheek.

"Oh my god, Jefferson Davis," I said so loud he jumped back, took the gun with him. Lucky he didn't shoot me in the process. "That's why you jumped off the roof. You really did try to kill yourself." I cried harder. "I'm so sorry," I said in a whisper. "I'm so, so, sorry."

"When I couldn't find my snake, I thought Dad got rid of it," he said. "He'd done it before with that first one I caught. It got too big, he said. So he shot it. I thought he'd done it again."

A flash of Jefferson Davis moping the day I went to get Hank's stuff from Margene came to mind. I'd taken the snake-in-a-box before I ever went to the door of the house.

"Well, it was a rattlesnake you—"

"When I heard Emily died of a rattlesnake bite—I knew. If I hadn't had that stupid snake to begin with you would never have thought of using one to kill Emily."

The inside of my chest felt weighed down by sorrow, guilt, fear. I couldn't find a way to sit that didn't hurt, the heaviness of all I'd done wrong could crumple me. "I honestly didn't think it would work."

"What wouldn't work?"

"The snake thing." My eyes burned. "There was a good chance it would've just slithered away."

"Why'd you do it if it wasn't surefire?"

"Because I was a kid—a scared, dumb kid who couldn't have gotten myself out of a wet paper bag." I laid my hand on his, the one not holding a firearm. "We all were, Jefferson Davis. All stupid kids who didn't understand consequences."

"Well, I wasn't as dumb as any of you thought." But he didn't take his hand away. "Not you, not my brothers, or my parents . . ."

If he was gonna give a rundown of all the people who'd thought him dumb as hair we'd be here until someone rescued me. I let him go on.

"Emily, Wanda—even that fucking Willy Wally," he pounded the butt of the gun on the grass. "Especially that fucking Willy Wally."

"Willy Wally?" I could feel the churning in my skull. Second time he brought him up. He knew about our affair. I remembered him shooting the pig with the gun resting on my shoulder, from behind. His crack shot. He never missed.

"You shot Willy Wally, didn't you?"

"Yeah, and I'd do it again, tomorrow." Jefferson Davis turned glassy eyed. "I knew he was messing around on Wanda." He jerked his hand away, turned to eye me. "When I found out it was you, I made up my mind to kill you both." His pistol rose up to meet me again. "I thought the world would be a better place without either of you in it. My world at least."

I decided not to ask how he found out. What difference did it make now?

"Were you gonna make the trip to the Valley to do it?"

Most of the highway folks never traveled that distance, to a place full of rich snoots, for anything, even killing.

"I hadn't thought it through, to be honest," he said, lowering the gun. "But that doesn't mean I wouldn't have," he said, gun up again.

"I'm sure." I wasn't going to argue the point.

"When I heard you planned to move back here it all fell into place with hardly any effort," he said. "And everything that happened after, my pushy mother dragging me out here, the pigs, me moving in, it all felt so right."

"Right. I suppose so."

"If you were so in love with Willy Wally, why Matthew too?" he said like he just realized I was screwing around with them both. "How many men do you need?"

"Willy Wally used me. I knew that. He didn't care about me anymore than he ever did. Matthew was just a stupid distraction. I grew so tired of all of it. The men, the wives, hating myself. So I did the only thing I knew how. I came home."

"Yeah, good job. You came home and I remembered how much I liked you," he said, gun down. "Then I felt so, so, right with you. Not like that stupid kid from years ago. But, like a man, a capable, needed, man. Shit, I started loving you. Even all the drinking I did didn't make me forget that I actually liked being around you. Christ, Dee, I've known you since I was seven years old." He lifted his lanky arm sideways to put the gun to my temple, gangsta style. "Every time I talked myself into forgiving and forgetting, I thought about what you did to Emily."

Despite the obvious peril I was in, I couldn't stop hearing him say he'd started loving me. Then I saw that damn gun.

"What about Doc? How'd you convince him?" I said, in a rush, hoping to distract him from ejecting a bullet into my brain. I thought I might piss my pants.

"Doc was thrilled," Jefferson Davis said, dropping his gun toting hand to his lap. "He's the one who told me Willy Wally was screwing around. I just led him to the obvious conclusion—except I never told him it was with you." He stopped pointing his pistol at me to draw circles in the grass with it.

"How'd you pull it off?" I figured I'd ask whatever I wanted, since it was probably my last night on earth.

"Easy. Me and Doc worked out where we'd go. I went up there first and laid low," Jefferson Davis waved his gun around, excited. "Doc brought him out there and I shot him with Doc's gun, from behind Doc. Doc had already taken a few fake shots at invisible deer so he'd have powder residue on his hands. We forgot Rusty wouldn't think to look. One clean shot, except the bastard moved and I got him in the neck. Worked though." He laughed, out loud for once. "Hell, I even got a deer. It was beautiful."

"It was hunting season, footprints all over the place, hunters all over the place," I said more to myself than him. "A perfect crime."

"Pretty much."

"Why is Doc at my house all the time?" Maybe he knew more than Jefferson Davis thought.

"Reckon for the same reason you called Karen to come over. He wants to know I'm keeping my mouth shut. As if."

Made sense.

The midnight sky turned a smoky gray, morning snuck up the mountains. I idly twirled the front of Philip's hair into a curl and pressed it into his greenish forehead. "If I could turn back the clock, I'd do everything different." I leaned my head back and felt my tears run down past my ears, resigned to my end. "When I think about it, and believe me, I try not to, I can't believe I did it, I never thought of myself as that kind of person, but here I am, that kind of person." I reached for his hand again. He let me. "I loved Emily. But not more than Fran."

"Well, none of us can go back," he said. "No reason to wonder."

"By the way, I would never hurt Leeann. She's up at Vi's."

I felt him relax. The gun fell off his lap. We stared at the gorgeous highway sky.

I squeezed his fingers. "I'll tell you this, Jefferson Davis. Killing is no good. You can shoot everybody who's ever done you wrong and unless you kill yourself while you're at it, it's no good."

He squeezed my hand too. I could see a tear run down his face in my periphery.

"The hurt still hurts. But then you're just a killer," I said. "You already know that though, don't you?"

We sat as quiet and still as Philip's head, for quite a while. I could hear Jefferson Davis's breath slow, the tension gone from his body. He wiped his eyes and nose. I didn't want to shame him by looking in his direction while he tried to stop crying. After what felt like forever, he unfolded his long legs to stand, his gun left to lie on the ground and started digging again.

"What are you doing?" I didn't grab for his discarded pistol.

"That hole wasn't deep enough. And show me where you put what's left of Philip."

CHAPTER FIFTY-SIX

"No news is good news," Fran said, a brown bag full of who-knows-what in her hands, her pants dusty, like she'd been digging for treasures at the bottom of a well. I didn't see the "Bad to the Bone" on her stained t-shirt till she turned her back to me.

"I guess," I said. "I'm sure Billy Dale won't give up any time soon."

"Jefferson Davis forgive you for Leeann now she's back here?"

I got up to get Fran some coffee. I thought hard as fast as I could. I stood in my kitchen, her cup in my hands. For once, I wanted the air to be clear between my mother and me. I wanted to love her without reservation, enjoy her funny barbs, her crazy shirts, her misguided but still thoughtful and kind gestures. Hey loyalty, her insistence on surviving, the bravery it took for her to live a life of her own choosing without apology. I wanted that Fran in my life. Not the woman who did the unthinkable. I wanted her to forgive me for knowing what she'd done and for what I'd done.

I brought her coffee out.

"Fran, let's talk."

Discomfort climbed all over her body. I could see it, feel it. I went forward anyway. I told her everything that happened with Jefferson Davis the other night, with Philip, all about Emily and what really happened with Willy Wally.

She didn't interrupt or interject. A few times I thought she might cry, even just a little, but she didn't. Fran was tough, through and through. When I finally got to the end, I stopped. She waited a minute or so then said, "Are you done?"

"Yes."

She reached for me. I didn't know what to do, she'd never put her arms around me before. She held me in her arms for a few seconds. I reveled in it. Then she stopped.

"Now, let's not talk about that again."

I could only laugh. Fran was still Fran after all.

****

Right away, I knew our relationship shifted. Too late to be what we could've been twenty years before—we'd become something different. Friends. We were just people now. Human beings with terrible flaws. We shared a history, admittedly an often painful, horrid one. But not every memory was sour. We could enjoy those now without the bad ones gathering like a swarm of bees.

I realized that years before, my insistence on doing anything to protect Fran was really to protect me. Sure, I didn't want anything horrible to happen to her, but as a kid, I worried more about what would happen to me if she were gone. I wasn't ready to live in a world without my mother in it. Even though I knew that feeling was pretty normal for a kid, I wanted to make up for it.

I wanted to love her in a way that was more about her, than about me.

We wouldn't, as she insisted, ever talk about any sordid doings in our past again. But, once was enough, wasn't it?

We spent a good hour laughing, remembering funny Arthur and Margene stories. Vi, back in the day. Family stories from way before the highway. I felt so good about my homecoming. We were gonna make it.

"Oh heavens," she smacked herself on the forehead. "You know I just came by to bring you a few things."

She reached into the bag. "Here's that scarf you wanted." She unfolded a yellow and blue paisley patterned, fringed piece of fabric, about four feet long, that I wouldn't be caught dead in.

"I didn't say I wanted it, Fran. I said I thought it was pretty." She cracked me up, didn't annoy me like she would've even yesterday.

"You want it, don't you?"

"Wouldn't pass it up for all the money in the world."

She reached down her backward shirt for a Marlboro and her lighter. I wasn't going to reprimand her (again) about smoking in the house. "Vi sent some hamburger."

"Hamburger?"

"You remember she bought a couple head of cattle to see if she could home grow her beef like you do your pork. Just butchered the first one. Well, one of the little presidents did it for us." Cigarette slung in her mouth, she mumbled, "Hope it didn't go bad with us yakkin' the day away. Oh, and some jelly. That grape mess Vi's always got in her cauldron. I hate that purple shit."

"Thank you, Fran. That was so thoughtful of you and Vi. Thank her for me too." I stretched out my arms and put a throw pillow under my head.

"Well, I've gotta take off before Vi sends the police, you know how she gets. She misses that damn pesky dog. Now she wants one. I want to ask Jefferson Davis about getting her one for a surprise."

As if he'd read her mind, in he came. Took his hat off right away, like the gentleman he always was. Said his hello to Fran.

"Fran wants you to get a dog for Vi as a surprise. One like Leeann."

"Sure. I'll go up to the turkey farm this afternoon. Just came to let you know I'm goin' into Kearny. Be back about two I think." He leaned down and kissed me full on the mouth. I'd discovered Jefferson Davis was the best kisser in the world. We kissed probably longer than was appropriate but I didn't want him to stop.

"See ya later, Fran." He flew out the door putting his hat back on.

I wish I'd had a camera to capture the look on Fran's face. Surprise wouldn't begin to cover it. Surprised, horrified, shocked, there it all played out across her face.

"Well, knock me over with a bulldozer," she said.

"Feather."

"Whatever." She shook her head as if to clear it. "I've gotta get home and lie down, I'm sure."

"Bye Fran. Love you."

She stopped, surprised at my endearment. "Now I'll probably have to take to my bed for days."

She stepped out onto the porch. I didn't follow. She could show herself out.

"Jesus, Mary and Joseph, how much food do you have in here?"

The hamburger. She'd taken it to the freezer.

"Fran, wait." I scrambled off the sofa.

"For heaven's sake, Delilah. You've still got Edith in here?"

CHAPTER FIFTY-SEVEN

"Delilah, we agreed you'd give this woman a decent burial."

"I know, I just couldn't bear to think about it. Besides, how could I get her out of there by myself? We could barely get her in."

Fran kept looking at Edith, frozen and white. "Even with all that weight she lost forgetting to eat, she could still crush a pony if she'd tried to ride one."

I slammed the thing shut. "Fran, it wasn't even necessary. She fell out the window. Everyone knew she wasn't right anymore."

"The Alzheimer's gave her loose lips, Delilah. I didn't tell you, but she kept talking about, well, what we already agreed we weren't going to talk about. The day she fell, she'd told Rusty all about what happened with Hank, said she told everybody. Who everybody was...well, who can know? She told me all about it too because she didn't remember it was me. I couldn't believe it. I didn't mean to yell at her, but I did. I walked toward her, yelling. She spooked, clutched at her chest, then ran backward through the glass."

"Oh my god, you didn't." Not more for Fran's body count.

"Not on purpose I didn't. I loved Edith and you know it. That's why I moved back to the house to take care of her. Make sure she wasn't talking about the wrong shit to the wrong people. And she really did need help. I think a heart attack killed her first, then she fell out the window. All that chest grabbing. It was awful. But how could I call Rusty when she'd told him, well, everything she told him? It would've looked bad and suspicious."

"Did Rusty say anything to you about what she told him?"

"Yes, if you can believe that shit. He got all cop like all of a sudden. After I supposedly drove Edith to her sister's in Portland. Even asked for her number. I made one up, but as far as I know he never called it, and never brought it up again. I know I worried for nothing, but what's done is done. If I could turn back the clock, well, we wouldn't be standing here in front of a goddamn freezer with a dead person in it."

"Does Doc know?"

"No. He thinks she's in Portland."

"Why are you mad at him, by the way?"

"I'm not. I just don't want him to see anything weird on my face that would give away . . . what I know about Willy Wally and you."

"I'm sorry Fran. I really am. He's your friend."

"I'm tired of Doc, truth be told. You're not the only one who wants a new life."

That I could believe.

"Well, I'll think of something to do for Edith. Don't worry."

"Please do, Delilah. She deserves a nice place under a tree or something."

"Will do."

I watched Fran roar out in the old Impala, an emphysema inducing cloud of smoke in her wake. Wait'll Jefferson Davis saw this. I'd have to tell him. He'd have to help me. Lots of beautiful spots around the ranch now.

What I wouldn't tell him, or Fran, or anyone, was Philip fell because he opened the freezer. The moron thought he could fix the loud motor and make points. He lifted the lid before I could stop him. I think he actually screamed when he saw poor Edith. He fell, hit his head so hard, bled like his throat had been cut. I wasn't sure he'd died. So I ran as fast as I could to the airplane hangar at his place to get the rat poison. Outlawed, but a lot of ranchers still used it to kill vermin, the snakes sometimes ate the vermin and it killed them too. Two for one, so to speak. Karen had been gone, I thought. I wasn't sure if she saw me running to and from the hangar, if she did, she never said. Anyway, I forced it down the unconscious Philip's throat. Before Karen barreled through the door, Philip was oh so dead.

It worked out for the both of us.

I made Jefferson Davis get Leeann to keep Karen or Penelope from poisoning me. Or worse. At least I'd hear them coming except Leeann was more worried about my yard than protecting us. But that worked out okay too.

In my zeal to get rid of Philip's body, I hadn't realized until too late—the arsenic would kill the pigs.

Now we'll never need to talk about that again.

CHAPTER FIFTY-EIGHT

"That was a beautiful spot you picked, Delilah. Edith would've loved it had she seen it," Fran said.

"It is," I said. "Jefferson Davis picked it."

"I can't believe he didn't squawk about the whole mess."

"Love forgives all things." Except the stuff you don't tell.

"Now you're scaring the shit outta me with all that sap."

She headed out to the porch to smoke. I couldn't believe it. First time she'd ever done that of her volition. Some things do change.

"Think anyone'll come looking for Edith?" Fran said.

"No. Her sister died eons ago. Who's left?"

"Lord, here comes Doc."

He slowed to a stop in his cherry red truck, rolled down the window.

"Where might I find Jefferson Davis?"

"One of the barns. Butchering pigs. The supermarket truck's coming tomorrow for a load." Off he drove.

"You think he's gonna worry about Jefferson Davis confessing forever?"

"Who knows?"

"You don't think he'd want to get rid of Jefferson Davis to make sure?"

"Jefferson Davis can take care of himself. No doubt. Besides, I think they've grown to like each other. Everyone's turning over new leaves."

"Nothing wrong with some of the old leaves, you ask me."

She flicked her ashes into the empty coffee can I kept on the porch for when I knew she wouldn't bother to go to the table for the ashtray.

"I appreciate all the help he gives us free, but something about Doc has always made my skin crawl." I didn't bring up the sedatives from years before.

"Doc's wife really suffered after her stroke," she said.

"I remember. What's that got to do with him making my skin crawl?"

"She was a young woman," Fran said. "Fat as hell, ugly as Wanda is now, but young. Too young for a stroke."

I knew something bad was coming. I steeled myself.

"Poor woman couldn't do one thing for herself. Couldn't talk, wore diapers, the only thing I ever saw her do was cry. It broke my heart. You can imagine what it did to Doc. Ugly or not, he really loved her. I used to help take care of her, as you know." She took a long drag. "One day, I walked in on him holding the pillow over her face. I walked out, pretended I never saw a thing."

"How horrible." And I knew from horrible.

"He knew I'd seen, came over crying, begging me not to tell. Of course, it wasn't about killing. It was about mercy. He showed her the mercy no one else would've had the guts to do. He did right by Angela. We've been friends ever since."

"I thought you were tired of him."

"I am. Even friends get tired of each other. Our lives, mine especially, are a lot different now. Still, I'd help him if he needed it and he'd do the same. He did do the same back when."

We didn't talk about that help.

****

Fran crushed out her smoke, gathered up her purse.

"I never wanted you to come back here, Delilah."

"I know," I said, opening the door to the porch, welcoming the warm sunshine on my skin.

"I didn't think you'd have a good life if you didn't get away." Fran took off her glasses to rub at her eyes. I felt stuck here, but you—you're smart enough to do anything you want. And you did. Look at all you accomplished. I'm so proud of you."

I swallowed the big lump of mama love that stopped up my throat.

"That reminds me. My agent called, finally found me."

"You're just now telling me?"

"Well, Edith took up a lot of my brain space ... anyway, I'm getting a new show."

"You are? That's wonderful." She clapped her hands, then her face fell. "But you'll leave."

I couldn't help but smile a huge goofy ear-to-ear one. "That's the beauty of it. They're going to film here, at the farm. It's a life-style thing. And Fork in the Road is an even more perfect name here."

"Wait'll I tell Vi. You'll quit there I suppose."

"The bar? No way. They'll film there too. Everyone will be stars." I laughed. So did Fran. "I better get me some new shirts. She looked down at her "I Fought the Law and Kicked the Law's Ass" t-shirt.

We made our way to the steps. From the porch I could see Doc and Jefferson Davis on the blue horizon. Surrounded by our porcine herd. They walked, close together, toward the farthest barn. Leeann pranced alongside.

"Vi loves that dumb new dog, by the way," Fran said. "She named her George."

"Of course she did."

"I'm glad you're staying. I hope you never leave," Fran said.

I knew I wouldn't. I'd been on the run the whole of my adult life. No more. Highway Fifty-three was my home. Why would I leave the place that shaped me, that place that had my back no matter what wrongs I committed, for somewhere else that held no affection for me, didn't know me, or anything about my life. All who lived here in this forgotten place were my people, an indelible part of me. Not flesh of my flesh, or bone of my bone, but still my own.

As he usually did, Billy Dale cramped my style by showing up. His Corolla peeled around the corner where it came to a stop behind Fran's ancient Impala. He bound out of the car, a dopey smile on his face, loping over like a Golden Retriever bringing back the ball.

"Hey, Matthew Hardy turned up," he shouted. "In Mexico." He got to the bottom of the steps. "Guess what else? Rusty's finally retiring. They're giving me a second chance. I'm taking his job up here."

Fran watched Billy Dale from the top step, instead of leaving she fished another smoke from the 7-11 in her bra along with her lighter.

"We're gonna need a new freezer."

The End

Read on for a preview from:

The Invisible Heiress

Dark, disturbing, deliciously inappropriate.

THANK YOU!

Thank you for reading my book. If you enjoyed it, please take a moment to leave me a review.

CONNECT WITH ME

Email: authorkodonnell@gmail.com
Facebook: facebook.com/kodonnellauthor
Web: http://www.authorkathleenodonnell.com
Twitter: twitter.com/authorkodonnell
Instagram: instagram.com/kathleenthewriter
Goodreads: goodreads.com/author/show/7200820
Pinterest: pinterest.com/authorkodonnell

PREVIEW:
THE INVISIBLE HEIRESS

Chapter One

Preston

I don't know which scene satisfied me most—my posh parents waiting in the concrete-walled visitors' room or me deposited in front of them by a uniformed guard.

They sat across from me at the Formica-topped table. My father's face was tight, eyes damp. Seeing him distressed kicked a dent in my smug demeanor, so I stopped looking at him, my eyes ping ponged toward my mother. Despite the sordid circumstances, she shone, her beauty ferocious, perhaps highlighted even more by the dour surroundings. Thick hair still a perfect shade of bombshell blonde, skin pale but flawless despite time's march, the blue of her eyes a perpetual shock.

So entranced I forgot to insult her.

Almost.

"My incarceration poses a real problem for you. Doesn't it, Mother? Harrison Blair doesn't sully herself with the downtrodden."

She shifted backward then forward quick.

"*You're* the problem, Preston. Downtrodden? That's how you think of yourself? You—"

"Harrison, Preston," Dad said. "Please. Let's start right. Preston, your mother and I haven't seen you in so long. Though God knows I've tried. Let's all make a real effort."

He paused, probably to steel himself for objections in stereo. None came.

Dad continued. "You're not incarcerated. You're hospitalized. Your new therapist what's her name." He squeezed his eyes shut like her name had been tattooed inside his lids. "Um, she, Isabel, says you've made some headway, participating in therapy now."

"Might as well," I said.

"That's the spirit. Won't be long until you're back home. You're doing so well considering how difficult, well you're done with that part of the, uh, the rehabilitation."

"You mean the sweating, shaking, puking, padded room part?" I said.

"You're sober. That's all I meant."

My mother's eyes popped like a kidnapper just yanked the hood off her head.

"Sober?" she said. "Doesn't that term apply to alcoholics? Surely they have another term for homicidal, drunken pill add—"

"She's clean, Harrison. That's all that matters."

Dad kept yanking on his tie. I thought he might hang himself with it right before our eyes.

"*All that matters*? Is that your idea of a joke, Todd?"

"Nice dye job, Dad. Only you'd believe those stupid commercials. So natural no one will—"

"*Darling*, stop," he said to Mother. "Of course sobriety's not all but it's a start. I think, *we* think enough time has passed. We should jumpstart our family therapy."

"*We* who?" I said.

The guard took a step forward, disapproving of my elevated tone. My father waved him back.

"Not *Mother*, I'm sure."

"Well, Isabel thought—"

"Just because I'm in the cuckoo's nest doesn't mean I don't have rights," I said. "Isabel shouldn't talk to you at all about me. I'm an adult. She's *my* shrink. Confidentiality too big a word?"

"Shrinks. Therapy," Mother said. "In my day you poured yourself a scotch and got on with it."

"You don't pour yourself anything. You hire that out," I said.

"Family therapy's part of the deal," Dad said. "The judge insisted—"

"*You* own the judge. *We* don't *have* to do anything. Remind him, Mother."

"You should kiss Judge Seward's robed ass," she said, hissing like a stabbed tire. "You'd be someone's bitch if not for his mercy."

"You mean, if not for *your money*. Don't pretend you did shit for me. You did everything for yourself, Mother, to stop the gossip. That's what you do."

With both fists, Dad twisted the tie he'd finally managed to take off.

"Preston, we hoped something good could come out of—"

"Todd, the only good that could possibly come out of this mess is if Preston stays *hospitalized* for the rest of her natural life."

"Harrison, please. We agreed—"

"*You* agreed. With no one but yourself."

"Hate to break up the party but I'm ready to go back to my room," I said more to the guard than my parents.

"Wait, Preston," Dad said, peering around the room, looking for his spine. "It doesn't feel like it now, but here's a chance for you and Mom to, I don't know what, start again, improve your relationship, even a little. That's what we all want, isn't it?"

"Steady on, Dad. The devil comes dressed as everything you want."

I let the guard take my arm, turned in time to see Mom lean her head back enough to dab at the scar under the collar of her ivory silk blouse, a scarlet line cut across her throat, not quite ear to ear, a vicious permanent necklace.

~~~End Preview~~~

Like *The Invisible Heiress?*

Read it now!

ABOUT THE AUTHOR

Kathleen O'Donnell is a wife, mom, grandmother and a recovering blogger. She currently lives in Nevada with her husband. She is a two time Book of the Year finalist for her debut novel The Last Day for Rob Rhino. You can find short stories and blog posts on her website: www.authorkathleenodonnell.com

CONTENTS

1985

2005

1985

2005

1985

2005

1985

2005

1985

2005

1985

2005

1985

2005

1985

2005

1986

2005